PRAISE FOR KERRY

"Laugh, cry, get angry, but most of all care in this wild ride of emotions delivered by Kerry Anne King. Brilliant prose inhabited by engaging characters makes this a story you cannot put down."

—Patricia Sands, author of the Love in Provence series

A compelling and heartfelt tale. A must-read that is rich in relatable characters and emotions. Kerry Anne King is one to watch out for!"

—Steena Holmes, *New York Times* and *USA Today* bestselling author

"With social media conferring blistering fame and paparazzi exhibiting the tenacity often required to get a clear picture of our lives, King has created a high-stakes, public stage for her tale of complicated grief. A quick read with emotional depth you won't soon forget."

—Kathryn Craft, author of *The Far End of Happy* and
The Art of Falling

"*Closer Home* is a story as memorable and meaningful as your favorite song, with a cast of characters so true to life you'll be sorry to let them go."

—Sonja Yoerg, author of *House Broken* and *Middle of Somewhere*

"Kerry Anne King's tale of regret, loss, and love pulled me in, from its intriguing beginning to its oh-so-satisfying conclusion."

—Jackie Bouchard, *USA Today* bestselling author of *House Trained*
and *Rescue Me, Maybe*

"King's prose is filled with vitality."

—Ella Carey, author of *Paris Time Capsule* and *The House by the Lake*

"Depicting the depth of human frailty yet framing it within a picture of hope, *I Wish You Happy* pulls you in as you root for the flawed yet intoxicating characters to reach a satisfying conclusion of healing. King's writing is impeccable—and her knowledge and exploration of depression and how it affects those it touches makes this a story that everyone will connect with."

—Kay Bratt, author of *Wish Me Home*

"Kerry Anne King's Rae is a woman caught between the safety of her animal rescue projects and the messy, sometimes terrifying reality of human relationships. You'll never stop rooting for her as she steps into the light, risking everything for real friendship and love in this wistful, delicate, and ultimately triumphant tale."

—Emily Carpenter, author of *Burying the Honeysuckle Girls* and *The Weight of Lies*

"Kerry Anne King explores happiness and depression; the concept of saving others versus saving ourselves in this wonderfully written and touching novel populated by real and layered people. If you want to read a book that restores your faith in humanity, pick up *I Wish You Happy*."

—Amulya Malladi, bestselling author of *A House for Happy Mothers* and *The Copenhagen Affair*

ALSO BY KERRY ANNE KING

I Wish You Happy

ALSO BY KERRY ANNE KING

Closer Home: A Novel

I Wish You Happy

a novel

wishing you happiness always

KERRY ANNE KING

LAKE UNION
PUBLISHING

Text copyright © 2017 Kerry Schafer

Published by Lake Union Publishing, Seattle

www.apub.com

Amazon, the Amazon logo, and Lake Union Publishing are trademarks of Amazon.com, Inc., or its affiliates.

ISBN-13: 9781477848869
ISBN-10: 147784886X

Cover design by Shasti O'Leary Soudant

Printed in the United States of America

For Jamie, a bright soul gone too early into the dark

Chapter One

The day begins with a pocketful of wishes, and not a star in sight.

Even though I know it's futile, I can't help voicing my requests.

I wish it wasn't Monday.

I wish I had air-conditioning.

I wish Oscar wasn't dead.

Wishes don't change anything, my mother always says, but sometimes they translate into action. And sometimes, every now and then, wishes are granted out of the blue, as if there really is a cosmic fairy godmother out there watching over me.

Oscar's death is not like that. It's not reversible. He's dead when I wake up in the morning, and he's still dead late in the afternoon. No wish is going to bring him back.

By the time I get into my car to drive to my weekly session with Bernie, I'm fed up with both wishing and thinking.

It's a blistering afternoon in late July. The air whistling through the vents of my elderly Subaru doesn't pretend to touch the heat. I drive with the windows open, for all the good it does me. Even the breeze feels thick and heavy and offers no relief.

An unnatural glare erases all shades of gray, turning the world into sharp-edged geometric shapes. Even the shadows look solid enough to touch. Storm clouds gather over the mountains to the north, brilliant white on top, black and ominous beneath. Maybe this is it, the apocalypse, ushered in not by smallpox or zombies, but a sun on nuclear overdrive, pouring out enough light to incinerate us all.

I navigate town on autopilot, aware of these two things: my sadness, and the brightness of the light, both of which are out of all reasonable proportion. Wedging my car into a too-tight space between an SUV and a pickup truck, I gather up the shoebox from the passenger seat and plod across the street into the waiting room of Your Mindful Self. Even this dim, shadowy refuge from the rest of the world seems far too bright.

Air-conditioning raises goose bumps on my sweat-slick skin; the cardboard is clammy and damp. I feel two-dimensional and unreal, as if an invisible camera is recording the details of me, disheveled and tearstained, the shoebox clutched in my arms like a talisman.

The small waiting area with its worn beige carpet and three green chairs is empty, except for me. According to the clock on the wall, I'm late, and Bernie comes to collect me almost at once, cool and serene as a willow tree in a floating green dress, her brown curls loose and long over her shoulders. With a murmured greeting, she leads me back to the inner sanctum.

Sinking into my accustomed chair I concentrate on my breath, the way I've been taught. But even my breathing feels sharp and wrong, and I open my eyes again and lock on to Bernie. My lifeline, my savior.

My paid friend.

Her words, not mine, and said tongue in cheek. A gentle reminder that she isn't my friend but my counselor, and won't be in my life forever. A catalyst, she says. To give me the momentum I need to get on with my life.

I've been steadfastly stuck now for five years, the weight of my determined inertia too much for even a force of nature like Bernie to budge.

I focus in on her face, the lines of kindness and humor, the curl dangling in front of her left ear, the green stone she wears around her neck on a silver chain.

I'm safe here.

With this thought, her image dissolves into a fractured kaleidoscope of colors. My face is wet with tears before I even know I'm crying. Bernie hands me the tissues, as bothered by my weeping as a tree would be by rain.

I relinquish my shoebox onto her desk while I mop my eyes and blow my nose.

"What did you bring me today?" Bernie asks.

"Wait." I grab for her hand, but I'm too late. She's already lifting the lid.

An instant of silence while she registers the contents, and then the peace is fractured by a piercing shriek. Bernie shoves her chair back, draws her feet up, and anchors them under her skirt. Her gaze is fixed on the box, eyes wide with horror, as if I've brought in a severed hand, maybe, or a skull.

"I don't do rats." Her voice jumps a full octave higher than its usual calm contralto. Her hands tuck the skirt in tighter around her feet.

"He's dead," I say, shocked out of my tears by her reaction. "It's not like he'll be jumping up into your lap."

"Still a rat, dead or alive." Her voice trembles. Her hands, too, are shaking.

"Breathe," I tell her, in my best imitation of her counselor voice. "In: two-three-four-five. Out: two-three-four-five." God knows she's used that one on me enough times to justify the little edge of sarcasm that's slipped past my guards.

She's not breathing, at least not in the mindful way, and the look she levels at me is one I'm pretty sure they don't teach in counselor training. "Why on earth did you bring that—thing—to my office?"

"It's not a thing. It's Oscar. He's dead."

"I can see that. What I don't see is why there is a dead rat on my desk."

I retrieve the box and cradle it in my lap, trying to understand her reaction. Oscar lies in a state on an old hand towel. It just happens to be Christmas red, and his white fur makes a dramatic contrast. His pink feet, which have always seemed like hands to me, are stretched out and open, as if he'd voluntarily surrendered when death came calling. His naked tail curls pathetically around his body.

"It's the tail," Bernie says. Her voice sounds a little better, and she's breathing again, but her feet hide safely underneath her skirt. One of her hands smoothes her hair. "Rat tails. Mouse tails. They're so naked."

I replace the lid on the box and let an edge of anger into my voice. "He was completely naked when he came to me. His mother was eaten by a family cat. My coworker brought him to me in a matchbox."

"And you took him home and saved his life." Bernie sighs, shifts her weight, and allows her feet to come back to the floor. Her professional skin is back on, but it doesn't fit quite right.

"Tell me about Oscar," she says, trying to take us back to our regularly scheduled counseling program. But the room is full of emotional fallout, and at least half of it is hers. Her eyes tell me that she sees this as clearly as I do.

"I wish you hadn't opened the box," I tell her.

"I wish you hadn't brought it." She takes a breath and softens her voice. "I thought it would be the usual. A wounded bird, motherless kittens. It never crossed my mind that you would bring me a rat."

Silence grows around us, pressing in on me. I try to swallow a golf-ball-size lump in my throat that refuses to go down. "It's *Oscar*," I finally manage to croak, willing her to understand the universe of meaning in my words.

"Oscar is a rat." Her voice is cool and relentless. "A dead rat." She doesn't say, *Get a grip, Rae,* but that's what she means.

She leans back in her chair, presses her fingertips together. "I wonder. Maybe if you had friends—real friends—your world wouldn't crash into pieces every time a small creature passes into the great beyond. This isn't the first time we've had this conversation, Rae."

Which is true, of course. I've wept in her office over kittens, birds, and bunnies. On those occasions she was warm and empathetic, but always the conversation comes back to this place. *What about people, Rae? When are you going to let some people into your life?*

"I've tried that," I tell her. "It never ends well."

"Try again. You know the definition of insanity, right?"

"Repeating the same action and expecting different results. Yeah, I know it. Which is why I don't do friends."

Her mouth opens, and I know what she's going to say, some sort of variation on doing friendships differently, using all of the tools in my toolbox, but then she shifts the gears on me and asks, instead, "How are your parents?"

Every muscle in my body tightens. "My parents are fine."

"You could change things up a little," Bernie says. "Call them tonight. Tell them your—pet—died, and you're sad."

It's not that my parents don't love me. The problem is that they are both what I call Highly Focused People, HFPs, while Bernie says I'm a Highly Sensitive Person, HSP. The disconnect caused by that one little letter—*F* versus *S*—puts us on either side of a vast communication chasm we've never managed to bridge.

They call me every Sunday afternoon, precisely at four, to inquire about my well-being and ask if I'm ready to apply to medical school yet. My mother asks if I'm dating, but weddings and grandchildren aren't really on her agenda. The only acceptable reason to call them on a Monday would be my impending death, or my long-overdue application to medical school.

Bernie knows all of this. She also knows this pattern is not about to change.

When she adjusts her necklace, leans forward with both elbows on the desk, and rests her chin in her hands, I brace myself for what's coming.

"When was the last time you went out? You know. Drinks. A movie. Dinner. Shopping."

"I hang out with people at work."

"That's work. You didn't answer my question."

Rule number one of counseling is that you can't run away during a difficult session. Letting go of the shoebox, I anchor myself to the chair with both hands. Bernie lets the silence grow until it is cosmic, then sighs, sinks back, and lets her hands fall to her lap.

The gesture does me in, it's so full of futility. Even Bernie doesn't know what to do with me.

"Your trouble, Rae, is that you only have two switches: full-on spotlight, or lights out. You need a dimmer switch. If you could modulate your emotional attachment to people—and animals—life would be so much easier for you."

I'm all about this easier life, and I think a dimmer switch sounds fantastic. But I've done the exercises and the journaling and the cause-and-effect chains and the feeling analysis. None of it works. Maybe because of this dimmer switch I'm missing, but also because everybody, including Bernie, lies about their feelings.

She doesn't want me to know what she's feeling. She wants to pretend that her emotional state is purely professional. But the acid wash of her anger and resentment swirls around in the pit of my stomach with my own anxiety and grief.

This is the thing she's never understood about me, as many times as I've tried to explain. I don't need body language or vocal cues to read her emotions. I feel them, just as surely as I feel my own. Her anxiety tightens my shoulders and quickens my breath. Her anger heats my blood. Right now, behind her oh-so-professional veneer, I know she wants this session to end as much as I do.

I need Bernie. I need these sessions. But it's not going to work with a morass of half-truths stretching between us. For the first time in years

I dare to speak what I'm not supposed to know, hoping against hope this time will be different.

"You're pissed at me. For making you feel vulnerable."

I don't need to see the infinitesimal lift of her eyebrows, the compression of her lips, the way her nostrils flare, to know I've crossed a line.

"What I feel doesn't matter right now," Bernie says, after a pause that is just a shade too long. "What matters is that you learn to handle your own emotions. Shall we go through a calming exercise? Perhaps—"

"No." I shake my head. "That doesn't work. I need to know what *you* are feeling. Right now. About me. About us. Are you hurt, pissed off, afraid? I bet you wish you'd stayed in bed this morning, or maybe called in sick."

"Rae, this isn't—"

"You keep talking about this dimmer switch thing. This is a perfect opportunity. Show me how it's done. Be real with me, Bernie."

For just a minute I think she's going to come clean. Her reserve falls away, anger firms the line of her chin. Her right hand clasps the stone at her throat. But then she takes one of those damned calming breaths and puts on a concealing smile.

"Deflection is a common defense mechanism," she says, far too gently. "I know this is difficult terrain for you, but—"

"I'm not deflecting." I get to my feet. "This isn't going to work, Bernie. I think we both see that."

"Rae . . ." Bernie stands and stretches her hand out toward me, as if she's going to touch my arm, grab my shoulder, reel me back in. She doesn't, though. Her hand drifts back down to her side. She doesn't say whatever she was thinking.

"Good-bye, Bernie." Tears distort my vision. I bump my hip into the doorjamb on my way out. Oscar's weight shifts in the box with a sick little bump and roll.

Bernie doesn't come after me.

Outside, the mass of clouds has grown darker. Thunder grumbles across the sky, and a gust of wind sweeps the pavement in front of me, raising a swirl of dirt and bits of paper.

Holding tightly to the box so the lid doesn't blow off, I bend my head and squinch my eyes half shut against the gritty wind. Once safely in the car, Oscar settled on the passenger seat beside me, I take three deep breaths before I turn the key.

Those breaths are Bernie all over again. Her words, her ideas, are embedded in everything.

I brush away tears. *Fuck Bernie. Who needs her?*

Me, that's who. I need her. I don't know how I'm going to manage without her, but I'm pretty sure I won't be coming back.

Chapter Two

Since I live in a rental house and lack a backyard for the purpose, I've taken to borrowing neglected graves in the Colville cemetery when one of my small creatures passes on. Nobody pays any attention to a sad-faced woman with a hand trowel planting flowers on an old grave. Most people look away, not wanting to see either grief or crazy, so it's never a difficult thing to slip a small body into the earth beneath the begonias or the petunias, or whatever flower I've chosen to commemorate the occasion.

If the storm holds off, I have just enough time before work to lay Oscar to rest. I've picked out the perfect grave for Oscar. It's away from the road, shaded by a tree. *Tom Childers, 1950–1956, May He Rest in Peace.* I figure Tom and Oscar can be company for each other.

In the back of my car, ready for the expedition, are my tools: a hand trowel, a watering can, and a pot of daisies. No need to bring extra fertilizer. The thought of Oscar as worm food twists my insides one more time. I pat his box again, this time to reassure myself.

A young couple saunters into the crosswalk, hand in hand, without even checking for traffic. I slam my foot onto the brakes. The car skids to a stop, momentum thrusting me forward against my shoulder belt. Oscar's box careens forward, slick as a toboggan on a sliding hill.

It tips onto its side. The lid comes off.

Oscar, stiff as a stone, rolls clear of his towel bed and out onto the floor.

I twist free of my shoulder belt and bend down and over to reach for him, but a horn blaring behind me jolts me upright. A man in a shiny sedan waves his hands, signaling for me to get on already. Glaring at Mr. Impatient in my rearview, I accelerate through the crosswalk, now clear, and on down Main Street.

Colville is a small town, and usually there's very little traffic, but today it seems the entire population has come out at once. Keeping one hand on the steering wheel, peering over the dash, I try to corral Oscar and get him back into his box, but I can't quite stretch my arm far enough while keeping an eye on traffic.

Approaching Third Avenue, I think I've caught a break. The light is red. I've got a right-hand turn. Just enough time to scoop up Oscar, and I'm off. But then a bicycle pulls up to the light beside me, and with it a whole new dilemma.

The woman on the bike, a sleek red machine nothing like the sec- ondhand object chained to my small porch, turns her head and makes direct eye contact. She's wearing a helmet, one of those trendy torpedo- shaped things, black and streamlined. Black spandex shorts and a mid- riff tank top expose a soft expanse of belly, burnt pink by the sun. Her face is flushed, strands of dark hair plastered to her cheeks with sweat.

Her eyes, for some reason, are hostile. They burn a hole through me, as though I'm an affront to her existence. Maybe I didn't see her and cut her off, maybe she's an environmentalist and objects to my rig, maybe she's just hot. Me, I've had about enough. If my being here offends her, she can get the hell out of the way. Holding her gaze, returning her glare, I miss it when the light finally changes.

Mr. Impatient, still behind me, leans into his horn. Clearly, he's not from here. On another day, maybe I'd ignore him. Who cares if I hold up traffic for a minute? So what if we all miss a light? Today I'm rattled and off-kilter. The sun glare is rubbing on my very last nerve.

I throw up my hands in a gesture of exaggerated frustration, then wave for the biker to go. I want to turn right. If I turn and she goes, we have a problem.

She just sits there. Still staring at me.

The horn behind me blares again.

I poke my head out the window and shout, waving my arm in an exaggerated sweeping gesture. "I'm turning right. Go already." When she doesn't, I throw my hands up in the air again, hit the gas, and accelerate into my turn.

The bike turns, too, keeping pace with me, as if we're a car-bicycle tandem unit.

I accelerate, wanting to rid my world of her.

The bike keeps pace, the rider bent forward over the handlebars, her legs pumping.

If she had superpowers I'd be on fire by now, the intensity of her gaze incinerating me from the inside out. My heart is beating way too fast, accelerating into warp drive. Everything else slows down. The houses, the pavement, the road ahead look flat as a painted canvas, stationary and unreal. All that matters is me, the biker, and Oscar, rolling gently to and fro on the floor.

The biker puts on a burst of speed, gaining on me. Her handlebars pass out of the frame of the passenger window, advancing on my front bumper. I ease off on the gas. The invisible band that ties us together stretches as she speeds up and I slow down.

Whatever that encounter meant, to her or to me, it's over. I draw a breath and let it go, checking my rearview for traffic.

Mr. Impatient is still right on my bumper.

I glance down at Oscar.

A dull thud, a jolt, a sound of metal on metal, snaps my eyes back to the windshield. The car lurches as the tires roll over something large before I fishtail into a skidding stop.

The street ahead is empty. All is quiet, peaceful. I can't see the bike.

A woman steps out of the apartment complex on the right, shading her eyes with her hand, staring in my direction. Her mouth opens and the screaming begins, high and sharp. Car doors slam behind me, voices shout.

I sit there, my foot frozen to the brakes, my hands welded to the steering wheel. If I uncurl one finger or move my foot a fraction of an inch, I'm certain the car will race away out of control and hurt somebody.

Kill somebody.

My insides quiver at the memory of the tires running over—something.

My door opens and Mr. Impatient's head pokes in. "My God. Are you all right?"

I should tell him I'm fine, but my tongue is stuck to the roof of my mouth, and I can't remember how to shape the word. "I've called 911," he says. "Sit tight. I don't see blood—are you hurt anywhere?" He sounds calm and in control, and that helps me take a breath. But then his face crumples. "My God. That poor woman." His hands start shaking. His head withdraws from my door, and a half a breath later I hear retching and a splatter of liquid on the pavement.

This is what shakes me loose from my inertia.

His shock. His reaction.

I don't need to ask what woman. He's talking about my road-rage biker.

My training kicks in. I shift the car into park and ease my foot off the brake. It takes three tries to get my seat belt unbuckled, but finally I scramble out into the heat and glare. Thunder rumbles in the distance, but the light is still overly bright. The red bicycle is crumpled and entangled hopelessly with my front bumper. I don't see the woman at first, but then my searching eyes find the crowd of bystanders.

Behind my car.

Behind my car. That bump I felt. That thing I ran over. My stomach contracts, and I almost join Mr. Impatient in a two-person vomiting brigade. Instead, I run toward the group with the sensation of running in a dream. It takes forever. I both want to be there and not to be there with equal intensity.

The crowd parts to let me through.

She's lying on her back, one knee bent, her head turned at an awkward angle. There's wetness on the pavement between her splayed legs. *Urine, not blood,* I tell myself. There is blood, though, beside her, behind her. A smear of it, like an abstract finger painting. Her chest rises and falls. She's breathing.

Irrational hope rises.

Maybe she'll be fine. It could happen. Knocked out, sure. A little road rash. A few scars. Someday she'll talk about them in a bar, tell the winning story of the time she survived getting hit by a car.

The tire track across her chest says otherwise.

I work with the elderly in extended care, not ER, but still my brain supplies me with what I don't want to know. Injuries will be internal, lacerations of liver or spleen. Ruptured bowel. Bladder trauma. Fractured pelvis. Not to mention her spine or her neck, for God's sake. She's probably bleeding out inside.

The woman makes a whimpering sound that brings me to my knees beside her. Her eyes are brown, wide open but blank and unfocused. A purple swelling disfigures her cheek. Blood smears her lips, and I don't know if it's because she's bitten her tongue or because of internal bleeding. I want to shift her onto her side so fluids can clear her throat and not choke her, but I'm afraid her back is broken.

"ABC," I remind myself. "Airway, breathing, cardiac."

She's breathing, or at least gasping, but her chest looks wrong. Part of it on the right side is doing its own thing.

Panic kicks in, my own heart trying to beat its way out of my chest.

I was driving distracted, and I ran over her. And now I have a chance to save her, but I don't know what to do. Looking up, scanning the crowd and hoping there's a doctor or an EMT just standing around, waiting for an invitation, my eyes meet those of people as terrified and incompetent as I am and then latch onto one familiar face. Mr. Impatient.

"You called 911, right?"

He nods, wipes his mouth with the back of one hand.

"Call them back. Ask ETA."

It can't be long. We're right here. Right in the middle of town. Any second the sirens will sound.

I go on with my assessment, as if I know what I'm doing.

Airway, clear. Breathing, for the moment. Don't think about if she stops, or if she starts to vomit or drown in her own blood.

Cardiac. Her heart is beating. Her pulse is rapid and fluttery but there.

I feel my way systematically down her body, checking for more broken bones. When I get to her hand, she grabs on and squeezes.

Her palm is scraped raw, blood smeared halfway to her elbow.

She's awake now, conscious.

"Hurts," she manages, between difficult breaths.

"The ambulance is coming. Hold on."

Her eyes, wide with pain and panic, encompass my whole world. Lashes thick and dark. Irises the clear liquid brown of a woodland stream, flecked with green. Eyebrows carefully shaped into the perfect arch. My own eyes burn and blur, but if I so much as blink I'm afraid she'll slip away from me. I stay with her, matching my own breathing to hers, holding her hand.

Her lips move, but the words are lost in the sound of a siren, loud and clear. A few seconds later booted feet and blue uniform pants enter my field of vision. Still, I don't take my eyes from my biker.

"How bad is it?"

The voice is male, young, not what I'd hope for from an EMT. He squats down across from me, face creased in worry. It's a cop, not a medic. Officer Mendez. His dad is a resident at Valley View, where I work.

"Ambulance is on its way," Mendez says. "They were out on another call. Probably fifteen minutes ETA."

I'm not sure we have fifteen minutes.

My biker's face is already paler. Her hand feels cold in mine. Her eyelashes flutter, the life lock between us wavering.

My fingers tighten around hers, and I touch her cheek with my free hand. "Stay with me."

Her eyes open again, but they are unfocused and blurred, and I'm not sure she still sees me.

"She's in shock," I tell Mendez, as if I know what I'm talking about. "We need to cover her, elevate her feet."

He's immediately on it. The crowd contributes useful items of clothing, blankets from their car trunks. Somebody hands me a first aid kit, the kind you can buy at the pharmacy for five bucks, filled with Band-Aids and a tube of antibiotic ointment.

"What's your name?" I ask, unfastening the biker's helmet, hoping that will ease her breathing.

"Kat," she whispers. Her eyes never leave my face, her hand locked so tight around mine my fingers ache with the pressure.

"Okay, Kat. Good. Officer Mendez is going to put a blanket under your feet, okay? Easy . . ."

The sound she makes when he lifts her feet tears through me. Her eyes close, her hand goes loose, and for a horrifying minute I think we've killed her. She's still breathing, though, her heart still beating.

I run my hands down her back, checking every vertebra in her spine, as if I'd know what a broken back feels like. When I get to her pelvis it creaks under my touch.

Kat whimpers. She's awake again, her eyes searching for mine, locking on, holding.

"Can't breathe," she says. Her lips are tinged with blue, maybe a trick of the light since the clouds have rolled over now. A fat raindrop hits my face, and then another.

"Yes, you can," I say, because she has to breathe. "Does this help?" I press my hand against her rib cage, stabilizing the fractured ribs.

"A little."

Rain is falling harder now. Somebody fetches an umbrella and holds it over Kat's head. Her breathing sounds wet, like she's filling up with water from the inside. Her eyelids flicker, then close.

"No, you don't." I squeeze her shoulders. "Kat. Come back here."

Her eyes open again, unfocused. Her hand fumbles blindly for mine, and again we're linked. Everybody else fades into the background, Mendez, Mr. Impatient, all of the bystanders.

"It hurts too much," she whispers.

"If you die, then I'll have killed you." It sounds selfish and brutal, given the amount of pain she's in, but it's the truth.

"No," she objects. "I . . ." She coughs, wet and ugly, fresh blood coloring her lips.

"Shhhh, don't talk. You're going to be fine. See all of these people? They all want you to hold on. Officer Mendez over there is going to be devastated if we lose you. Paperwork and guilt, probably forever, and he's got a wife and new baby to take care of."

Improbably, the corner of her lip moves in what might be the ghost of a smile, and I go on.

"That's Mr. Impatient, holding the umbrella. He was on his way to somewhere very important, but look at him, hanging around here to make sure you make it. Because you are more important than anywhere else he needed to be. So you can't make him waste his time. You see?"

This time I'm so engaged I don't even hear the sirens. There's a hand on my shoulder and then a uniformed body beside me, edging me out of the way. Kat won't let go of my hand, and they work around me. IVs and EKG leads. A backboard. When they lift her up onto the stretcher and into the ambulance I lose her.

Rain washes over me, drenching my hair, soaking me to the skin, but it doesn't cleanse away the blood from the pavement or the dirt ground into my knees. There's still a bicycle twisted under my car; there's still a dead rat in need of a burial.

All I can think of is that I can't drive anywhere until I move the bike. I grab the bent handlebars and give a tug, but it's trapped beneath the bumper.

"Hey, don't touch that."

It's Mendez, his hand on my arm like a band of iron. The teamwork we shared during the crisis is past. His face is set in hard lines I don't understand. *Crisis aftermath*, I tell myself. *Like Bernie and the rat.*

I try to twist out of his grasp, reaching for the bike. "I'm late for work."

"I called in for you. Your car's not going anywhere until we've done a scene reconstruction."

There's a slight hesitation before the word *scene*, and my heart takes an elevator trip down into my toes as the missing word shapes itself in my mind.

Crime.

Crime belongs with scene like toast belongs with peanut butter and ham belongs with eggs, but it has nothing to do with me. I've never even had a parking ticket.

I stare up at Mendez, trying to connect the dots. "Are you going to arrest me?"

"Should I?"

That hideous moment of impact, the wheels passing over something large and soft. I shudder, wrapping my arms around my chest.

"Hey." The voice belongs to Mr. Impatient, who moves his umbrella over my head, even though it's way too late to save me from the rain. "This woman is a hero. What the hell do you think you're doing?"

"My job. Do you have a lawyer, Rae?"

My whole body is shaking now, with chills, or reaction, or both. Of course I don't have a lawyer. I'm going to have to call my parents.

Mr. Impatient unbuttons his coat and drapes it over my shoulders. "I saw what happened," he says, holding the umbrella over both of us. "The bicycle swerved right in front of her. There was no way she could have stopped. Nothing she could have done. Did you ask any of the other drivers before leaping to your grand conclusion?"

I clutch at his words the way Kat clutched at my hand. Are they true? I play through the crash in my head again. The bike beside me. The rearview mirror. The glance at Oscar. That was the moment it all went wrong. I took my eyes off the road. Whether Kat crashed into me, or I crashed into Kat, it happened when I wasn't looking.

Mendez shoots Mr. Impatient a dirty look. "Thank you. If you would care to make a statement to Officer Jenkins over there, that would be immensely helpful."

"Fine. If you would care to hold this umbrella and maybe get this woman some medical attention, that would also be helpful." My protector hands over the umbrella and stalks off to a police car angled behind mine, lights flashing.

"Come on," Mendez says. "Let's get you out of the rain."

I follow him to a second squad car and climb into the back when he opens the door for me. At least I haven't been cuffed or read my rights. Jail seems a small punishment for having killed somebody.

If she dies.

Please don't die. Please.

"So?" Mendez says, sliding into the front seat and turning to look at me. "How did it happen?"

"I don't know. She was riding on the side of the road, just in front of me. I glanced down and . . . crashed . . ."

It's warm in his car, but I can't stop shaking. My stomach won't stay still, and I'm afraid I'm going to puke. I press the back of my hand against my mouth and try to breathe.

Mendez sighs. "Is there somewhere I can take you?"

"We're not going to jail?"

"No. Not today, anyway. There were four witnesses, including your bodyguard with the umbrella, and they all tell the same story. Nothing you could have done. The crime scene guys will have to do their thing, though, so your car stays here."

"Please take me home."

"Are you sure? Is there a friend you could call? Family?" He looks more like the friendly guy I've always known, now that he's done playing hard-ass, but it's too late for him to offer me comfort, and he knows it.

"Home," I say again.

All the way there I breathe against the nausea, holding the pieces of myself together. He walks me to my door, and as soon as I'm inside I lock it between us. I'm halfway to Oscar's cage, seeking the comfort of rat snuggles, when I remember. No more Oscar. I stop short in the middle of the living room floor, rainwater puddling around my feet, thinking about what the crime scene investigators are going to find in my car.

Chapter Three

My house feels wrong, as if somebody has come in and renovated in my absence. I stand still, breathing, shivering, dripping, trying to connect with my surroundings. There is my thrift store couch, shabby and stained, but broken in to fit my curves. My Nikes on the mat by the door. My poster prints on the walls—Monet and Chagall intermingled with surreal photomontages.

It's dark and stifling, all the blinds and windows closed up tight. My teeth begin to chatter despite the heat, my jaw and shoulders aching with the effort to contain my shivering.

I discard my soaking clothes in the middle of the floor. Rain has diluted the stains on my T-shirt into pale pinkish splotches that look more like Kool-Aid than blood. My jeans are ruined, gravel and tar ground into the knees. They cling to me like a second skin, leaving a rusty streak on my right thigh when I peel them away. Blood is caked beneath my fingernails and smeared up my arms to the elbows.

Shock.

My brain isn't working right, but I latch onto that one word. I need to move. I need to do something.

Get clean. Get warm.

The legs that carry me into the bathroom don't feel like mine, and the face gazing out at me from the mirror belongs to a stranger, ghost pale, blue eyes shading into gray. When my hand rises to touch the blood speckled on my cheek, the hand in the mirror does the same. Both the mirror woman and I are shivering, our blonde hair plastered to scalps and shoulders.

Turning from the mirror I strip out of my bra and panties and climb into the shower. But this is a cold that hot water can't begin to touch. By the time I give up and get out, the bathroom is full of steam, but I'm still shivering.

I pull on an old pair of sweatpants and my favorite oversized sweatshirt. Wrap myself up in a blanket. Something needs to be done with the heap of ruined clothes on the living room floor, so I stuff them into the trash can, get them out of my sight. But no matter what I do, I can't get warm and I can't stop the movie replaying on an endless loop inside my head.

Kat's eyes, inexplicably angry as she pedals along beside me. Oscar rolling around on the floor mat. The lurch of my car as the wheels roll up and over something in the road.

A person.

Kat.

Make it stop. Please, make it stop.

Maybe music will help, something light and catchy. I settle for Taylor Swift and turn it up good and loud, trying to drown out the noises in my head. Since I'm already as miserable as I think I'm capable of being—*unless she dies, unless she dies, oh God, don't let her die*—I tackle Oscar's cage. It hasn't always been Oscar's cage, of course. I've used it for a succession of small creatures.

This time I want the cage gone. Out of my room. Out of my house. Out of my memory.

Gathering up the bag that holds my clothes in one hand, and Oscar's cage in the other, I lug everything out to the trash cans. The rain has passed; the sun is breaking through the clouds. It's still well above the horizon, but the light has softened. The air smells of rain and grass.

For the first time since the accident I'm able to draw a deep breath. I stand there, barefoot in the wet grass, eyes closed, letting the sun warm me. The sound of a car interrupts my solitude. I ignore it, pretending it isn't there, waiting for the driver to either move on or turn off the engine, but the idling continues.

When I open my eyes, Mendez is watching me from his patrol car. My stomach lurches.

The world spins, and I brace myself on the trash can. There can only be one reason he's back so soon. Kat's dead and they've come to arrest me for vehicular homicide.

But when Mendez opens his door, it's not to read me my Miranda rights and put me in handcuffs.

"We're done with your car. Figured the least I could do is give you a ride over to get it."

My throat is dry as a bone, and I can't speak or swallow.

"Rae? You okay?"

I manage to nod but can't get out the question I need to ask. Maybe he sees it in my eyes. "She's in surgery," he says. "Some sort of internal laceration. You don't look so good, Rae. Maybe we should get your car another time."

I shake my head and manage to croak, "I'm fine. I'm good. Let me get my keys."

Shoes would be good, I remind myself, as I scoop up my house keys from the table. Maybe some clothes that don't make me look like I'm homeless. But I'm just going to get my car and come right back, so I shove my feet into a pair of sandals and call myself good to go.

Mendez opens the front door of the police cruiser for me, making it clear I'm not a suspect anymore. He tries to make small talk on the way, but his words are little more than a buzzing in my ears. I hope the listening noises I make are adequate and I'm not accidentally admitting to a crime.

When we reach the scene of the accident, the bicycle is gone. My car sits by the side of the road. From the back it looks innocent and normal. I wonder if there's blood on the tires or paint on the bumper.

"There was a dead rat in your car," Mendez says, opening my door for me. His voice is unusually tentative. "We took care of it. Figured you had enough to worry about."

A wave of gratitude takes me by surprise. Even knowing that Oscar is decaying ignominiously in a nearby dumpster, all I feel is relief that his interment is no longer on my worry list.

My car has been sitting in the heat with the windows closed, and I can tell by the smell that the rat removal wasn't immediate. My hands start shaking again, my whole body reliving the sensation of that bump in the road, solid and soft.

I start the car. Open the windows. Turn on the radio.

Mendez waits, watching, and I signal and pull away, watching in my rearview until he pulls a U-turn and heads in the opposite direction.

As soon as he's gone I want him back. Freedom sucks. I need purpose and a place to be.

I arrive at the hospital parking lot without conscious intent. I'd meant to go home and don't remember the turns that brought me here. But if Kat is dead, I need to know. If she's going to make it, I need to know that, too. Everything in my life teeters on the fulcrum of this important information.

Mount Carmel Hospital is familiar territory; most of the employees know me. I worked here for a couple of years when I first moved into town, before shifting to extended care as a better fit. I smile at Liz, behind the registration desk. She smiles back, but tentatively, staring at me as if I've grown antennae or turned green overnight. Gossip runs quick, and I figure she's already heard about what happened.

In the waiting room next to the surgical suite, a man sits in one of the chairs. There's a laptop open on his knees, but he's staring at the clock, not the computer screen. I take him in with one quick glance.

Dark hair in tight curls over a well-shaped skull, gray at the temples. Tailored suit, dirty at the knees and damp at the shoulders. A leather briefcase at his feet.

"Mr. Impatient," I say aloud, before I catch myself.

His eyes brighten in recognition; his lips curve in a tight smile.

He gets to his feet and holds out his hand. "Mason Montgomery."

"Rae."

"You don't look like a Rae."

"I don't?"

His hand is warm, but he ruins the shake by putting his other hand over mine, like a preacher or a politician.

"I've been calling you Barbie all afternoon."

"You have got to be kidding."

Surely the man isn't trying to flirt with me, not with Kat dying or maybe dead just beyond the forbidding double no-admittance doors that separate us from the operating room.

His eyes travel over me—crazy hair, baggy old shirt, sweatpants, sandals—and a spark of laughter lights his eyes. "Well, maybe Finger-in-the-Light-Socket Barbie."

My rising anger collides with the taut anxiety that underlies his awkward humor. I yank my hand away and take the chair on the far side of the small room.

"What are you doing here?" I ask. His presence feels like an intrusion, as if Kat belongs to me and I'm the only one who has a right to be here.

He shrugs. "Same thing you are. Guilt. Responsibility. I couldn't rest until I know if she's okay."

I remember the creaking of her pelvis under my hands, the deformed rib cage, the blood on her lips. She's not going to be okay for a good long time, if ever.

Mason glances down at his laptop screen and taps a couple of keys. I hope he's going to ignore me now, but no such luck. "I had a job interview. That's where I was going."

"Did you get it?"

"What? The job? I missed the interview."

He doesn't look like the sort of guy who would be interviewing for anything in Colville. That low-level anxiety wafting off him is at odds with his big-city persona, but then anybody would be rattled by watching somebody get run over.

"It doesn't seem to matter, does it?" His right leg bounces, jarring the laptop so he has to steady it with his hands. "A woman very nearly died. What's an interview in the balance of that?"

A rat.

An interview.

A woman's life.

Priorities and perspective. The man grates on my nerves, but I feel a weird connection to him, like we've known each other for years, not just a couple of hours.

"How is she? Have you heard anything?"

"Nothing, other than that she's in surgery. She was still in the ER when I got here. I told them I was a friend, but they still wouldn't let me in. Then the doc came out and said they were taking her to the OR. Bleeding internally. Fractured pelvis. Broken ribs and a flail chest, if that means anything to you?"

"How long has she been in surgery?"

"Three hours, ten minutes, and about fifteen seconds."

A quick jerk lifts the corners of his lips, as if he's given himself instructions to smile. Another couple of taps on his keyboard, and then he closes the lid and shoves it into his briefcase without powering down. "Who am I kidding? I can't work. I keep seeing her go down in front of your car. Horrible." He shakes his head and repeats himself. "Just horrible."

This is not helping my own nerves at all. I wrap my arms around myself to head off another bout of shivering, realizing as I do so how frayed the cuffs of my sweatshirt are. It's also three sizes too big and sports a skull-and-crossbones logo. *Great.* I've come in a ragged grim reaper outfit to a death vigil. No wonder Liz looked at me that way when I came in. Mason hit the nail on its proverbial head with that whole Light-Socket-Barbie thing.

"Hey," he says, concern in his eyes. "You okay? How about I get you a cup of coffee. I'll be right back." Without waiting to hear whether I want coffee or even like coffee, he's off, leaving his laptop in my keeping.

The level of implied trust alarms me. What makes him think I won't just take it and run?

I can't sit still, and I'm pacing the small space when he returns with two Styrofoam cups. "Forgot to ask what you like," he says, handing me one. "So it's got cream and sugar in it. Figure it's got to be swill, right? So I doctored it up for you."

His laugh is nervous, his movements tight and jerky. He's as rattled as I am. What I can't figure out is why. He didn't run over anybody. All he's guilty of is big-city driving in a small town. The coffee is bitter and burned, but at least it's hot. The cup warms my icy hands.

Mason sits, holding his cup but not drinking. While he was talking, his voice irritated me and I wanted him to shut up. Now I can't stand either the silence or the unspoken horror that tethers us together.

I make an attempt at small talk. "So, where are you from?"

"It's that obvious, huh? That I'm not from here?" This time, his smile is real. It softens his face, brightens his eyes. "Born and raised in Chicago."

"What on earth are you doing here?"

His right hand combs through his hair and then scrubs at the side of his jaw. "Running away."

"Aren't you a little old for that?"

"Family is family, no matter how old you are."

"Me, too," I say. His eyebrows go up, and I clarify. "Running away from family, I mean."

I ran away nine years ago, on my twenty-first birthday. Colville was meant to be a way station, a short stop on my way to freedom, but somehow I got hung up and never kept going. As places to be trapped in go, it's not half-bad. I love the mountains and the trees, and the people are generally good at minding their own business.

"Is that ruined now?" I ask him. "The running away? Seeing as you missed the interview and all."

"Rescheduled it for tomorrow. Couldn't have made up a better excuse." He sets the coffee on the table beside him, untouched. "God, watching her disappear in front of your bumper like that . . ."

My insides turn over at his words. Coffee and acid burn the back of my throat, and I can't quite swallow it all back down.

"Oh God. I'm sorry," he says, in a voice that means it. "I shouldn't have said that. I can't even imagine how you must be feeling."

"Like I ran over somebody. That's how I feel."

"Nothing you could have done," he says. "Like I told the cops. She turned right in front of you. A woman on a mission like that, you can't . . ." His voice chokes off. He pulls a tissue from his pocket and coughs into it, then blows his nose.

Time slows. His words refuse to make sense. His face behaves strangely, moving in and out of focus. There's a tiny black spot just above the bridge of his nose. A blackhead, maybe. Or a bit of dirt. I can't decide.

"What do you mean, a woman on a mission?" My lips feel numb and stiff, like I've been to the dentist.

"You didn't . . . nothing," he says, wadding up the tissue and using it as an excuse to turn his back to me on the way to the trash can. "Never mind."

"What kind of a mission? What are you talking about?"

Kat's face as she pedaled beside me. Kat's eyes, drilling into me. Kat's body . . .

I press the palms of my hands against my eyes, making bright-white light to burn out the images.

"God," Mason says. "I'm sorry. Me and my mouth. I thought you would have seen it."

"I didn't see anything. I glanced away, and then . . . I thought she'd lost control of the bike. Hit a pothole. I don't know." My mouth is dry, my voice muffled by my hands over my face. I don't want to look at him, don't want to hear what he is saying.

"I'd think you'd be relieved," he says. I hear the guilt in his voice, though. He's looking to make me feel better, not so much for me as to relieve himself from responsibility for the blunder. "To know it's not your fault. I mean, if it wasn't you, it would have been somebody else."

And that's when it all comes clear. By somebody else, he means him. He would have been the one with a bicycle crumpled under his bumper. It would be his tire that rolled a dirty tread track over Kat's shirt, broke her ribs, tore up her insides. His guilt, instead of mine. Anger burns through me, sudden as lightning out of a clear blue sky.

"Well, it wasn't you. It was me. Maybe if you hadn't been tailgating, I'd have been driving slower. Maybe I wouldn't have hit her at all."

Maybe I'd have taken time at the corner, picked up Oscar, and put him in his box. Kat and her bike would have been way ahead of me, and she could have wound up under somebody else's tires.

"You still don't get—" His voice cuts off sharp as a razor's edge.

Footsteps in the hall, a man in the doorway. He's still got a surgical mask hanging around his neck and has forgotten to take his paper booties off. Otherwise, he looks like some ordinary guy you might see hanging around the hospital, visiting relatives or waiting to be seen in the ER. I happen to know better.

Dr. Maxwell Klemmer, fantastic surgeon and all-round nice guy. He's also the inspiration behind Bernie's dimmer switch lectures.

"Rae." Max smiles at me, then fades to seriousness. "Oh no. It was you?"

"She turned right in front of my car. I couldn't stop."

"Poor girl." He doesn't specify which one of us he's talking about, but his hand descends, warm and comforting, on my shoulder. "Surgery was a success, you'll be happy to hear."

"She'll make it, then?" Mason breaks in, coming to stand beside me. He smells of deodorant-masked sweat. That, and fear. The deodorant commercial people are missing a market with that campaign.

Will your deodorant stand up in court?

Max looks from me to Mason and back again. "Friend of yours?" he asks me.

"Friend of Kat's," I clarify. "That's her name. Kat."

"I'm a witness," Mason says. "Driving just behind Rae. I saw everything."

"He helped save her," I add. Then look up into Max's face. "We did save her, right? She's going to be okay?"

"Stable for now. Unless something goes south, I think she'll do quite well. We're moving her to ICU. I think we can keep her here, rather than life flight her to Spokane. How she recovers depends partly on how her lungs hold up. And that flail chest—breathe, Rae. Don't pass out on me."

His hands grasp my shoulders and push me down into a chair. I drag a breath into my lungs and push it out again.

"Have you eaten today? You're pale as death."

I pull my hands up inside the sweatshirt sleeves and hug my arms over my breasts. "Can I see her, Max?"

"Not now," he says, as if I'm a child clamoring for a treat. "Tomorrow, maybe. Go home. Eat something. Get some sleep. This has all been a shock for you."

When I don't budge from the chair he stashed me in, he sighs, squats down in front of me, and takes both of my hands in his. "Rae. There's nothing you can do here. Take care of yourself first, and then you'll be up to visiting her in the morning. If she takes a turn for the worse, I'll call you. Deal?"

I nod, past words for the moment.

"I've got another emergency surgery. Gotta go." He smiles one more time, then leaves me, cold and very much alone.

My fault, as usual. I refused the second date, and with it, the possibility of building something with Max. What would it be like, now, to have a man who would hold me, shelter me, comfort me?

"Let me buy you dinner," Mason says. "Please."

Mason is not promising in the comfort-and-shelter department. I shake my head. "I don't think I can do food."

Even as I say it, my stomach does an empty wobble. I trace back through the events of the day, realizing that I haven't eaten so much as a breath mint. Breakfast was preempted by Oscar's death, which feels like days ago, rather than hours. I missed lunch because I was late for Bernie, and then there was Kat.

"A drink, then," Mason says.

Maybe he's hitting on me, but all my radar is picking up is an uncertain relief, an emptiness, a restless irritability that might be mine or his. My emotional super sensors feel fuzzy and full of static, blown up by a volume overload.

"You'd be doing me a favor. I don't want to be alone." The cuffs of his tailored pants are deformed by water and mud. There's a grass stain on one knee. Despite the graying hair he looks young and vulnerable, as much in need of comforting as I am.

"Do you always travel without your wife?" I glance pointedly at the white line circling his ring finger.

"Divorced." There's a hitch in his voice, and my heart softens. I've never bought into the opinion I hear from other women, that divorced men are dangerous, hormone driven and desperate. It's the emotionally available men who scare me.

Decision made, I stretch and push myself up out of the chair. All of the tension has drained out of my body, leaving me floppy and limp. "Want me to drive?" he asks.

I shake my head. "I'll meet you there. Sports bar, next to Benny's Inn."

We walk in silence out of the hospital and into the cooling evening air. I feel incomplete and unfinished, like I've walked away from work in the middle of a shift. I sit there long after Mason's rental turns out of the parking lot, my mind looping over and through the events of the day, caught up in a futile search for meaning.

~

The bar is loud and crowded and drowns out the thought loop in my head. Normally this sort of crowd is a torment for me, my emotional radar system picking up emotions faster than I can process them. But tonight, numb as I am, I find the press of bodies and clamor of voices unexpectedly comforting.

Mason has commandeered a small two-person table at the far edge of the room. I order nachos and a beer, but Mason starts in with whiskey, straight up, and keeps them coming.

"You driving far?" I ask, watching the second shot vanish down his throat in two long swallows.

"Staying right next door at the inn. Figured I might as well."

Relieved of the potential responsibility of driving a drunk home to bed at the end of the evening, I pick at my food and sip at my beer pretty much in silence. It's not until Mason is on drink number four and I've reached the bottom of the bottle that I dare to ask him what's on my mind.

"What did you mean, earlier, about Kat?"

"What about her?" His eyes are fuzzy. His hair, short and tightly curled, still manages to look rumpled. His tie is crooked.

"A woman on a mission, you said."

Mason under the influence is no longer a man in a hurry. He adjusts his little paper coaster so it's in the middle of the table and sets his empty glass down with a little thud.

"I'm going to tell you a thing," he says, wiping his mouth with the back of his hand. I wish he wouldn't, but I can see there will be no stopping him. When the waitress swings by I ask for another beer. I figure I'm going to need it.

Mason leans in closer, his tie dangling nearly in my nachos. "Truth time. It was my fault my wife left."

I steel myself for what I'm sure is coming, wishing myself well away from here. I should have known better. I did know better.

"You'll have noticed I'm an obnoxious asshole," he continues. "I drink too much. I work too much. She was my second wife, another failure in a long list of disasters. Plus, she went for the jugular with her financial demands, and she had a shark attorney."

"You were cheating on her, then."

"What?"

"She wouldn't have gotten your money if you weren't cheating on her. Or beating her. Were you beating her, Mason?" Alcohol seems to have unleashed my own mean streak, and I'm a little shocked to hear the words leave my mouth.

Mason laughs, though, as if I'm being charming and witty. "Work is my mistress," he says. "Who has time for two women? Or the energy. I don't know how men do it. Nope. Never said she got the money, just that she went for it. It was ugly."

I'm still waiting for the punch line. "And?"

"I let her have the house. I moved into this hotel in Chicago, working, drinking. Drinking a lot, to be honest. And it gets to where there doesn't seem to be much point to anything. You know? One night I take a good look around me. The room is sterile and cold and empty. I've got nobody. My exes are teaching the kids to hate me. Nobody loves me or would care if I was gone. This is what I told myself, anyway. And so, I pull all the towels out of the bathroom and lay them out around a chair. Get out my handgun, load it, and actually hold it to my head.

"That's a strange sensation. Where do you put the muzzle? I've heard horror stories about guys who meant to take themselves out and blasted off their jaw or half of their face, and failed to die. I try it under my jaw. In my mouth. At my temple. Nothing feels right."

"And then?"

"And then nothing. I went to bed. Woke up in the morning, put the gun away, and went on with my life."

He pauses to take a swig out of his new glass and catches the expression on my face.

"Don't look at me like that. You've thought about it. Fess up. Not a gun, maybe. But something. Everybody's got a method in mind."

"I don't."

"Sure you do. Everybody does."

He believes what he's saying. I can see that. But I have never in my life had the idea of killing myself so much as drift through my head. I can guess where he's going with this confession, and I don't want to hear it. Too late.

"Take this Kat, now," Mason says. "She had her own method. Not quite as sure as a gun, but these things aren't logical, you know?"

The only thing I know is that I need to get away before I come unglued.

I shove my chair back from the table. "Thanks for dinner. You've got this, right?" Not waiting for acknowledgment or a good-bye, I work my way through the crowded bar, my eyes focused on the door.

It's dark outside, cool now, with a breeze that smells of grass and dust and distant rain; I click the "Lock" button on my key fob, leaving my car where it's at and heading home on foot. Beer and nachos slosh around dangerously in my stomach. I don't realize I'm crying until the breeze picks up and chills my cheeks. I brush the tears away, feeling anger well up again to overtake the grief.

Out of all of the other cars and drivers on the road, Kat chose me. Used me.

Who does a thing like that?

Well, if she wanted somebody to take her out, she picked the wrong person. If there is one thing at which I excel, it's deflecting other people's plans for me. For the first time in this long and crazy day, I feel free, the righteous tide of anger clean and bracing as a north wind. Tomorrow I will shake off this whole thing. No thoughts about Mason or Kat. No visits to intensive care. Just my usual routine, and maybe I'll take on the orphaned kittens I told Jenny I couldn't handle a couple of days ago.

By the time I reach home, I've managed to convince myself that nothing in my life has changed.

Chapter Four

By morning, all of my good intentions are undone. At 10:05 a.m. I show up to ICU with a get-well-soon card and a bouquet of flowers.

"How is she?"

Van, the nurse on duty, looks like the wrong side of a night shift. His hair stands up in a bush on top of his head; a beard shadow darkens his jaw.

"Hey, Rae. Wondered when you'd be up."

"News travels fast."

"News of this kind, for sure. How are you?" He emphasizes the *you*, giving me the benefit of his full attention so that I know he's really asking, not just throwing me casual politeness.

I smile, to demonstrate how well I'm taking everything. "I'm good. A little sleep and some coffee cures everything. You, on the other hand, look like hell."

"Short-staffed again," he says. "Day shift couldn't make it in. I'm working 'til they find me a replacement. Last I heard, that might be by noon."

While I feel for the guy, I'm grateful he doesn't have the energy to challenge my own story. In reality, I slept restlessly and woke repeatedly to the sound of twisting metal, moans of pain, and the sensation of running over a human body. What I saw in the mirror this morning was not advertisement material for beauty sleep.

Van looks back at his screen, clicks a button, types a few words.

"She's critical, but stable. We've got her on oxygen, but no need for intubation, at least not yet. Urine was bloody, but now it's running clear. Vital signs are stable. Her head CT came back okay, so that's good news. Head injuries take out more bikers than anything else."

"She was wearing a helmet."

"Not much protection if the head gets squashed or hit hard enough. Anyway, she was lucky."

My mouth tastes metallic, an unwanted image arising in my brain of Kat's head popping like a squashed grape, and I swallow, hard. "Did we find her family?"

"Not yet. No ID on her, and she's been too sedated and out of it to talk to us. The cops are trying to trace her. Nobody in Colville seems to know who she is."

"Kat," I tell him. "Her name is Kat." From the desk I can look through a glass wall into a room where a slight figure lies inert, hooked up to monitors and IVs.

"We got that much," Van says. "Ambulance crew said you might have saved her life, you know."

"I didn't do anything. Look, Van, can I go see her?"

"I don't know why not. She probably won't know you're there."

All at once I'm not sure I want to see her. I could leave the flowers and go. Nobody would judge me. Nobody except me.

Coward, I tell myself, and tiptoe through the door into Kat's room.

It's hard to see the woman for the tubes. Tape distorts one side of her face, anchoring a suction tube in her nostril. The other cheek is the color of a ripe plum. An oxygen mask covers her nose and mouth. Her blood pressure and oxygen levels are stable. The EKG beeps out a reassuring and steady eighty beats per minute. Like Van said, the urine flowing into the catheter bag is clear.

Both hands rest on top of the sheets, bandaged, and I remember her hand and mine sealed together with the warm wetness of her blood, the way she wouldn't let me go.

Anger is easier than grief, Bernie always says. It's true. Guilt settles down on my shoulders as my anger dissipates. I pull a chair up close to the bed and lay my hand gently over her bandaged one.

"Hey, Kat, it's Rae. You know, the one who ran over you. Can you hear me?"

Her eyelids flutter, but her eyes don't open. She doesn't move. I bolster myself with Van's report that there's no brain injury. Pain and medications. That's all. I can't imagine how her body must hurt, from head to toe. My own joints ache, my knees bruised from kneeling on the pavement.

I clear my throat and move my hands to my lap. "Well, okay, then. I just wanted to make sure you're doing all right. The nurses are awesome here. Get well, okay? I'm sorry about your bike."

I sound like a babbling idiot.

As I start to shove the chair back, her lips move, but I don't catch what she's saying. The oxygen mask obliterates everything. Her eyes open and focus on me, and she lifts a hand to paw at the obstruction.

I ease her hand back down onto the bed. "Easy, you need that. Your lungs have been hurt."

Her lips move again, and this time I lift the mask away, just for a minute.

"Stay," she croaks.

Alarms go off all over the place. Oxygen level falling, heart rate rising. Something has kinked in the IV tubing, and the pump starts beeping. Van comes running in to see what's going on. He replaces the mask, adjusting the strap that holds it in place. Kat's eyes, panicked, cling to mine, and I pull my chair close again.

"Easy," I tell her. "You're going to be fine."

"Visitors might not be the best idea," Van says, frowning at the monitor. Her heart rate has jumped up over one hundred.

Kat's right hand wanders to rest over the broken place in her ribs. Her left reaches for me. I lay it gently down on the bed and place my own over top of it, weighting it there. Her eyelids drift closed, and she slips back into unconsciousness.

"She was trying to talk," I say. "I won't touch anything again. I swear."

"Nurses are the worst," Van mutters, walking around the bed, checking all the tubes and monitors as if he suspects me of tampering. "You know better. What did she say? Anything about family? Someone we could call?"

I shake my head, not wanting the sound of my own voice to cover the memory of hers.

Stay. That one whispered word breaks through every one of my carefully built barriers. Kat has nobody. No family, no support, barely even a voice just now. Warmth fills my chest. There's no more room for anger and confusion, only the certainty that if she needs me, I'll be here.

~

All that morning I sit by Kat's bed, soothing her when she stirs, watching the monitors and tubes and machinery as if my will alone can keep things operating smoothly. The day nurse, a woman I don't know, works around me like I'm part of the furniture.

Twice Kat wakes up, thrashing around until her wild eyes find mine, then sinking back into the dark. By noon I'm stiff from sitting. The nurse comes in to do procedures and kicks me out for a bit. I'm reluctant, but she's insistent.

"Go eat something. You have to take care of yourself, too."

I'm not hungry, but I head toward the cafeteria anyway, remembering when I'm halfway there that I'm expected at work in a few hours. The thought of getting myself from here to there seems unrealistic and unreasonable.

My cell phone will never hold a charge, but by some miracle it has one bar of battery left. I stop in the lobby to call in sick. At least I try. Jeannie is sympathetic, but sounds a little desperate.

"Are you sure?" she says, her voice pitched high with tension. "We've got nobody, Rae. Corinne worked a double yesterday to cover for you. She can't do it again."

Silence stretches while I search for an excuse that will work, some way to explain my situation, and that gives Jeannie time to latch onto her position of authority.

"I'm sorry, I'm sure you're shaken up from yesterday. But we need you."

Need again. This time being needed feels like duty and obligation, not a wonderful infusion of warmth. But responsibility is a huge motivator, and away from the bed and the monitors and the evidence of the damage done to Kat, it seems a little weird even to me that I'd skip work to stay with her.

"All right. I'll be in."

I'd meant to go back to Kat, but there isn't time. I'll have to go home to change. I still haven't eaten, and there's nothing in my fridge to take for my work lunch. I'm not hungry, but I grab a prewrapped sandwich and a bottle of water in the cafeteria and take it to the tables outside. The sun is hot, but it feels good on my cramped muscles. The cellophane wrapping on the sandwich has sealed itself so tightly at the seams it's going to require an act of God to get it open.

"Hey, Rae. Mind if I join you?"

The voice belongs to Cole Evans, LMHC, DMHP. A mental health crisis worker, and one of the people in town whose job it is to send the dangerously mentally ill or suicidal off to a locked unit for supervision and care. We've worked together on a few cases over at the nursing home.

I can't think of a word to say, and he takes my silence as permission, setting his tray on the table and sliding into the chair across from me.

He's casually dressed in faded blue jeans and a collared T-shirt. Dark hair with just a hint of a wave grazes his collar. His eyes are dramatic and vivid, a light brown that borders on amber. He also has a quiet intensity that makes me feel like those eyes are seeing more than I want to show him.

"You probably know why I'm here."

"You mean you're not just stalking me for the pleasure of my company?"

"That part is the bonus." He grins and stabs a straw through the top of his plastic drink container.

I can guess only too well the reason why he's here, and I don't want to talk to him. Gathering up my ill-fated sandwich, I shove back my chair and get to my feet. "I was just leaving. Sorry. I don't mean to be rude, but I have to get ready for work."

"When can we talk?" He transfers his lunch from the tray to the table. Salad. Vegetables. A big slab of roast beef flooded with gravy. Then his gaze arrests me again. "There's no urgency, since she's still mostly unconscious, but I'd appreciate your input."

I seem to have grown weights in my butt, and I plunk back into my chair, elephant heavy. He has hawk eyes. That's what they are. And I'm a squeaky, quivery little mouse without a hidey-hole. My hands are shaking again. I want to squeeze them together between my thighs, anything to make them stop, but they are still clutching a sandwich destined never to be eaten.

A fierce loyalty to Kat swells up inside me, bracing my spine. "Maybe it was an accident. It's all speculation, isn't it? Until she wakes up and can tell us herself."

"Right," he says, around a mouthful of roast beef. He pauses for a minute, chewing. "This is delicious. I had no idea. Is the cafeteria food always this good?"

"I don't eat here."

"I see that. You come here to play with the food. Maybe you could make a sculpture out of that."

My gaze travels to what I'm holding in my hands. The bread is flattened, mayonnaise oozing out and smearing onto the cellophane. A limp bit of lettuce is turning black around the edges. Another casualty of my life. A dead sandwich.

It takes me longer than it should to see that he's teasing. He doesn't smile, but his eyes have shaded into laughter.

"Here's the concern," he says. "Accidents aren't always accidents. Say maybe she did really want to die. When she wakes up, what's she going to do? It's my job to evaluate the risk."

It's also his job to send people off to a locked psychiatric ward. I've seen that happen, and it's not pretty. Colville doesn't have its own unit, and transport is done by a sheriff's deputy. I try to picture Kat in handcuffs, being marched down the hall to a cop car and then locked up somewhere with a bunch of crazy people.

The idea is ridiculous. She's not going to be walking anywhere for a long time.

"Pretty hard to kill yourself in an ICU unit," I tell him.

"It's been done." He sets down his fork and focuses his attention on me. His hands lie still on the table. His eyes are on mine. Every inch of him—body, mind, and soul—is listening to me. And every inch of me feels like it's burning. I've never been the subject of anybody's fully focused attention before, at least not like this.

I gulp water from the bottle to cool the heat.

"I don't have anything to tell you. I was driving, and then there was a bicycle under my tires. Maybe the witnesses saw something. There was this one guy—"

"Mason. Yeah, I talked to him. He claims she pedaled past you on purpose and turned right in front of your car. Definitely on purpose."

"He's biased."

"How so?"

"Tried it once himself and thinks everybody is walking around dreaming up ways to kill themselves. I'm not. I don't, I mean. Do you?"

"More people do than you'd like to think."

He says it with a dark twist of humor, but I recognize deflection when I see it. Like Bernie. All of the heat flows out of me, leaving me shivering again. I'm so utterly weary of games and deflections and parlor tricks.

Maybe my sensors are still on overload, because I can't read him. Gathering up all of my energy, I put my elbows on the table, rest my chin in my hands, and level a gaze on him that is as direct as I can make it. "You. Specifically. Do you walk around thinking about killing yourself?"

I wait for him to evade, for his intensity to waver, for him to hide behind his own professional creds, like it's a virtue or something. Counselors are good at using their licenses like armor. Bernie's not my first go-round.

He shifts in his chair. His right hand plays what looks like a short piano riff on the table. Here we go. What will it be?

This isn't about me.

My personal experiences are irrelevant.

His hand stills once more. "Once," he says. "When I was sixteen. Once was enough."

My emotional response is a mixed bag of shock, curiosity, sympathy, sadness, and a small, shining light of joy that he has chosen to be a human being with me. I can't tell him any of this. Can't think of a single appropriate response. So we sit there, silent, with the cafeteria noise wafting out through the open doorway, the sun overhead, the soft breeze blowing, and the knowing that he, Cole, the DMHP, has played with death, while crazy, scattered, messed-up Rae has never even thought about it.

After a long moment, Cole picks up his fork and pushes the food around his plate, not eating.

"How's the rat?"

"What?" I blink, disoriented by the shift.

"Last time I saw you, you had a baby rat. At work. Did he make it?"

"Oscar."

"That's right. Oscar. Perfect name for a rat."

"I was on my way to bury him when I . . . when Kat . . . when it happened."

The transformation on his face is like the shift from harsh daylight to dusk. A softening of all the edges, a gentleness that feels like a cool evening breeze on my hot forehead.

"Rough day" is all he says, but it feels like maybe he understands. He doesn't ask if I'm okay. Doesn't do gushing fake sympathy or treat me like a five-year-old who has just lost a goldfish. This quiet acknowledgment of the difficulty of yesterday soothes something inside me I didn't even know needed soothing.

But then he ruins it all.

"Her name is Katya Manares, by the way. She arrived at the bike hostel up Hotchkiss day before yesterday. There were a couple of other bikers there, who said she was quiet and polite but didn't really talk to them. Yesterday, she left all of her belongings there—backpack, wallet, and this."

He reaches into a briefcase and pulls out a folded square of paper.

The way my stomach responds to the tone of his voice and that piece of paper, it's a good thing I never got around to eating.

My universe narrows down to the paper and his hands. They are nice hands, sun browned, strong without being meaty ham fists. Hands that might play the piano or craft jewelry. There's a small gold ring on his baby finger and no white line where a wedding ring would be. He holds the paper delicately at the edges, unfolding it one square at a time and smoothing it on the table. Notebook paper. College ruled. He turns it so I can see.

The words blur in and out of focus, and I realize I'm crying again.

Cole passes me a napkin, and I blot my eyes and blink the tears away.

43

The note is written in blue ink. Cursive. Neat and flowing, totally unlike my own wild scrawl.

Tom,
None of this is your fault. I'm so terribly sorry, but I just can't do it anymore. I can't try again. I don't know how to be happy or to make you happy. You're better off without me.
Live and be well.
Love, Kat

There's no denial I can make in the face of this kind of evidence. My fingers feel numb as I refold the paper, hiding the words I don't want to see. Cole says nothing, waiting for me to process. When I slide the note back across the table to him and my eyes finally rise to meet his, I can't read his expression at all.

"I wanted it to be an accident," I whisper.

"I know. But you can't wish somebody happy, Rae."

I can, I want to tell him. *I do. Every day.* Not that it works, as far as I can tell. But it's something, the only response I can make to the heartbreak and suffering floating around in the emotional atmosphere.

"I haven't talked to her yet," he says. "So I don't know. But in case we need to send her somewhere to keep her safe, I need you to help me make a case. Just write up your impression of what happened that day. Not right now. You can give it to me later. It's the best thing you can do to help her."

Personally, I can't imagine how being locked up somewhere is going to help any suicidal person feel like life is worth living, but I find myself nodding in agreement.

Cole pushes back his chair. He hasn't eaten half of what is on his tray. Maybe talk of suicide kills his appetite, too, even if he does deal in it for a living. I'm busy slamming all of my inner doors on him and feeling manipulated. That honesty thing was just a trick to gain my cooperation.

But then he pauses in the act of getting to his feet and asks, "So where did you bury him? Oscar?"

I swallow the golf ball that appears in my gullet and shrug, aiming for a light response. "He was disposed of by a helpful cop. Whatever that means."

Tears again. I'm starting to hate them, but they have a will of their own, and what I want has nothing to do with their behavior. I smear at them with the back of my hand, waiting for some sort of condescending platitude to emerge from Cole's lips.

"Oh shit," he says. "That sucks big-time. Hey, maybe a memorial service is in order."

Now I think he's the one that's crazy. Either that or he's mocking me.

"I've got this," he says. "You have plans for Saturday night?"

Those are date words, and I stare up at him in confusion and suspicion, so many other emotions swirling around inside me that I can't begin to name them. He doesn't look like he's joking.

"I'll get some people together, and we'll commemorate."

"Like, in a church?"

He grins. "I was thinking marshmallows and beer. It will be good. You'll see. Call me when you've got your statement written, and we'll confirm details."

A business card drops on the table in front of me, and he walks away.

I watch him until he's gone, and then my eyes drop to the beige rectangle on the table. Just a business card, and not even a personal one. There's the counseling center logo on the left-hand side. The name: Cole Evans. Even the phone number isn't really his. If I dial it right now I'll get an answering machine at best, at worst a cool and efficient front-desk receptionist.

It's not like he's scrawled his phone number on the back of a napkin and tucked it into my hands with a meaningful leer. He's not asking me out on a date, just being ridiculously understanding about how I feel about losing Oscar. But then, he's a mental health counselor, and they're weird that way. Getting back to him about Kat would be the right thing to do. Still, when I get up to toss my mangled sandwich into the trash, I leave the card lying where he left it.

Chapter Five

I take a wide detour on my way in to work, following Highway 395 to Kettle Falls and then up toward Marcus. Another turn onto a little-used gravel road takes me to my wishing place.

Parking the car in a pullout, I skitter down a steep bank, holding on to trees and branches for balance, ending up on a small, gravelly beach.

Nobody ever comes here, at least not that I've ever seen, and I think of this place as mine.

Amid the gravel here I can always find stones that are small, flat, and perfect for skipping. There's a touch of magic, to my mind, because no matter how many stones I throw, the next time I come back there are more, and I'm sure they are new and different. I'm too old to believe in a stone fairy replenishing the supply each night, but I still watch for her out of the corners of my eyes, just on the off chance there's a better reality than the one I've been forced to accept.

Some days, when I have all the time in the world, I'll take hours selecting the perfect stone for my purpose, but today I don't have that luxury. A gray oval will do for starters. Nothing fancy required.

Standing at the edge of the beach with my toes not quite touching the water, I close my eyes and fill my body with the smell of river and trees and sunshine. Only when I feel like I am partly made up of river, stone, and sunlight, do I summon the image of Mason as I last saw him, more than a little drunk, hair disheveled, the pain naked in his eyes. Letting down the barriers a little more, I let my memory of his emotions flow through my own body.

Shame and failure, a hollowness in my belly.

Loss, an empty dullness in my chest.

Anxiety, a clammy dampness in my palms, a tightness when I take a breath.

I open my eyes on bright sun and sparkling water, superimposing the river world over the image I've built of Mason's pain.

"I wish you happy," I whisper, then send my stone skimming out over the water with my wish. It skips one, two, three times before sinking. As the ripples fade, I draw another deep breath, then release Mason from my consciousness.

Kat's stone needs to skip far and light, and I take my time, despite the uneasy pressure of work and the probability I'll show up late. I walk the entire beach, end to end, twice over without success, until I finally see the stone I want, submerged in water at the river's edge. I close my fingers around it, hefting its weight, checking the balance. It shines in the sunlight, black and lustrous.

The stone feels right, but when I open myself to my memories of Kat, it's all too much. Her pain is bigger than I am, and even the perfect stone is inadequate to carry the weight of my wish.

Keeping my eyes closed, I peel off my shoes and socks and stand on the sun-heated gravel, anchoring myself in the pain of each sharp fragment burning into the soles of my feet. Breathing in the sound of flowing water, the faint kiss of a breeze, I open myself wider, reaching for the essence of what makes up Kat.

And again, she is too much for me. When I bump up against the image of her eyes as she lay crumpled on the pavement, darkness blots out my web of connection to river and earth and sky, threatens to blot out *me*.

Gasping, I open my eyes, reorienting myself to the river world while retaining what I can of Kat. Knowing it won't be enough, I shout, as if volume will help me, "I wish you happy!" and loose the stone.

It slips from my fingers in the instant of release, and I know my throw has gone wrong. Still, I hold my breath as it strikes the surface of the sparkling water, waiting, hoping, but my wishing stone sinks like any ordinary rock. The breeze picks up, blowing my hair into my eyes, ruffling the surface of the water and turning it from blue to gray. I glance up at the sky, thinking a cloud must have drifted across the sun, but there is not a cloud to be seen.

Shivering a little in what is now a brisk wind blowing in straight off the river, I shove my damp, gritty feet back into my shoes and scramble up the bank to my car. When I turn the ignition and the clock comes on, I can see that I'm already late, but still I sit there, getting a handle on what has just happened.

The last time I missed a throw, Jenny's dog was sick and maybe about to die. Nothing horrible happened, I remind myself. The dog recovered. Jenny got a kitten for good measure. My wishing game is nothing but a childish superstition, something I do to make myself feel better, and in my head I know this.

Still, I'm shaken.

"Not my problem," I tell myself, out loud. "Not my circus, not my monkeys."

Even as I say it, I know these words are a big, fat lie. Kat and I have been tied together from the moment her eyes met mine through the window of my car, the bond deepened during the time I tried to hold her away from death. We are blood sisters now, and there's no point fighting the inevitable.

~

By the time I run down the hall into the office, I'm more than a little late. Corinne has already changed into her civvies, her purse waiting on the desk beside her, ready to roll. Her fingers fly over the screen of her cell phone, texting with an enthusiasm that I'm pretty sure is born of annoyance.

"I'm sorry, I'm sorry, I'm sorry." I slide into a chair and give her my best apologetic smile.

She flies up out of her seat, flings her arms around me, and envelops me in a hug that smooshes my face into pillowy breasts. When I try to breathe, one of the frills of her silky blouse sucks up against my nostrils, blocking airflow.

I flail with my arms, trying to find purchase somewhere to push her back, my hands sinking into the softness of her belly. She hugs me tighter, and I start to panic and laugh at the same time, picturing suffocation in her sympathetic bosom.

But she releases me before my air hunger grows dire, and steps back to look at me, keeping her hands on my shoulders. I luxuriate in breathing, welcoming in even the dubious odors of nursing home life, mingled with the perfume-scented sweat emanating from Cor.

"You're okay!" she says, as if I've been to the moon and back in a damaged spaceship. "You're never late. I was worried. I'm so sorry I couldn't work tonight. I'd have done a double again, only I'm watching the grandbabies tonight, and they don't have another sitter. Is it true, what happened?"

She steps back, keeping her hands on my shoulders. "Are you sure you're all right? You look shell-shocked. Like one of those refugees on TV."

"Finger-in-the-Light-Socket Barbie. Thank you so very much." I feel like that invisible camera is watching me again, feeding footage out to a critical audience.

Rae, shaken and unsettled, returns to her natural habitat. The struggles of the past twenty-four hours are clear in the bags beneath her eyes, the windblown hair. Is it a trick of the light, or are those nursing scrubs looser than usual? If she grows much thinner, she may fade away altogether.

Corinne makes a clucking sound with her tongue. "Don't be silly. You're beautiful, like always. Just—here, let me fix you." She proceeds to gather up my hair and smooth it into a braid, talking all the while.

"I just can't believe it. So sudden. So unexpected. Don't you worry, I've told the rest of the staff all about everything. You won't have to do a thing."

"I won't?"

"Just this once, let us take care of things for you. I'm in charge of food. Tia will handle the service. Does Saturday evening work for you? It's good for the rest of us. Don is working, but we wouldn't want him to come anyway, so that's perfect."

Cor unearths a hair tie from her pocket and secures my braid, then straightens my scrub top and removes a smudge from my cheek with her thumb.

I blink at her. "Wait—what are we talking about, exactly?"

"The memorial service, honey. You need some closure, and we are all here for you."

"But she's not dead," I say, as the panic threatens to knock me off my feet. Maybe Kat took a turn for the worse but nobody called. Maybe nobody wanted to tell me. My heart drops like a stone. "Oh my God. Did she die? Did I kill her?"

It's Corinne's turn to stare, her mouth open but no words coming out, a highly unusual state of affairs. "Kill who? Oh, you mean that woman," she says, as if this thought had never occurred to her. "No, of course not. Or at least I haven't heard anything. I'm talking about Oscar. We're all so sad. We had a part in his life; he spent so much time here with us when he was tiny."

"Cole talked to you."

"Nancy Weathers. I mean, yes, Cole was here to talk to Nancy. We've got her on a watch of sorts. She's been talking about dying all weekend, and today we found a little hoard of pills in her bedside drawer. Poor thing. She just broke right down and wept when we took them away from her, said she didn't want to spend another day in this horrible place and why won't we just let her go home? We've got her on watch. Everything sharp has been cleared from her room, and when Chris hands out meds, make sure the old dear hasn't cheeked them. Oh my. Look at the time. I have got to get out of here. Let's do report, shall we? Mostly there's nothing new, but . . ."

I lose track of her voice as she goes through the report book, staying just tuned in enough to register a shift in tone when she mentions something important. Cor is a wonderful human being, but if I try to listen to everything she says, meaning gets lost in an ocean of words. Besides, I'm busy trying to sort out how I feel about a party commemorating Oscar.

Shared grief is a novel idea. Who knew Oscar had so many friends? I'd thought of him as mine. This infusion of Cor's sympathy, the idea that the rest of my coworkers might feel sad, punctures a little hole in my dark bubble of grief, shifting it from something that was mine alone into communal property. I feel lighter. I also feel a loss.

Corinne slaps the report book closed and plunks it down onto the desk beside me. "Well, there you have it. Nothing new, apart from the thing with Nancy, so you're all set, and I'm off home to the grandbabies. We'll bring things we can roast over a campfire, okay? That was Cole's idea. Marshmallows and such. I wonder if Oscar would have liked marshmallows? Probably not good for rats, but who knows? Seems like it doesn't hurt the wild ones any. I was in Seattle once, and two of them ran right past my feet. Big as my cat, can you believe it? And sleek and shiny. Life's just not fair, at all, with those nasty things living forever and probably carrying plague, and poor little Oscar taken so early. All right, then, I'll just be going. I'll see you tomorrow. Take it easy tonight, if you can. The CNAs can do almost everything."

She's already down the hall and into the lobby before this speech is over, and she turns to wave at me before heading for the door.

Despite Corinne's parting advice, there's no taking it easy. The pace here is always hectic. A lot of the residents need help with the most basic daily living activities, so there's a round of getting dressed and cleaned up and pointed toward the dining room, for starters. I help with this when an extra pair of hands is needed, besides dressing the wounds that so easily develop on fragile skin, checking blood sugars, doing assessments, and a myriad of other tasks.

When I run out of legitimate excuses, I drag myself into Nancy's room, determined to do a safety check and get away clean without any conversations about death. I've had my fill of that topic for the rest of my lifetime.

Although I know Tia got her up and put her in her wheelchair, Nancy is lying on top of the bed, flat on her back, hands loosely clasped on her breast with a single red rose placed artistically between them. She doesn't move when I call her name.

"Nancy!"

Not so much as a twitch.

Her eyes are open, staring up at the ceiling. I can't tell if her chest is moving.

Shit. Is she a code or a no code? I can't remember. I shout for help and dash toward the bed. Just as I reach out to put a hand on her chest, she sucks in a breath and turns her head in my direction. Her angular face cracks into a grin.

My heart stumbles over itself, trying to figure out what it's supposed to do, and I can't quite catch my breath.

Nancy sits up, laughing so hard the tears run down the grooves life has carved into her cheeks. "You should have seen your face!" She slaps her thigh with a blue-veined hand. "Priceless."

"You're trying to kill me," I say, sinking down in the wheelchair parked beside the bed.

"No, I'm trying to kill myself." She adjusts her face into a mournful expression, droops her shoulders, transforming from gleeful old vixen to a poor pitiful crone in a matter of seconds. "No hope. No point. Why won't you people let me die in peace?"

When I continue to stare at her without response, she lays the back of one hand across her forehead dramatically and drifts back onto the bed, emitting a tremulous little moan. She's the perfect picture of a lady suffering an attack of the vapors, and I remember, a little late, that she was an off-Broadway actress before the stroke that confined her to a wheelchair a few years back.

I get up from the chair and pick up her untouched dinner tray. "I guess you won't be needing this, as you're actively dying. I'll just take it back to the kitchen."

"Hey, I want that!"

I turn around and glare at her.

"You're no fun." She sits up and smoothes her hair, disheveled by the theatrics. "Bring me my tray. It smells amazing. You took forever to come in, and there I was, knowing all of that good dinner was getting cold."

Leaving her sitting on the side of her bed, I pull over a table and set up the tray.

"Want to tell me what this is all about?"

"I'm bored," she says, diving into the food. "This is delicious. Although, what I really want is a good restaurant meal, you know. Mexican, maybe. Why do they never do Mexican?"

"Because everybody gets heartburn."

"And gets the shits," she says, grinning at me. Her eyes in her wrinkled face are dark and clever, still sparkling with laughter at her own prank. "Is there even Mexican in town? Because somebody could bring me some. I'm not given to getting the shits.

"That was a hint," she adds, when I don't answer her. "No reason you couldn't stop by and bring me some enchiladas or some such. Is there? Death by cheese would be infinitely preferable to me overdosing on pills."

"You weren't ever going to take those pills, were you?"

"Are you crazy? Here? That would be the stupidest thing ever. A body is barely allowed to breathe without somebody watching. I've had my stomach pumped once before—I'm not bored enough to do that again."

She waves her fork at me. "I don't blame you, dear. Bureaucracy, that's what it is." She shoves another bite into her mouth and chews thoughtfully. "I heard about the demise of the rat. Can I come to the memorial thing?"

"I'm not sure there's going to be a memorial thing."

"Oh, my dear, you can bet your sweet bottom there will be a memorial. It's not a thing anymore, either, it's an Event. Taken on a life of its own. I've heard about it from the bath aide, the janitor, Tia—oh, and Corinne, of course."

She's crazy, I tell myself. *Faking suicide.* Why am I going on as if this is a rational conversation? I've checked on her. I can get up now, leave the room with a clear conscience.

My butt stays firmly planted in the wheelchair. "They can't possibly all care about Oscar."

She looks at me like I'm the crazy one. "Of course not. I told you, it has become an *Event.* Events have a life of their own. Same reason some people go to church services or like to attend funerals. They don't give a rat's ass about God or the deceased; they just want to eat good food, see what everybody's wearing, and dish out some gossip."

"You are a piece of work," I say, getting to my feet, but I can't help my lips quirking up into a smile.

"Did you like what I did there? The rat's ass thing?"

"Brilliant. I've got to get back to work." I'm trying with all my might to hang on to the heaviness of my grief, but my heart feels almost buoyant as I head for the door. I have an unreal sensation, as though my feet are barely touching the ground and I might lift off and float down the hallway.

"So can I come?" Nancy calls, just as I reach the door.

I turn around to look at her. "Maybe. I don't know. It depends where it is. Your chair has to be able to get there."

"I'll continue to be suicidal if I don't get to go."

"You're not suicidal."

"Nobody knows that. You can't prove it. I'll say you didn't check on me, and they'll find me in a heap on the floor, oh-so-pathetic. Your word against mine."

"Blackmail, now? Isn't that a little beneath you?"

"I'm a desperate woman, Rae. Come on. I never get out." She tips her head to one side, and her eyes go dreamy. "Although, being suicidal has its perks. That Cole is a beautiful man, don't you think? Almost worth a stomach pumping to spend another hour with him."

"Oh my God. You are incorrigible."

"So I can go?"

"If there's a thing. *If.* I'll try. No promises."

"Oh, there'll be a *thing,*" she says, mimicking my tone. "An *Event* is not a thing. Two very different creatures, I'm telling you."

Outside the door I very nearly collide with a slightly built man, shorter than my five foot six, with a kind face and tired eyes behind wire-rimmed glasses.

"How is she?" he asks, helping me steady the tray. "I heard all about it. Poor old dear. Life can be so hard for the elderly. I'm beginning to have some aches and pains myself. Slowing down a little, but there are miles on the old rig yet."

He's got to be seventy, minimum, and he's in for trouble if Nancy heard him refer to her as a poor old dear. But his age and manner make him the perfect chaplain for Valley View.

"She's fine, really," I tell him, starting off down the hall. "But I'm glad you're here to talk to her." I raise my voice, using distance as an excuse. Nothing wrong with Nancy's ears, and I want her to hear me.

"I'm sure she'd be delighted if you would pray with her, maybe read from the Psalms."

"Oh, Rae?" he calls after me. "I'm sorry to hear about Oscar."

He's got his sympathy face on, the one I've seen him wear when he's consoling the family after a resident's death. He clears his throat. "If you'd like, I'd be happy to say a few words at the memorial. Even rats are God's creatures, after all."

"That would be . . . great. Thanks so much."

See? Nancy says inside my head. *An Event. Not like a thing, at all.*

Chapter Six

Where Monday was all bright light and sharp angles, Wednesday is shaped like an amoeba—an amorphous, gelatinous sort of day full of guilt and inertia. It's eleven o'clock before I finally climb out of bed, and even then I feel sluggish and heavy. By the time I've managed to get ready for the day, I have just enough time to go see Kat before heading off to work.

I'd meant to bring flowers, but there's no time for that. By the time I drag myself into the ICU guilt might as well be my middle name. There's not a nurse in sight at the desk, so I bypass checking in, relieved not to have to speak to anybody, and let myself into Kat's room.

She's not alone.

A man sits in the chair beside her bed, one ankle crossed over his knee. His shoes are black and polished to a mirror shine. The socks are black and long enough to cover the expanse between the shoe and a pair of black slacks. His head is bent over a magazine in his lap. I can't see his face.

Her husband, I think. *Tom. Come to comfort her, encourage her, take her back home. Whatever drove her away, he's here to make it right.* A whole romantic movie episode plays through my mind, complete with full orchestra scoring and a sunset over ocean waves in the background.

The imaginary camera zooms in.

"I'm so sorry, my darling," movie Tom says, cradling Kat in his arms as if she weighs no more than a child.

She wears a dress, something flowing and white. Her head rests on his broad chest. "I'm the one who's sorry, my love. I'll never leave you again."

"Here, you can have the chair. I should be going, anyway." A man's voice jars me out of the daydream. It does not belong to the Movie Husband of the Year. Instead, Mason stands looking at me, one hand resting on the back of the visitor's chair, the other gesturing toward it. My eyes flow over him and then past to the woman lying on the bed.

"Are you okay?" he asks, the tone of his voice shifting to alarm.

"What's wrong with her? What happened?"

The bruises on her right cheek are ghastly today, a dull greenish black. Her eye is swollen shut, the lid purple and grotesque. That's to be expected. The oxygen mask is gone, replaced by a nasal cannula. The suction tube is no longer taped to her nose. These are good things.

What's bothering me is her hands, bound to the railing with soft restraints.

Her good eye flickers open.

She tugs at the restraint closest to me. "Please," she croaks through dry lips.

"What the hell?" I ask Mason, my hands already undoing the release. I glare at him, as if he's the one who has tied her up.

"Now you've done it." He reaches out to stop me, but it's too late. Restraints are easy to undo if you know the trick.

Kat flexes her fingers, as if they are stiff, and detaches a strand of hair that has stuck to her lower lip. "Thirsty," she says.

There's a carafe of ice water beside her bed and beside it a half-filled glass with a straw. Between that and the absence of the tube into her stomach, I assume they're allowing her liquids.

"Just a sip," I say, holding the cup and putting the straw between her lips. She holds it with the free hand, lifting her head a little from the pillow and sucking down water.

"Easy," I tell her. "You don't want to be sick."

Restlessly, she gropes for the release of the other restraint.

Mason grabs her hand and holds it back. She fights him a little, grunts with pain, and gives in, letting her arm flop back onto the bed. The beep of the EKG monitoring her pulse accelerates. With each breath she gives a tiny moan, as though it hurts her.

I glare at Mason and he releases his hold, raising both hands, palms up. "Hey, don't shoot me. There was a sitter here when I showed up. She asked if I'd watch while she went out for a smoke. She specifically said not to undo the restraints."

"That's crazy." Still, I hesitate to undo the ties on Kat's other hand.

"Not so much. Apparently, Kat pulled out all the tubes—the one from her stomach, her catheter, something in her chest. So they sedated her and put her in restraints. They're waiting to see if they need to put any of them back in."

He's overdone the cologne, and it smells expensive and demanding, taking control of my olfactory senses whether I like it or not. I don't like the way we're talking about Kat as if she's inanimate, so I turn my attention back to her.

"Lots of people get confused on pain meds. That must be what happened to you. I'll talk to them about the restraints."

Her gaze sharpens, lasering in on Mason. "Why are you here? Go away," she whispers. "Please."

Her free hand drifts to the broken place in her ribs, splinting them to ease her breathing.

I glare at Mason. "You heard her."

"She's not making sense . . ."

"Does it matter? You're disturbing her. You need to go."

"Fine. But let me tell you something." He beckons me to the door of the room. I sidle after him, crab-like, reluctant to take my eyes off Kat.

Mason stops in the hallway. He drops his voice to a whisper, but it's still too loud. "What I told you the other night . . ."

"Right. You told me so. I don't want to talk about it."

"That's not what—"

"Look. I have just a few minutes to visit with her, and then I have to go to work. Can we have this conversation later?"

A light dawns on his face, and I see my mistake. He's not a man to accept a brush-off. He'll hold me to that.

"Sure," he says. "Maybe over coffee or dinner."

"Right. Some time when I'm not working." I back into the room, drawing the curtain behind me to shut him out.

"I don't know why he comes here," Kat says as soon as he's gone. "What does he want?"

And as irritated as I was with Mason a minute ago, now I find myself defending him. "It was hard to watch, you lying in the road like that. He wants to see that you're okay."

"He didn't run over me. What's he feeling guilty about?"

"I'm not here because I feel guilty . . ." I begin, but stop on the lie. There are other emotions to sort, but guilt tops the list. When—*if*—I go to see Bernie next week, she'll make me tease them out, one at a time. "What color is this emotion?" she'll ask me. "What does it feel like?"

No color at all. Not white, made up of all the colors but black. Raven's wing black. That should be a crayon color. Maybe another shade called "bruised." Bloodred probably already exists.

With a little sigh that goes straight to my heart, Kat lets her eyelid drift closed. She lays the back of her hand across her forehead, as though it aches. "I remember him. From the accident." She licks her lips, and I hold the water for her again. "I bet he's the one who talked to that crisis guy."

"A crisis guy? What crisis guy?" I'm sure she can hear the guilt in my voice. I make a point of wiping up the ring of water on her nightstand left by condensation.

"Maybe I dreamed him. But it seemed real. He came in here, asking all these questions, like he thinks I did this on purpose. The nurse made him go away."

Her hand drifts back down to her side. Her eyelid opens, and she pins me with a direct question. "Was I dreaming? Was he here?"

I pull up a chair to the bedside, using the motion and the time to avoid her gaze. I don't want to tell her that I've spoken with Cole. Just the fact that I was civil to him now feels like a betrayal.

"He might have been here," I say, cautiously. "What do you remember?"

"He was here," she says. "He brought my backpack from the hostel. He thought I might have done this on purpose. This!" Her hand hovers over her bruised cheek, the fractured ribs, bandaged belly, broken pelvis. "Who would do a thing like that?"

Silence grows between us. Before it can flourish into a jungle of doubt, I ask, "Do you remember what happened?"

"I remember you. In the car. Glaring at me through the window like I was a mosquito you'd like to squash. And then I remember waking up in the street with your face looking down at me. I thought . . ."

Her head moves restlessly on the pillow. "The crisis guy—he says I turned right in front of your car. That there was nothing you could have done. Other people said the same."

We sit with this, neither one of us able to supply a memory blazoned with the label *What Really Happened*. We're stuck with accepting other people's versions of an event so earth-shattering neither one of us will ever be the same.

"They found a note," I blurt out. "To your husband."

Kat's forehead creases. "I don't understand."

"With your belongings. At the bike hostel. They found a suicide note . . ."

"I never wrote such a thing. How could they say . . ." She pulls on the bed rail with her free hand, tries to sit up, and falls back with a groan. Sweat beads her forehead. Her face has lost all color.

"But there was a note," I insist. "To Tom. From you."

She focuses on breathing, her hand pressing against her ribs, and I think she's not going to answer. Finally, she says, "Not a suicide note. Just . . . I meant to leave that for him when I left. So he wouldn't worry. I didn't, I guess."

Relief floods through me. I review the note in my mind. There's no mention of suicide, or death. It could easily be a good-bye note. Cole, Mason, they're both jumping to conclusions.

"It was an accident," I tell her, finally. "That's all."

"It's a nightmare," she whispers. "I want . . ." Her voice fades, and I think she's drifted off again.

"I know." I wish I had magic hands, that I could trace my fingers over the damage to her face, her body, and undo what has been done.

"Don't let them," she says, and now her hand fumbles for mine and grips it. "Don't let them lock me up."

I swallow something in my throat. My pulse sounds like dark wings beating at my temples.

"Please."

"All right. I won't let them." The words have a leaden finality to them, as if I've signed and sealed some sort of deal.

"What did you do?" a voice demands from the doorway. It's not a soft, sick-room voice at all, and it belongs to a woman in uniform. She's as large as her voice, tall and broad beamed, solid rather than fat. With her there is no hesitation. She comes to the bedside and gestures for me to release Kat's hand.

"You should go," the sitter says. "Let me fix this."

I wait for Kat to say something, but she just lies there, eyes closed. She releases my hand. A tear glimmers on her lashes, then glides down her temple and into her ear. I want to wipe it away, but I've been dismissed. When I get up, the sitter drops into the chair with a little grunt, immediately redoing the restraint.

Out in the hallway, I blink in the fluorescent lights, dazzled and confused. The nurse is back at the desk, typing something into the computer. Her eyes drift up when I stand there, waiting. "Yes? Oh, it's you. Rae, right?"

"Are the restraints really necessary?"

"We'll reevaluate."

"Surely, with the sitter there . . ."

"Last night we weren't able to restrain her. Patients can be crazy strong when they get agitated. Was there anything else I can do for you?"

Another dismissal.

Not wanting to wait for the elevator, I make my escape down the stairs. In the lobby I run into Mason. I'd forgotten about him, that he might be waiting for an opportunity to speak in a low voice about how horrible it is, that a woman would want to take her own life. So young. So beautiful. So sad.

Only now I can tell him that he was wrong. The note is wrong. Only, if this is true, why does the darkness continue to weigh me down?

"I thought you'd be long gone" is what I say. I don't want to stand around and be polite, and there's nothing I want to hear from him. I head across the lobby, toward the door.

Mason follows. "Business."

"Wasn't your interview yesterday?"

"I'm waiting to hear. They said I was overqualified."

"For what, exactly?" I immediately wish I'd bitten my curious tongue, but I can't imagine what he's planning to do in Colville with his Chicago impatience and his fancy suit and expensive shoes.

"Selling real estate."

Maybe he's kidding. I stop to take a long, hard look. Nope. Dead serious. I try to picture him showing a mobile home plunked down in the middle of forty acres of nothing to a guy in a dusty pickup truck, and fail.

"It's, um, sort of a specialized market around here," I say, cautiously. "Not exactly what you're used to."

"That's why I'm here. What I want. A slower pace, a different life. Besides, my mother is here."

That makes more sense, then. He could be a dutiful son, maybe, although I give him about a week as a real estate agent in this town. We've reached the front doors and my freedom.

"Well, good luck with that. Have a great day!"

"I gave a statement." He stands still, holding the door, but his words follow me. "To that guy. Cole. That's another reason for the sitter."

My steps slow, my feet mired in the implications of what he's saying. I could tell him what she said about the note, but I don't stop, don't look back.

In my car, though, the memories thud against the inside of my skull, laundry spinning in a drier, around and around and around.

Kat's eyes burning into me.

Her fragile-looking hands tied to the bed rails.

Her words. *Don't let them lock me up.*

Her lips moving silently just before the ambulance showed up. I've told myself over and over that I couldn't hear her. The siren was too loud. I'm not a lip-reader. But I understood her perfectly well. *Please. Let me die.*

I lean my forehead against the steering wheel, letting the heat burn into my skin. *It was the pain talking,* I tell myself. *Fear, maybe.* People say these things all the time, even when they're just sick with the flu. The note could easily be just what she said.

But my promise feels heavy. If she's lying to me, if I don't say anything and she manages to kill herself even in ICU, it will be like I've killed her twice.

Tearing a sheet of paper out of the coiled notebook I keep in the car, I write the date at the top, and then *To Whom It May Concern.* My fingers twitch with the desire to crumple it up, toss it in the backseat, but instead I keep the pen moving, writing out my statement for Cole. I include that Kat on her bike looked angry, not frightened or grief-stricken. I write what she told me about the note just now, and I write what she whispered before the ambulance came. I state my opinion that it's all kinds of wrong to put her in restraints. I sign my name at the bottom, and after a brief hesitation, I print my full legal name along with the date. Elizabeth Leila Blackwell Chatworth, a.k.a. Rae.

My plan is to drop it by Cole's office and leave it with the receptionist. But when I start my car and see the clock I realize that I'm already going to be late for work. Again. No time for detours. I could fax it to his office. I could call and ask him to pick it up.

After a silent war with my conscience I decide that karma has stepped in and saved me from my complicated loyalties. When I pull into a parking spot at Valley View, I fold the paper in half and stash it in the glove box.

Chapter Seven

I'm only five minutes late, but that's enough to throw off the flow, mine and everybody's. Corinne, oblivious to my difficulty tracking report, is all over the place, mixing stories about her grandbabies in with the medical condition of the residents and leaving me wondering whether Neil has really been spitting pureed peas across the dining room while Corinne tries to bandage a blister on the baby's heel, or whether this happened the other way around.

As she's leaving she turns back with a parting shot.

"Oh, I almost forgot! How could I forget, when it's so important? The Remember Oscar Event is moving down to the river. We were going to do it at Cole's place, in his backyard, but I think there might be too many people, and besides, he says the terrain is too rough for Nancy's wheelchair. It's supposed to rain this week, so all fingers crossed there won't be a ban on open fires. I'm making posters. Oh, don't look like that, honey. The grief will pass. That's what we're all here for." She trots back up the hall, purse swinging, bosom bouncing, and grabs me for a hug.

For the next couple of hours I don't have time to think about anything besides work. One of the CNAs calls in sick. All of the residents seem hell-bent on being difficult. At dinner, it turns out that it *is* Neil who was spitting peas, or, in this case, chocolate pudding. Usually dinner is when I catch up on paperwork and do some charting, but since we're down a staff member I help out, taking it in turns to feed a couple of the residents who are too far gone with dementia to feed themselves.

Neil behaves himself all through the main course of ground beef and gravy, the mashed potatoes, the soup. We're late. Meds are due. I still have a couple of foot ulcers to bandage and skin checks to do. I'm careless and in a hurry. There's a little more than a normal-size spoonful left of chocolate pudding. I pile it on, a heaping, gelatinous mound.

"Open extra wide," I tell Neil.

He complies, his toothless mouth stretching into a wide oval. When I remove the spoon, the pudding leaves a brown smear on his upper lip. He freezes, cheeks bulged, lips pursed. Before I have the sense to duck, he puckers and spits. The whole wet, warm mess hits me full-on across the face. Even with my lips sealed against it, I catch a taste of chocolate.

Neil bursts out laughing, a toothless cackle that rouses the other resident at the table, who has been nodding off over her plate. She takes one look and joins the laughter. Even Tia, who rushes over with a cloth to wipe my face, is laughing.

I glare at her.

She schools her face into a sober mask, but the laughter creeps up despite her best attempts. "Be thankful it's not what it looks like." She blots at my scrub top, which has also been liberally spattered. "Much better tasting than the alternative. Smells better, too."

Her laughter warms me like sunlight, seeps in through my pores, and teases the dark knot clenched in my belly. My own answering smile eases an ache in my cheekbones I hadn't known was there. I breathe in a deep, chocolate-pudding-scented breath and relax back into the chair. My body feels loose, disjointed, and all I want to do now is close my eyes and drift on a warm wave of letting go.

Which, of course, is impossible.

"Party's over," I say, getting to my feet, noticing again how much my body aches. Images of Kat's battered body swarm, unsummoned, into my brain, chasing away the warm lightness of laughter. "Let's get the show back on the road."

When I pop into Nancy's room, I hear male laughter before I get into visual range. She'd said something about her son visiting, and I walk into the room, wondering how far the apple falls from the tree. I have him in my head as an actor. Probably gorgeous, gay, and impeccably dressed. But the man sitting in her visitor's chair is not some stranger. It's Cole. He's wearing jeans and a black T-shirt and looks more like he's visiting a relative than doing an evaluation. His long legs are stretched out, comfortably, and he holds a paper coffee cup in one hand—the good stuff, from the Ritzes kiosk. My body goes into instant craving as the rich smell of it finds its way through my nostrils and all the way into my belly.

Nancy has been entertaining him. She's sitting up in her recliner, dressed in a sparkly black tank top with a rope of pearls around her neck. She's done up to the nines, hair curled, makeup perfectly applied, and looks every inch a star, albeit an aging one.

Her wicked old eyes narrow as she inspects me head to toe and back again. "What happened to you? Bring somebody Mexican food?" She actually has the nerve to sniff, loudly, like she's a hunting dog catching the scent. "Doesn't smell like shit," she says.

She, too, has a coffee cup in hand.

"That better not have sugar in it," I say, inserting a test strip into the glucose meter.

"I'm old," she says. "Better my blood sugar kills me than I kill myself."

"You didn't tell me you were diabetic," Cole says to her, and then turns to me. "Sorry. I should have asked."

"She's of an age to make her own decisions."

When I reach for her hand, she tucks it down along her thigh and gives me a mutinous look. "Let me do it. You'll hurt me."

I roll my eyes, used to her theatrics but self-conscious with Cole watching. Nancy's more than well aware of my discomfort; I can tell by the way she tilts her head to the side, glancing up at me sideways.

"Fine. Shoot yourself."

"How can you say that to a suicidal woman?"

Setting her cup on the bedside table, she takes the lancet and deftly pricks her finger, producing a perfect drop of blood.

"She's no more suicidal than I am," I tell Cole, touching the test strip to the blood drop. "She's just bored. Two-eighty. How much sugar is in that coffee?"

"Never you mind, dear. That's my business. That's what the insulin is for."

There's no point preaching at her. I've learned that much.

"My son is in town," she tells Cole. "I'll bring him to the Event. For the rat. I can come, can't I, Rae? You got that set up?"

"Ask Cole. It's out of my hands."

There might be an edge to my voice, because Cole glances up, his eyes asking a question I don't know how to answer. His intensity makes it difficult to focus, and I check the insulin dosing and what I've got in the syringe twice, and then once more for good measure.

"Told you," Nancy says. "An Event. Has a life of its own. You'll have to leave now, my beautiful young man, because she's going to stick that needle in my belly, and that's a thing you don't need to see."

"Yes, ma'am." He unfolds himself from the chair, then totally surprises me by bending down to kiss her cheek. Mental health people of my acquaintance don't act like that. Maybe a professional pat to the hand, not this gentle, half-mocking affectionate behavior. It sets me off guard, and the smile he turns on me doesn't help.

"I need to talk to you," he says. "Will you have a minute?"

"Maybe one. We're having quite a night."

"I see that." His gaze drifts down to my scrub top and back. He's not checking out my breasts; he's looking at the chocolate pudding stains.

My cheeks heat, and I turn my back to open an alcohol swab so he can't see my face. "Let me get this done, and then I'll meet you outside. I'm due for a break."

This is a stretch of the truth. True, I am due for a break. We're supposed to get three of them during a shift, in addition to a half hour for lunch. Most nights this is a joke, the truth being that there is always more work than can possibly be done. *But I do need to talk to him,* I tell myself. *For Kat.*

"Don't blow it," Nancy says, just before I inject her.

We both know she's not talking about the shot, but I ignore her insinuations. "The Event, thanks to you, will be held down by the river. Do I need to arrange transportation?"

She chuckles. "You mean, do you need to pick me up? So kind of you to offer, dear, but my son will bring me. Hey, I just thought of something. We could call this the Oscar. Right? Maybe I'll wear a dress."

"It will be cold. On the beach. By the river. At night. Wear sweatpants."

She gasps in true horror. "Be seen in public in sweats? My darling girl. Where do you get these ideas? Now go, your young man is waiting for you."

My young man is indeed waiting for me, swatting at a cloud of mosquitoes that has seen dinner and will not be deterred. They're more interested in him than me, so I don't offer the reprieve of moving back inside.

I fetch the statement from my car, first things first, feeling like Judas. I half expect him to hand me thirty pieces of silver in exchange for the folded paper, but he only folds it one more time and tucks it into his back pocket without even taking a look.

"You can take Nancy off the watch list," he says, smashing a mosquito on his forearm. It leaves a smear of blood, and he picks it up between thumb and forefinger and wipes it on his jeans.

"So you *are* working, then?"

He flashes me a disarming smile. "Hey, she was much more open to conversation than when I came in last time for a formal evaluation. No way will she be killing herself—at least not until after Saturday night. She will not miss the Oscar Event for love nor money."

"Seems a little unfair."

"All fair and aboveboard. I read her the riot act last time. She's a sharp old bird—she understands exactly what I'm doing here, no doubt about that."

"You're not like any counselor I've ever met."

"Thank you?" He crooks his right eyebrow upward in a question mark.

I wave my hand in his direction, lacking the words to describe the way he feels human. Immediate. Real. "You're so comfortable with her. Laid-back. More like you're a favorite grandson come to visit than a crisis worker here for an evaluation."

"I've always been a fan of Carl Rogers. I guess it shows."

"I thought his name was Fred."

His laughter is clean and warm, with no undertone of meanness or ridicule at my mistake. "Not that Mr. Rogers, although they preached pretty much the same doctrine. Carl Rogers the psychologist, the person-centered psychology dude."

Will wonders never cease. I consider myself pretty well informed when it comes to counseling. Cognitive behavioral. Mindfulness. EMDR. I know about Freud and Jung and the behaviorists. I don't know this Carl Rogers guy.

"Basically, he figured it's okay to be yourself with clients. No need to hide behind a wall and pretend you're not human. People thrive in an atmosphere of unconditional positive regard, as he called it. So yeah. Our Mr. Rogers had it down."

So that's it. Cole is treating me like one of his clients with the whole human act. It's a good one, I'll give him that, but the idea sets all my fur standing on end.

"And that reconciles for you with the job of locking people up?"

I'm sorry the minute the words are out of my mouth. I feel them thud into him, and stick, like a handful of mud or a mouthful of chocolate pudding. He finishes his coffee and walks away from me to toss it in the trash can outside the entrance door. I know this move. He's an honest guy. It will take him time to think of an evasion.

He gives me a half smile and a shrug. "Call me the Cognitive Dissonance Guy. It doesn't reconcile. People have a right to their own path, and I respect that. Maybe it's this. Suicidal people aren't thinking straight. They're in a dark, distorted head space, and death looks like the only thing. Maybe it's not. I buy them time to maybe get clear, to see a different perspective. Does that make sense?"

It makes more sense than I want it to. I feel a connection, a sort of alignment, between his energy and mine, something more subtle and dangerous than chemistry.

"What about Kat? You really think she should be locked up somewhere?"

"I'd rather be talking to you about Saturday night and Oscar, but Kat is really why I'm standing here volunteering as a feast for mosquitoes." He squashes another one, this time on his face. "I talked to her husband. It didn't go well."

"What do you mean?"

"I was hoping he'd come get her. That she could go home to mend and he'd take on a crisis plan. According to him, she's been depressed for months, years even; he's not at all surprised if she tried to kill herself."

"So the note . . ."

It could still be true, what Kat told me. Just because she's been depressed doesn't mean she's suicidal. Lots of people are depressed. Lots of people have suicidal thoughts. Both Mason and Cole have driven that point home. Not everybody acts on it, though, or we'd have bodies all over the sidewalks and nobody left to run things.

"It could be what she says," Cole says, quietly. "But desperate people lie. To themselves, as much as to people around them."

It's warm out here, but sweat is cold on my back, and I cross my arms over my chest to hold myself together. "So you're going to lock her up, then?"

"I don't know." Conflict is plain on his face. "It would help if she'd be honest with me."

"Should you be telling me all this? Isn't there some confidentiality clause, or whatever?"

"You are way too easy to talk to." He makes it sound like a compliment, which confuses me for a minute. I've heard a lot of "you are way too" statements in my life, generally followed by one of my flaws or deficiencies. His tone of voice and the expression on his face indicate something other, and I don't know what to say.

"No need to worry," he says, after a small silence. "She gave me permission to talk to you. Technically, I should have a written release, but I'm going with a verbal okay. Kinda hard to write when your hands are tied to the bed."

I can see that he doesn't like this part any better than I do. His face closes, the intensity factor ratcheting up a couple of notches. A minute ago I was shivering, now I feel overheated and out of breath. This man is altering my personal weather system. To borrow from Nancy, he is an Event, like a hurricane or a tropical storm.

"Will you be there again tomorrow?" he's asking, and I bring my drifting attention back. "I'm going to be meeting with her at ten. I'd like for you to be there."

"I already gave you a statement. Isn't that enough?"

I don't want to be there for the interrogation, don't want to see the betrayal in her eyes when she realizes what I've told him. Most of all, I know I have no defenses strong enough to shield me from what she's going to feel.

"She could use an ally," Cole says. "And I'm afraid you're all she's got."

When he puts it that way, I don't see that I have a choice. "All right. I'll be there."

"Great. Tomorrow morning, then?"

I hesitate. I've already promised Kat I won't let anybody lock her up. And now I'm promising to help the man who has the power to do that. I'm hopelessly tangled in a web of conflicting loyalties that threatens to tear me apart.

"Tomorrow morning," I say, dread squeezing my heart like a fist.

Chapter Eight

I'm smack-dab in the middle of a convoluted nightmare when my land-line starts to ring. The harsh trilling levitates my sleep-heavy body off the bed before I can get my eyes open.

Just the phone, I tell myself, staggering out of the bedroom to answer, but there is no *just* when the landline rings at six o'clock in the morning. Nobody calls this early with good news.

Kat, I think. *Something horrible has happened to Kat.*

As it turns out, it's not about Kat at all. The caller is my mother.

"Leila?" she queries, in response to my breathless hello. "Are you all right? You sound out of breath."

"It's six a.m. It's Thursday." I'm breathless, all right, the sort of breathless that happens when the hot water runs out in the shower and an icy deluge pours over my head.

"Oh, were you sleeping? That's right. I forgot about the time zone. I must be slipping."

My mother, a.k.a. Dr. Angela Masterson-Chatworth, doesn't slip, and she doesn't make Thursday-morning phone calls. She's as well known for her theories on routine and time structuring as she is for her skills as a pediatrician. Her last book, *Parenting on Time*, hit the *New York Times* bestseller list and spawned a circuit of conferences and seminars. Routine is the most efficient way to accomplish anything from parenting to conducting business, she says, and she has always followed her own doctrine down to the tiniest detail. Everything has its time, and everything in its time.

This early-morning call can only mean disaster.

"Is Dad okay? What's wrong?"

"Nothing's wrong, dear. I just wanted to tell you that we're coming to visit. Leila? Are you still there?"

I press my hand over my chest, as if the gesture can slow my racing heart, help me catch my breath. "It's Rae, Mom. It's been Rae for years."

My parents never come to visit. I fly home every year for Christmas, but in the nine years I've lived here they've never once talked about coming to see me.

"I am sorry I woke you. But I couldn't wait to tell you the news. We're going to be teaching a workshop in Seattle, and we thought we'd drop in and see you on the way."

I wander into the kitchen and look longingly at the coffeepot, wishing I'd preloaded it last night. I'm going to need all of my brain cells for this conversation.

"Colville isn't exactly on the way to anywhere," I tell her.

"Oh, nonsense, dear. Everywhere is on the way to somewhere. There's a perfectly serviceable airport in Spokane. We've already booked our flights. We'll be there next week. Thursday."

Frantically, I run my schedule through my head. "I have to work. The airport is two hours from here. I don't think I can get the time off, so there's no way I can come and get you—"

"We can rent a car and drive from the airport. It will be an adventure. YOLO, am I right?"

That does it. This is not my mother. I shake my head to clear the buzzing in my ears. I'm dreaming. That's it. I must be dreaming.

"Mom?"

"Yes, dear?"

"What are you talking about?"

"YOLO is an acronym, honey. For 'you only live once.' I thought all the millennials were using that one. Maybe it's only the younger set. The older I get, the harder it is to keep you all straight."

"I know what YOLO means. I just don't know what it means coming from you."

She laughs, as if I've said something hilarious. "I forgot we hadn't told you! It's a new theory your father and I are working on. There's going to be a new book. It's very exciting, and the Seattle trip is our very first seminar on the topic. We'll be teaching it together, doesn't that sound fun?"

"What happened to *Parenting on Time*? And you always do your teaching in the summer. You know, winter is for flu and colds and medicine, and summer is for travel."

"Oh, but that's the beauty of *YOLO for Seniors*. I had an epiphany. Time scheduling is for younger people. Those of us who are close to the death deadline need to shake our lives up a bit, do things differently. We've already *been* productive, so now it's time to live. It makes brilliant sense, don't you think?"

I don't think. I'm like a tiny little boat, adrift on an uncertain sea. I don't have the heart to tell her that her acronym is already out of date, not that it would make any difference.

"Did you want to talk to your father?" Mom asks. "He's right here."

"Maybe not right now I—"

"Elizabeth."

"It's Rae, Dad."

"To me, you will always be Elizabeth. We can't wait to see where you've been living all this time. Quite rustic and backwoodsy, from what I can see on the Internet. Should we book the Benny's or Comfort Inn? So interesting that you have only two hotels."

I should invite them to stay with me, but I can't make the words come out of my mouth. What they will think of this house I live in, with its secondhand furnishings and the posters on the walls, I can't begin to imagine. Maybe I have time to get more chairs for the kitchen table before they come. Some real wall art to replace my posters.

"I imagine all of this change is a little disconcerting for you," my father says, into my silence. "We've been growing into this new philosophy for several years, and now we've dropped it on you all at once."

"It does seem a little—sudden." I feel dazed and off balance, as if the sun had decided to stage a sunrise in the west, just to shake things up a bit.

"We'll talk more when we see you," my father says. "It will be late when we get in, so we'll go straight to the hotel. Let's plan on breakfast Friday morning? We love you. You do know that, right?"

"I love you, too, Daddy."

Long after the phone starts beeping to remind me to hang up, I'm still standing in the kitchen, the receiver digging into my cheek, wondering about a world in which even my parents can make a dramatic change while I'm still running as fast as I can, just to stay in place.

~

I can't go back on a promise, even one I'm loath to keep. My heart feels like ten pounds of cement when I drag myself into the hospital for the meeting with Kat. Maybe Cole won't be there. I wish several small disasters on him, everything from a minor cold to a flat tire, but he's there, waiting for me at the nurses' station. His smile is direct and bracing. "I was afraid you might bail."

I try to smile back, but to my horror I feel tears pricking at the backs of my eyes instead.

His smile fades. "What's the matter, Rae? Are you all right? You look pale as the dead."

"Fine. I'm fine. Sorry to keep you waiting." I brush past him. Might as well get this ordeal over with.

Kat is sitting up in the chair. Her hair has been washed and combed. The swelling around her eye is retreating, although the green and black has an added tone of yellow, and the abrasion on her cheek has crusted into a scab. I'm conscious of Cole entering the room right behind me, as if we've arrived together and are in league against her. I make a point of putting distance between us, crossing the room to sit on the edge of Kat's bed and letting him pull up the visitor chair.

"Your blinds are open," I observe, trying to soften the hard mask of her face with small talk.

"The light's too bright," she replies, in a brittle voice. "I've asked them three times to close those blinds. They seem to think I need sunlight. Like I'm a plant."

Cole is the one who responds to her unspoken request, crossing the room to adjust the blinds. He doesn't quite close them, letting sunlight fall in bars across the bed, across my lap and hands.

"The two of you didn't come to discuss my room lighting. To what do I owe the pleasure?"

She's gone ridiculously formal, every word enunciated, her hands folded in her lap. She holds her head like a queen, bruised as she is, despite the blue hospital gown, the white blanket draped across her legs.

Cole is not relaxed today, like he was with Nancy. There's no casual slouch, no laughter. He's got a briefcase with him, and he hands her a sheet of paper.

She glances at it, then up at him. "What's this?"

A thunderstorm is brewing in this room, the barometer dropping, dropping.

"When I first came to talk to you, I explained your rights," Cole says. "Do you remember?" I can't hear any conflict in his voice. He's made his decision already. This interview is a formality.

I can feel his determination in my bones, warring with Kat's rising anger. There's no way to modulate any of it, except to breathe, to accept, to try to tell myself the war I feel within my body doesn't really belong to me.

A lie, but a comforting one.

"So you're going to drag me off to an asylum?" Kat shoots a dirty look at me, a reminder that I promised to help protect her from this. "You've been hovering like a vulture, just waiting for me to be well enough."

"That's the very last thing I want to do, or that the law allows me to do. If we can make a workable crisis plan that you agree to, then we'll do that. I want everything to be aboveboard. I don't want you to think I tried to trick you. So you need to know that it's in your best interest to talk to me, and to be honest. But at the same time you need to know that statements you make can be used as evidence to place you on a seventy-two-hour mental health hold."

A small pounding begins in my head, right at the base of my skull. With my eyes I plead with Kat, try to make her understand without words that I'm not part of this, that we're not allied against her.

Kat's eyes shift away from me, a clear dismissal. It's too much. I can't be here.

"Maybe I'll just wait outside." I push myself up to my feet, my body buzzing with the energy emanating from the two of them.

"I'd like you to stay." Cole's tone, more command than request, triggers my contrary streak, and I get halfway to the door before Kat stops me.

"It's the least you can do." She still won't look at me, but the words invoke my broken promise.

"As for you," she says to Cole. "You've already warned me. Twice now. I don't understand what has changed."

"I talked to Tom," Cole says.

Kat's hand goes to her cheek, as though he's struck her. Some of the stiffness leaches out of her spine. But her voice remains perfectly level and her eyes are a warning.

"And? What does Tom say?"

"He says you've been depressed for years. That he wouldn't be at all surprised if you'd turned in front of Rae's car."

"And of course his word is worth more than mine. The word of a man over the word of a woman."

"When I put his words together with those of the witnesses, and the note you wrote, yes."

"I am not crazy. I would not do this to myself on purpose."

"This?" Cole's voice gentles, a thread of compassion winding into it. "No. I don't imagine this was what you intended."

My breathing hitches in my throat. I want her to deny it. I want her to have words that lay all of Cole's certainties and my suspicions to rest. I want her to say it was an accident. But the sadness rolling off her is a thick, dark fog that dims the colors of the room to shades of gray.

"Tom says this isn't the first time. I looked up records."

"He says I've ridden into a car before? That's ridiculous." But she sounds tired now. Defeated. Her hands come together in her lap, clasped as if in silent prayer.

"No. The last time it was a razor. You did a pretty good job of it, he says. If he hadn't forgotten his lunch and come home for it, you wouldn't still be with us."

I watch her struggle to hold his gaze. Watch her eyes fill with tears, her head droop like a wilting flower as the tears spill over and splash onto her folded hands.

Anger stirs in my belly—*mine,* I think, though I can't be sure. I want to throw things at Cole, to shout at him, drag him out of this room. Fair or not fair, rational or not, I don't care. He's a bully operating under false pretenses. Any decent human being would never do this job, breaking people down like this. Pushing Kat into this sort of a corner. I turn to snap at him, only to see that his eyes are luminous with unshed tears, his face lined with sadness.

"Let us help you," he says to Kat. "Dying is not an answer."

"You know nothing of my life, and my death is none of your business," she fires back at him. Her voice is thick with tears, but there's as much anger as grief in it. "Who are you, or Tom, to say what value my life has in this world? You don't have the right to stop me."

"But I do have the law," Cole says, still very gently.

"Ah yes. The law. The government. Controlling who can die. Go ahead, then. Lock me up. You can't stop me forever."

"No," he agrees. "But I can give you time to think."

"You think I haven't thought already? That I drove in front of Rae's car on some random whim? *Whee, it's a beautiful day; I think I'll crash my bike.* Thinking does nothing. There is no *hope* for me." Her voice breaks on the word *hope*, and she buries her face in her hands, the tears falling between her fingers, her breathing ragged and harsh.

My body is carved from stone. If my heart is beating, I no longer feel it. Kat drops her hands and glares at me.

"You promised," she says. "You promised to help me, and now you're here with him. You want me to go to the hospital?"

No words will come when I first try to speak. I manage to swallow. Once, twice, and then again. "I don't want you to die," I finally manage, my gaze locked with hers.

Kat does not release me. "My life," she says. "My choice. And if you both think that seventy-two hours in the loony bin is going to fix me, you're crazier than I am."

Guilt weighs heavy on me. An obligation. As if, having almost killed her, now I am responsible for both her sanity and her safety.

"I'm afraid it's not that easy," Cole says. "The hospital is not an option just now."

Kat laughs, a harsh sound, far from mirth. "Make up your mind. What exactly do you want from me?"

"Your safety," he says. He rubs the back of his neck with one hand and stifles a yawn with the other. "Sorry, been up all night. Here's the thing. None of the hospitals seem to be able to care for somebody with your injuries. Sacred Heart is really the only one that might be able to handle it, and they're full. Eastern has beds, but they won't even think about taking you, not with the medical follow-up and the fractures. So we're back to making a crisis plan."

"You appear to have given it plenty of thought," Kat says. "What do you propose?"

"Tom was willing to have you come home. Just to heal, he said, to be clear."

"No."

Cole's lips curve in a rueful smile. "He also said you would say that. Any other family you could stay with? Parents? Siblings?"

"Let me be clear."

Kat has mastered her tears. She looks cold and remote, her lips move stiffly. "If you send me back to live with my husband or my family, I will kill myself. Sooner, later, there will be no if. Do you understand this?"

"The only other option I have is the crisis house."

"What is that?"

"The agency I work for has a safe house. It's staffed around the clock. You could be there on observation, although we also are not equipped to deal with your injuries."

"She can stay with me." The words are out of my mouth before they've even connected with my brain.

Both of them stare at me, Cole and Kat, as if I'm speaking Sumerian.

Silence grows around us, and I fill it, the words coming from somewhere that has nothing to do with logic or sense.

"You can have the bedroom. I'll sleep on the couch. I'm a nurse; I can help with your care. It's small, but better than the crisis house, right?"

"I'm not sure that's a good idea," Cole says, slowly. I can't read him, can't identify the emotion emanating from him, but it grates on my skin like sandpaper.

"Do you have a better one?"

"Give me a bit. She's not being released today. There's time—"

"Hey," Kat interjects. "Over here. Do I get a say in this or is it just between the two of you?"

"Sorry. Of course." Tearing myself away from the target lock I have on Cole is a physical jolt. Even when I'm not looking at him I can feel his energy so different from Kat's. Hers dark and secretive, his fierce and bright.

"I don't need handouts—" Kat begins, but I cut her off.

"Let me do this. I ran over you. So you turned in front of my car. I wasn't looking. I glanced away. Maybe I could have stopped. So it's my fault, too. Let me give you a place to stay until you're mended."

My words hang between us all, and I realize I'm holding my breath, waiting for judgment.

Neither of them says a thing.

"I promised," I say, glancing at Cole out of the corner of my eye and then away. "I told Kat I wouldn't let them send her to the hospital. And I promised you I would help you. We're all in this together now."

"Rae," Cole protests, "I don't—"

"You wanted me to be here. I'm here. You want a safe place for her to stay. I'm as good as it gets."

He runs both hands through his hair, standing it on end. Dark stubble shadows his jaw. I'm still furious with him, but I also want to smooth his hair, want to make that bright flash of a smile appear on his face.

"If you're sure," Kat says. "Since Cole will never just let me be."

"I'm sure. What do we have to do?"

He doesn't like it. He really doesn't like it, but he doesn't argue anymore. Extracting a folder from his briefcase, he selects a sheet of paper and fills in some blanks. Then he passes it to Kat.

Her brow creases as she reads.

"I have to do counseling? Please tell me you're not serious."

He answers her with a look.

"Oh, for God's sake. I've done so much counseling I could be the counselor."

"I can keep looking for a hospital bed. There's also the option of trying for a single bed certification—keeping you here with the sitter until you're judged to be no longer a risk to yourself."

"You're a bastard, you are." But her eyes go back to the paper. "Fine. Hook me up with a counselor. Give me an antidepressant. They don't work, just so you know." She initials boxes as she reads. "Yes, I will stay with Rae and advise her of my whereabouts should I ever be well enough to go somewhere on my own. Yes, I promise not to kill myself or commit any acts of self-harm for"—she looks up at the ceiling for inspiration—"for two weeks. Sorry. That's all I will promise to."

"I'm good with that," Cole says, quietly. "Much better than promising the moon with no intention of keeping your word."

She signs with a flourish and passes the paper to me.

"Your turn."

The paper has an official agency header and two columns. One is for Kat's responsibilities. The other is mine. I'm promising to lock up all sharp items, to manage any and all of Kat's medications, to assist her in getting to counseling and medical appointments, to let Cole know the minute she breaks her end of the bargain or if I'm worried about her.

I hadn't realized, quite, what I was committing to when I blurted out my impulsive offer for her to come and live with me. She's not a motherless kitten or a bird with a broken wing, or even a naked rat too young to fend for himself.

She's a human being with a history I don't know—a history that includes enough desperation to carve into her wrist with every intention to die, to turn her bike in front of a car. My hand is shaking by the time I've initialed all of the items and moved to the binding signature at the end.

I'm committed, though. I've stated my case. I've talked myself into this corner. And I am not about to let her kill herself, not if I can stop her.

I sign and pass the paper over to Cole. His eyes are dark and resigned and sad, all of which are emotions I don't want to equate with him.

The tension between the three of us wraps around my lungs and makes it hard to breathe. I need to get out of this room. Away from Kat and her darkness, away from Cole and his conflictedness, mostly away from myself, but there is no escape from that.

A nurse comes in and saves us all from any ensuing awkwardness.

"You've been up quite long enough," the nurse says to Kat. "It's past time for your pain meds. Do you two mind?" Her lips are pursed in disapproval, of what I'm not certain, but I'm glad for the excuse. Cole follows right behind me.

"You all right?" he asks.

"Not exactly." I keep walking. He keeps pace beside me.

"I had no idea you were going to do that."

Despite the fact that I had no idea, either, I turn on him. "What did you expect me to do? Why did you ask me to be there, if that's not what you had in mind? Looked to me like you had no plan at all."

"I thought . . . she might listen to you."

"Yeah. Well, it looks to me like she needs somebody to listen to *her*. What's wrong with her husband, anyway? Why isn't he here? What kind of man doesn't come see his wife when she's been run over by a car?"

He doesn't answer, probably maintaining some idea of confidentiality. *Well, it's a little late for that.*

"A lot can change in a couple of days," he says. "Listen, about the Oscar Event."

My footsteps slow, waiting for the punch line.

"My schedule got changed. One of my coworkers had a family crisis out of town, the other one is sick. Looks like I'm on call Saturday night."

As excuses go, it's a decent one. I didn't want the Oscar Event. I check myself for relief, but what I feel is disappointment.

"Nancy will be devastated."

"She'll be fine. We'll just have to shuffle it off to the next weekend. It will give her longer to live." The flash of humor is back in his voice, side by side with exhaustion and determination and the lingering disapproval.

"You're not cancelling it?"

"You can't cancel an Event."

"What about Kat? Don't I have to watch her every minute?"

"Were you planning to not go back to work?"

My feet stop of their own accord. Cole stops, too. This forces me to look at him, to make the eye contact I've been avoiding. The intensity of his gaze makes me feel dizzy, and I look away. "I have to work. I was thinking—if I secure her meds and the sharps—there's not too much she can do to hurt herself."

I expect he'll argue, tell me I'm not a fit watchdog after all.

What he says is as unexpected as my mother's late-life crisis.

"It's really just a formality, all of this planning. We can't stop her, if she's hell-bent on doing it."

Images throng the movie theater in my head. Kat dead on the floor, my paring knife lodged in her chest. Kat hanging from the ceiling. A tiny Kat curled up in Oscar's cage, one hand resting on the exercise wheel. This one is bizarre, even for me, and I shake it off in favor of reality, even though in this case reality means Cole and the darkness in his voice just now.

"I don't understand you, at all," I tell him.

I'm rewarded with a flash of his smile, a little subdued but still bright, still there, not at all altered by the depth of the sadness I pick up from him at the same time.

"That makes two of us," he says. "I'll call you."

Chapter Nine

Kat comes home on Sunday.

We ditch the nurses at the station, and I roll her out to the car myself in the wheelchair. It's an absolutely gorgeous day. Warm, not hot, with a clear blue sky you could get lost in, and a gentle breeze blowing away the besmirching pain-racked atmosphere of the hospital.

"Stop," Kat says, the minute we clear the doors.

I think maybe she's changed her mind about going home with me, but she leans her head back to get the sun on her face and makes a sound that is half purr. "You forget, locked up inside, what sun feels like," she says.

I know what she means.

For my sixteenth birthday, I got the measles.

I'd had all of my immunizations right on schedule. My mother, a firm believer in the infallibility of vaccines, felt personally betrayed when the damning red rash erupted on my itchy skin. She drew the blood for the confirmation test at home, herself, rather than allow a display of my immune system's failure at the clinic.

Of course, I was never dangerously ill, or I would have been whisked off to the hospital forthwith. As it was, I didn't leave the house for two weeks, not until the last, lingering vestige of rash was gone.

I remember with crystal clarity that first breath of fresh air when I stepped outside. The movement of a breeze on my face, the expanding world with all of its smells and colors and changing rhythms. The sensory impact nearly knocked me off my feet. So I do know something of what Kat is feeling, and I wait until she says, "Okay, let's go," before I resume our progression to the car.

They've pronounced her pelvic fracture as stable and not in need of surgery. But the bone is still broken. That and the staples in her belly make moving agony for her. By the time I have her stowed in the car her skin has blanched white, the bruises standing out in garish contrast.

"No seat belt," she says, when I reach for it. "Ribs," she adds, as if she knows I'm wondering about her death wish. "Belt would do more damage than good."

She's probably got a point. It's only a few blocks to my place, anyway. I drive like I've got an unbuckled baby in that seat, feathering the brakes at every intersection, double- and triple-checking for oncoming traffic, accelerating at a pace that makes even the elderly gentleman behind me lift both hands in the air in a *what on earth are you doing?* gesture of frustration.

Finally, though, we reach the moment I've been dreading.

I get her out of the car and into the chair, then roll her in through the front door. I try to see the house through her eyes. The tiny front room, with my secondhand couch and armchair, the overflowing bookshelves, the clean white walls with the poster print décor. The kitchen with the scarred wooden table and two old chairs. And then on into the bedroom, which I've arranged for her with clean sheets and a new comforter. A bouquet of fresh flowers conceals the water marks on the dresser, and a small bedside table covers the spot where Oscar's cage used to be.

There's just enough room to roll the chair up to the bed.

Kat waves off my attempt to help. "I can do this," she says. Bearing all of her weight on the good leg, she pivots, balancing on the arm of the chair. A gasp of pain escapes her as she sinks down onto the mattress, and she sits like a statue, eyes closed, barely breathing.

This time she doesn't object when I kneel down to take off her shoes and then help her swing her legs up onto the bed. I dispense an oxycodone, bringing her a glass of water with a straw so she doesn't have to sit up. It's stuffy and a little too warm, so I open the window and turn on the fan to get air circulating.

"You've thought of everything," Kat murmurs, lying back with her eyes closed, as if all of the energy has been sucked out of her. "This is lovely."

She says nothing about the shabbiness or the posters or any of the other shortcomings that I fear my mother will go on about. Back out in the living room I flop down onto the couch, hoping this isn't all a terrible mistake.

It's not forever, I remind myself. *It was the only option.*

But my living space feels heavy and claustrophobic, an energy of pain and sadness permeating the atmosphere.

While Kat rests and recovers from the trip, I spend my time figuring out how to honor my part of the crisis agreement. All of my sharps, not that I have many, go into a locked box I picked up at Walmart. Kitchen knives, scissors, razors. Now I add in Kat's medications. The pain pills. Vitamins. Her hospital discharge instructions from the physician, the list of exercises from her physical therapist. With some dismay I realize she has a lot of appointments. A follow-up with the orthopedic surgeon. A follow-up with the general surgeon. Physical therapy twice a week. Counseling isn't set up yet, and we'll have to wedge that in somewhere.

Just getting her to appointments is going to be a logistical challenge, given that I will still have to go to work.

The anger I feel toward her husband wells up again. He should be here. He should come and take her home. Unless, of course, he's an abusive asshole. Maybe he beats her. Maybe her whole existence has been one of gaslighting and verbal abuse, and the whole reason she's been suicidal in the first place is because of him.

Protectiveness of Kat fills me with a dark energy. I will take care of her. Forget wishing. I will find a way to make her happy.

~

By the time Kat wakes up from her nap, I'm ready with a plan. The pain pill is doing its job, and we get her into the wheelchair and out to the living room without too much trouble, taking a detour to the bathroom.

"I can manage this," she says.

There's no room to get the wheelchair in and close the door, so I walk away to the kitchen to give her privacy, wincing at a couple of thuds and a stifled groan. There are also reassuring sounds. The toilet flushing. Water running.

"Well," she says, rolling herself out to the living room, "that was an adventure."

"It will get easier. Hungry?"

She shrugs. "I guess."

Pain meds, inactivity, and depression don't make for a healthy appetite. I, on the other hand, am starving, and she needs to eat so her body can heal. Martha Stewart I am not. In fact, as I carry out two bowls of tomato soup and a plate of grilled cheese sandwiches, I realize that I eat like a college student.

"I'll go shopping tomorrow," I tell her, setting the food on the coffee table and drawing over my old TV stand to set it up in front of her wheelchair. "I tend not to cook, since it's just me."

Kat leans forward and inhales a little too deeply, her hand going automatically to her side to brace her ribs. "I love tomato soup. Just like this. Out of the can. Tom didn't—" She stops midthought. "Anyway, this is perfect."

She sounds like she means it, but I'm still braced for criticism. I realize I don't know her at all—what she likes or dislikes, what interests her. The only bond we have is pain and death, which is great for cosmic moments but not so much for an evening of togetherness in a small and confined space.

"Would you like to watch TV? Or read, maybe? I have tons of books."

"I noticed." A smile takes the sting out of what might have been sarcasm. It's the first time I've seen her smile, and my heart grabs on to hope and runs with it. "How about a movie?"

"Sure." We scan through Netflix and select *Sleepless in Seattle*.

"I've never actually watched this," I confess as I cue it up.

"Me, either," she says. "Why, I wonder?"

I know why. I've started watching it twice, and bailed within the first thirty minutes. It's not just the grief of Tom Hanks and his young son at the beginning, it's the knowing that people have relationships like that. So deep, so connected. It makes me feel alien and alone.

This time, watching with Kat, I make it all the way to the happy ending, but the cloud of emotion Kat and I have generated by then is so big I get up to open windows to let it dissipate a little.

"It's warm in here, don't you think?"

It is warm. I don't own an air conditioner. Most people here in Colville don't. It cools off enough in the evening that my system of opening the windows and turning on fans as soon as the sun goes down is sufficient for cooling. But opening windows and turning on fans also gives me a chance to hide my face and dry my tears.

My father's voice drifts through my head. "It's just a movie, for goodness' sake. They are actors. You're not a child anymore; surely you can cope with this reenactment."

The last time I attended a movie theater, I went with a group of college friends. It was some lighthearted flick, or meant to be, but by the time the credits rolled I was a sodden mess. My date was clearly repelled. My girlfriends laughed at my distress, though they offered tissues to blot my streaming eyes.

My emotional control hasn't gotten any better with time, and this movie has done me in.

Kat's face, too, is wet with tears.

Her lips twist in what is meant to be a smile, and her hands flutter, like they are trying to speak for her; then one of them presses against her mouth. A sob slips past it, and then another. Breath keens in her throat, and her face twists.

"Sorry," I say. "So sorry. It seemed like a good idea at the time."

She tries to say something, but the shape of the word is lost in her weeping. One hand braces her ribs, the other goes to her belly, and I'm lost, with no idea how to ease her.

"What can I do?" I ask, kneeling in front of her. "You'll hurt yourself, with the crying. Here, use this." I fetch my pillow from the couch and press it against her belly and around the broken ribs. "Use that to splint. Better?"

Kat nods and manages a full breath.

"From now on, you are not allowed to cry. No sad movies. Or funny ones, either, probably. I guess we're stuck with *Law & Order* reruns."

Her lips move. No sound comes out, but it looks like it might be *sorry*.

"Are you kidding?" I tell her. "I am such a wuss. I can't even watch commercials. Movies always make me cry. Movie dates? Terrible things. Makeup smeared everywhere. People turning around to stare at me and tell me to shut up. Snot bubbles coming out of my nose . . ."

A choking noise makes me think maybe I'd better call 911, but it turns out it's laughter, doing battle with the tears. She manages to drag in a full breath, and then another. The sobs ease, little by little, and she leans back, limp and white and exhausted.

"That little boy," she says. "The thing with the apple, how his mother always peeled it . . ."

My eyes water and I blink, hard. Tears are contagious, and I'm not about to set her off again.

"I can't have kids," she says. "Did they tell you?"

It's the way she says it that slows the world down; the way she glances up at me and then away. Who would say anything to me about whether she can have kids or not? Unless, unless . . .

"There was damage, I guess, internally . . ." She lets go of the pillow and buries her face in her hands.

I stay where I am, balanced on my knees, my hands still clutching the pillow.

Kat can't have babies now, because of me.

My car did all of that. Broke her pelvis. Tore her uterus. The extent of this loss detonates an emotional mushroom cloud that sucks my capacity for speech out the windows in its wake.

"I always thought I'd have a bunch of kids," she says, her voice muffled by the hands still covering her face. "Three boys for Tom, and three girls for me. As if life ever lines up like that. He said two would be plenty. He said . . ."

I want to say something comforting, something to lessen the impact of this. Maybe she could tell me she didn't really want kids anyway. Or I could bring up adoption, but I know better. All I can do is stay here with her, to hold the grief in my body instead of walling it off. Maybe that's no comfort to her, but it serves as penance for me.

"You wanted a big family; he didn't. Is that why . . . why you don't already have kids?"

She doesn't answer that. "How come you don't have any?" she asks me, after her breathing steadies.

"Are you kidding? Look around. I can barely take care of myself."

She gives me an assessing sort of look. "You seem to be doing fine."

I don't answer. This is complex, boggy ground, the thing about me and kids, and I am not going to venture into it. Not now. Probably not ever.

After a long moment her eyes drift back to her hands. "God. Tom," she says, in a tone that might be prayer or curse. "I can't tell him this. Do you think he knows? How damaged I am?"

"Cole told him about the accident, because of the note."

"That stupid note. I should have shredded it. Better, I should never have written it."

I picture Kat's house.

Something urban and modern, with shining tile floors and granite countertops and a stainless-steel fridge and stove, polished to a mirror shine. Tom doesn't fit. He wears a half-buttoned shirt and has a beer belly and a scruffy beard, because he's too lazy to shave. He lounges around the house while Katya works her fingers to the bone. She fastens the note to the fridge with a little heart-shaped magnet, one she bought to hold pictures of the babies she will never have.

"Why didn't you leave it for him?"

"I forgot." Her hands twist together in her lap. "When I decided to go, it was—sudden. I packed while he was at work, only what I could carry on the bike. All I could think of was getting clean away before he got home. So I wrote the note, and then I must have stuffed it into my bag instead of leaving it. I was so afraid he'd find me, before—" Her voice breaks on a sob, but her eyes are dry and she doesn't weep anymore.

In my mind Tom morphs. The beer belly contracts into washboard abs. The half-buttoned shirt changes into a tank revealing muscular pecs and biceps. He's handsome, but his eyes are cold. He beats her, careful not to leave bruises on her face where they can be seen.

I put my hands over both of hers. "You're safe here. You don't have to go back. You don't have to tell him a thing."

"You don't understand. How could you? He's my husband."

"I understand that you are your own person. He doesn't get to control you or tell you what to do. Okay?"

She nods. Her hands don't cling to mine, but she doesn't pull away, either. "It was nice," she says, after a minute. "Watching a movie together. Maybe we could try again. I promise not to have another meltdown."

"Yeah, well, I'm capable of meltdowns over slapstick comedy. It's a curse."

A ghost of a smile crosses her face, but her eyes have that pinched look that lets me know she's hurting. Time for pain meds and to tuck her into bed.

"Tomorrow I have to work."

"I can manage."

"I'll set everything up before I go." Already, I'm running lists in my head of what needs to be done. An easy dinner she can manage by herself. An appointment set up with a counselor. I'll need to run to the grocery store.

At the back of my mind my parents' impending visit looms, but I push it away while I get Kat settled for the night. When I snuggle up on the couch with a blanket and a pillow I feel complete, as if all of the missing Rae pieces have assembled themselves and conglomerated into a whole being without any work from me. Sleep comes quickly and gently and carries me away.

∼

It hits me midmorning, while Kat is giving herself a sponge bath in the bathroom and I'm washing our few dishes in the kitchen.

It's Monday. Monday means Bernie.

In five years, I have never missed a session.

I'm not going today. I won't be going next week or the week after or the week after that. No more Bernie. Ever. That disastrous last session is clearly marked *The End*.

I feel every letter in those two words as if they are etched into my flesh. What will my world be like without Bernie in it?

When the answer comes to me, I'm shocked to discover that the loss isn't monumental after all. Six days and twenty-three hours of my week will be exactly the same as they've always been. For all the real estate I've given this relationship in my head and my heart, that's all the time it gets. One hour, one day a week.

"Are you all right?"

Kat's voice startles me. I release the breath I've been unconsciously holding and shut off the water. The sink is full nearly to overflowing, suds bubbling up level with the counter.

"I'm fine. I'm good. Daydreaming. I do that. Listen, are you going to be okay if I go to work? I can still try to find someone to cover."

"Relax a little," she says. "I'll be fine."

"Promise?"

"Cross my heart and hope to die." She accompanies the words with a macabre grin, and we both laugh a little, but I'm still uneasy.

I leave her with a list of phone numbers. Valley View, Cole, the crisis line. She's got sandwiches and salad and plenty of water. I dispense the pain pill that is due, and set another one out for later. Two, I figure, can't be enough to kill her. The key to the locked box goes with me.

But I can't shake the worry.

I call home twice to check in. Has she eaten? Did she take the medications I left out for her? The first time around she sounds happy to hear my voice. When I call at nine I pick up an edge of irritation.

"I'm fine. Ate my dinner, brushed my teeth, said my prayers."

"Sorry, I just—"

"You're hovering," she says.

"I worry. You being there by yourself."

"About which thing? That I've fallen and can't get up? Or that I've laid my wrist open with the secret razor blade sewn into the seams of my backpack?"

I hadn't even thought to worry about either of these things, but now I do. "Do you? Have a secret razor blade?"

"Rae." She says it like my mother when she thinks I'm out of line. "Would you stop? I'll be here when you come home. Alive, breathing, and hopefully asleep. All right?"

Some sort of background noise has been trying to make itself heard around the noise of my worry and doubt. "What's that sound?"

"What sound?"

"It's a sort of squeaking."

"I've got the TV on. Some sort of commercial about cat food. I'm going to bed in a minute. All the doors are locked. I'm all right. Stop worrying."

Stop worrying.

I repeat this to myself over the rest of my shift like a mantra. The universe plays along. Nancy has unearthed an old Bobby McFerrin CD from somewhere and is practicing wheelchair dance moves to the tune of "Don't Worry, Be Happy" when I enter her room to give her insulin.

Half a candy bar sits in plain sight on her bedside table, and her blood sugar makes it clear that she's the one who ate it. My attempt to lecture her is met with an "Oh, honey, please. I'm going to die of something, I might as well enjoy it."

The delay of the Oscar Event is a sadness to her, but only a small one.

"I'm going shopping for something appropriate to wear."

"You're remembering this is all happening on the beach. At a campfire."

She waves a bejeweled hand dismissively. "My son is taking me shopping in Spokane. Where else will I wear new clothes?"

All of the staff is buzzing about the Oscar Event. Some of them are also discussing wardrobes. My own emotions are all over the place, and when I catch myself thinking about what I could wear and whether Cole will like it, I'm ready to concede that the world as I know it has gone mad. By the time my shift is over, I want only to get home, crawl between the sheets, and obtain oblivion as rapidly as possible.

My key is in the lock before I remember that I'm sleeping on the couch, and that Kat will be in my bed. A brief longing for my old life flickers through me, forgotten the instant I step into my house and discover that my couch is occupied by my roommate and a litter of mewling kittens.

Kat is a mess, and the kittens are no better.

Tears streak her face. Her hair sticks up every which way. Five tiny, blind kittens lie on her abdomen, every single one of them squeaking out a story of hunger and despair. On the floor beside the couch, a kitten-size bottle lies on its side, slowly dripping milk from the nipple.

"Some lady named Jenny brought them," Kat says, in answer to my unspoken question. "I've tried to feed them, but they wouldn't drink and they won't stop crying."

I stand frozen in the doorway, calculating the impact of a new batch of kittens on the chaos I'm already trying to navigate. They're not a thriving bunch; I can see that from here. Too thin. Their protests about the harsh world they've been born into are feeble. They aren't all going to make it.

My lips feel numb. "I can't do this right now. I told Jenny that."

"Because of me, right?" Fresh tears streak down Kat's face. "The woman said nobody else would take them and they'd have to be put down. So I said I'd help, and she said great, only then she took off before telling me what to do."

There's only one thing to be done, of course, which is to go into full-on kitten-saving mode.

"Which formula are you using?"

She looks at me blankly. "There was milk in the fridge. I found the bottles in the cupboard. Did I do wrong? I did. I can see that."

"Kittens can't drink cow's milk." I pick up the bottle and carry it to the sink, dumping it out and letting it soak in hot water and soap while I blot at the couch. "You've got milk in your hair."

Her hand explores the stiffened locks and she sniffles, looking as forlorn as the kittens. "It got everywhere except in the kittens. I'm sorry, I should have said no. Will they die anyway, now? Because I did everything wrong?"

"You didn't do everything wrong. You kept them warm. Jenny didn't bring any formula?"

She shakes her head.

"Never mind. I think there's some left over from last time." Digging in the storage cupboard turns up a large plastic bin full of supplies. Another bottle and a set of nipples, a can of formula, and a heating pad. There's also a set of syringes, needles, and a bag of Ringer's lactate for administering fluids to dehydrated kittens.

It's been a long time since I've accepted a litter. Since before Oscar, in fact. Not that there haven't been plenty of motherless kittens, but it seemed inconsiderate to invite a troop of cats into his home, given the circumstances of his mother's demise.

"The woman who brought the kittens—Jenny—said you would want them, now that the rat was no longer a barrier. Is that some sort of code? God, I do wish they would hush."

"They're starving. Why didn't you tell me when I called?"

"I wanted to help. To show you I could be something other than a burden."

"They could have died." I kneel down beside her to assess the unhappy babies. All of the crying, while irritating, is a good sign. They still have enough energy to complain. The one that worries me most is the smallest, a gray tabby. He's not meowing. His sides suck in with every breath. When I pinch his skin it stays where I put it, loose and wrinkled.

"What's wrong with him? Have I killed him?"

"Dehydrated." I don't have time to reassure her, not if I want to save him.

Weary as I am, my hands perform the necessary tasks without much guidance from my brain. I've done all of this a hundred times, often in the middle of a night of highly disrupted sleep.

Filling the bottle with warm formula, I get one of the kittens started suckling and then hand the bottle to Kat. The kitten is tentative at first, but rapidly figures out he's on to something. His little paws begin kneading. I pick up the little tabby and wrap him in a washcloth. He doesn't fight, doesn't try to get upright, and my heart sinks.

I don't bother with a bottle; he won't have the energy to suck. Instead, I draw up some formula into one of the syringes and dribble a few drops into his mouth. He swallows, the first good sign I've seen so far. I give him a few more drops, then set him back down on Kat's lap to keep him warm while I draw some sterile fluid from the IV bag.

"What are you going to do?" Kat stares at the syringe in my hands, her eyes wide with horror. "You're not putting him down?"

"He's dehydrated. It's life-threatening for a baby this tiny."

"You're starting an IV? On a cat?"

"Nope. Just injecting into the space beneath the skin. He can absorb it from there."

"I think he's full," Kat says as the little kitten she's feeding releases the nipple. He's no longer crying, and his belly is rounded.

"Now you have to burp him."

"You're messing with me."

"Nope. Bottle-feeding makes air bubbles. Hold him up against your shoulder and just rub his back."

She handles the little bit of fur as if it's made of glass, lifting it up to her shoulder. It attaches to her shirt with all of its claws, clinging, and she gently taps its back. Her face softens, the lines of worry easing, a slight smile curving up the corners of her lips.

I dribble more formula into my little patient's mouth until his belly, too, is rounded and full. He seems to me to be breathing more easily. Taking a cotton ball I massage his lower belly and his genitals, as his mother would do with her tongue. He pees in response, only a tiny amount, but if his kidneys are working there is hope.

When I set him down on the heating pad he makes a tiny squeaking sound and curls into a ball. Detaching the kitten from Kat's shoulder, I rub him down and set him beside his brother. She picks up another kitten and manages to get it started sucking. I fill the second bottle and sit down beside Kat on the couch, bringing another one of the kittens into my lap.

By the time we have a nest of sleeping kittens sprawled on the heating pad, Kat is smiling, but her joy fades when she glances up at me. "You're so tired," she says. "Taking care of me, and then a long shift at work. When do we have to feed them again?"

"In a couple of hours. And you're supposed to be sleeping. You need rest to heal."

She shakes her head in denial. "I shouldn't have opened the door. I don't know why I did."

I stretch and laugh, leaning back against the couch to close my gritty eyes. "It takes a strong woman to say no to Jenny and a batch of motherless kittens. Stronger than I am, anyway. Better sleep while we can. How much are you hurting?"

"I forgot about it for a few minutes." She straightens up, tentatively, splinting her side with her hand. When she yawns, it's followed by a small sigh of pain.

"Let's get you to bed. We'll talk kittens in the morning."

"You'll wake me?" Her lids have fallen half closed over her eyes, and her movements, as I help her up from the couch and into the wheelchair, are slow and clumsy. She means for the next feeding, but I deliberately misinterpret. She needs her rest.

"I'll wake you."

Given her pain and fatigue, everything takes extra time. A two-minute trip to the bathroom takes fifteen. Getting into the tank top she sleeps in and from there into bed takes ten. By the time I dole out her pain pill and set a glass of water by her bed, I've only got an hour before the kittens will need feeding. It's really not worth going to sleep. I'll just lie down for a minute, to rest, before I check to see how the weakest of the kittens is doing. If he's dead, which is highly possible, I don't want to know. Not. Just. Yet.

~

An unidentified sound wakes me from an uneasy dream. Already memory is slipping away, but I think it was about a baby. Kat's, or mine, here in the house and then gone missing. The sound is persistent enough to drag open a pair of stone-heavy eyelids.

For a minute I don't know where I am, and then it all comes back. Home. Couch. The sound is the meowing of hungry kittens.

Groggy and disoriented, I roll off the couch onto my hands and knees as the easiest way of getting my body into an upright position. This puts the heating pad right in front of my nose. One of the kittens is crawling determinedly toward me, drawn by scent or body heat, I'm not sure. In the dark I can't tell which one until I pick him up and turn on a night-light.

It's the once-half-dead tabby, now mewing and butting his blind face against me, seeking milk.

"Hey, Pipsqueak. You're tougher than you look."

I don't need lights to make formula and fill a bottle. This time he's strong enough to suck. I sit down on the floor, cross-legged, my back against the couch, and stroke his tiny head with one finger while he nurses. I've learned from experience not to be lulled into false confidence, and he gets a very careful burping and rubdown, before I settle him onto the heating pad. I feed his more stalwart brothers and sisters two at a time, and within half an hour I'm crashed out on the couch, my hand trailing down onto the floor where it rests protectively over a tiny kitten.

~

"You look exhausted," Cole says.

I can't imagine what he's doing here, wherever here is. My eyes jerk open, my neck snaps upright.

Cole's attentive face is directly across from me. The chair he's sitting on is not one of mine, and the space around us is hospital cafeteria. My hand still circles the triple-shot latte I was drinking before I drifted off.

My morning is such a sleep-deprived fog that it takes a minute to remember how I got here. Tuesday morning. Kat. An appointment. God, I should not be driving.

"Better talk to management," Cole says. "They're leaving the caffeine out of the coffee again."

I run a hand through my hair, but it catches on tangles, a problem that brings me awake enough to remember leaving the house in a hurry, no makeup, hair smoothed but not properly brushed. Words are still not forthcoming, and I suck up coffee through the straws to give myself time.

"Either that, or they're adding extra tryptophan to the milk."

He grins. "Or, in an alternate reality, Rae is not getting enough sleep. How's Kat?"

"It's the kittens that are the problem," I explain, and then realize it's no explanation at all. I go for more coffee, hoping it will defuzz my laboring brain.

"Kat is here for physical therapy. The kittens are at home. A batch of rescued babies. They keep me up at night."

"One Kat was not enough for you?" He says it lightly, but that singular intensity of his makes me defensive.

"She wanted them. Kat did. You know about the injury? They told her she probably can't have children. So motherless kittens . . ."

"You can't fix everything, Rae," he says. "You're going to wear yourself out."

"I'm fine."

"Clearly."

Something about the way he says this doesn't feel like criticism. It warms a cold place inside me, and I realize I'm smiling when he smiles back.

"I've got a counseling appointment set up for her. Thursday at eleven. Does that work?"

"Maybe?" There are too many appointments to keep track of in my head, especially sleep deprived as I am. Physical therapy. Primary care doctor. Surgeon. Orthopedic specialist for her hip. I've got it all written out in a planner that I pull out of my purse.

"Haven't seen one of those in a while," Cole says.

"Yeah, me and electronics aren't friendly."

His eyebrow goes up in a question mark. Something about Cole invites the truth, although I immediately want to snatch it back.

"I kill them," I tell him, flipping to Thursday in the planner and frowning at the logistics. "Smartphones. Watches. Laptops. Continual malfunctions, and the batteries are always dead. Thursday she has a doctor's appointment and physical therapy. She's free at eleven if I can find somebody to feed the kittens."

"Saver of small abandoned creatures, destroyer of all things electronic?"

"Pretty much." I shrug, searching his face for the inevitable *this woman is weird* expression.

"Let me help," he says, placing his right hand on the table next to mine. It lies there, palm up, open. It looks like an invitation, one I can't accept.

"With the electronics?" I close up the planner and return it to my purse, folding my hands in my lap for safekeeping.

"I was thinking kittens. Either that or taking Kat to the appointment. Name it. I'm there."

"Kat isn't overly fond of you."

He grimaces. "Kittens it is. You'll have to show me what to do."

Up to this point, at least to my knowledge, he doesn't know where I live. My heart flutters at the thought of Cole in my house, but it's not like I'll be alone with him. I can't think of any good reason to tell him no; I can't afford to turn down help.

I glance at my watch, half hoping it's time to go pick up Kat, half hoping it's not. Small talk isn't something I know how to do, and we've exhausted kittens and my electronics-killing powers. Or at least I think we have.

"My grandma's like that," Cole says. "With electronics. Can't wear a watch for more than a day. She swears she blows out light bulbs, and that's why she still likes to sit and knit by candlelight."

"For real?" I'm interested, despite a suspicion he's making things up. I have a deep fondness for candles, myself. "Are you close with her?"

"Closer to her than my folks, really. She half raised me. My parents divorced when I was ten. Looking back, I think it messed them both up royally. My mom was always working after that. Dad had a second family. I was horribly jealous of the new siblings."

"And your grandma understood things?"

"Better than I wanted her to. She told me I was acting like an obnoxious little brat."

I'm indignant on his behalf. "You were just a child!"

"Oh, sure. But she was right. Thing is, she could say things like that, and it didn't make me believe I was a bad kid."

Now I'm the one who is jealous. "I never knew my grandparents. They were all dead before I was born."

Cole leans forward, elbows resting on the table, doing that thing with his eyes that makes me feel like the most important being in the universe. It's a counseling trick, and I know it, but I still want to fall for it. I want to tell him all about my childhood and my failure to grow into the successful poster child for *Parenting on Time.*

Instead, I drain my coffee and shove back my chair. "Time to go pick up Kat. They were going to start her with a walker today. She'll be wiped."

He stands up and walks to the door with me. Even when I don't look at him I can feel him beside me, a pleasant heat, like a campfire.

"So, an address, then?" he asks, when we get to the cafeteria door.

I tell him, feeling like I've crossed a bridge from somewhere to somewhere, although from where to where I haven't got a clue.

"What time should I be there?"

I calculate the probable kitten-feeding times, how long it will take to teach Cole what to do, the distance to the counseling agency, the time to get Kat in and out of the car, and alarm bells go off in my head.

"Nine a.m. ought to do it."

"I'll be there." He flashes me that smile, the one that is a slice of pure, uncomplicated joy, and strides away, leaving me to stare at his retreating back and appreciate the fit of his T-shirt across broad shoulders, the way his jeans ride low, but not too low, on lean hips.

This man, who sets my heart to thumping and my knees to shaking for reasons I haven't begun to sort out yet, will be coming to my house on Thursday morning. Kat and kittens aside, I am in a whole lot of trouble.

If I live that long, which my current level of fatigue is leading me to doubt.

~

Wednesday night I take the carrier full of kittens to work with me. Kat protests that she can manage them while I'm gone, but exhaustion and pain have etched lines around her eyes that should not be there, and her cheekbones look sharp enough to cut.

She'd hoped to come home from physical therapy with crutches. What they've given her is a walker.

"The ribs," she explains. "They were worried about the ribs."

I wince, just thinking about the pressure crutches would exert on her rib cage. "Well, at least you're up and moving. Better than sitting in that chair."

"Maybe. I feel like my old granny. Buy me a cotton dress and a kerchief and call me Babushka."

"You're Russian?"

"Oh, you have no idea how Russian." She gives me the ghost of a smile. "I'm still offering to do kitten duty."

"Go to bed. Maybe tomorrow."

I can see she wants to argue, but she shuffles off to bed. From behind, she does look a bit like an elderly woman, her shoulders slumped, her feet encased in hospital slippers, shoving the walker along. But she's up. She's moving. And this is a good thing for both of us.

It doesn't take me long to pack up the kittens. I have a whole mobile nursery unit ready to roll. The heating pad goes in the cat carrier. I'll plug it into a socket in the staff room. I've got a diaper bag for formula and bottles, cleaning rags and cotton balls.

"Oh," Corinne coos when I stagger in, cat carrier in one hand, backpack weighing me down from behind, diaper bag slung on the other shoulder. "They are adorable."

She opens the carrier and takes the whole nest of them into her lap. "Have you named them yet? This big one looks like a Henry. I had a cat named Henry once. He was the hugest tom you ever saw. Oh, you could name one Oscar! Maybe Oscar the Second, just to keep things straight. This white one would be perfect."

The tiny kitten hisses at her when she picks him up.

"Oscar the Grouch would be more like it. Let's get through report, Cor. They're going to all be hungry in a minute."

But she insists on handling every one of them, stroking them while she talks. I'll admit that they're adorable, but the attention wakes them up and makes them hungry so that they're all crying by the time Corinne is packing up to leave and I have work to do.

"Want me to stay and help?" She would, I know, but she's tired and has things to do at home.

"I've got a plan."

"Of course you do." She draws me into a warm hug, but I'm forewarned and able to keep my face clear of her breasts.

Once she's gone I take the kittens straight to Nancy. She needs something other than the Oscar Event to look forward to. She can start by feeding kittens.

To my surprise, her response to them is horror. She backs away, climbing up onto her bed.

"What are those, rats?"

"No, they're kittens. They've lost their mama, and you get to feed them while I do rounds."

"I'm allergic."

"Doesn't say anything about allergies in your chart."

She pulls her legs up into the bed, much in the way that Bernie tried to get away from Oscar. "I'm allergic to responsibility. Why are they making that noise?"

"Because they're hungry."

"How did you know? Did he tell you? Why would he do that?"

For the first time since I've known her, Nancy looks her age. The sparkle has died out of her eyes, and her body looks frail and tired.

"I'm not sure what you're talking about, Nance. Are you feeling okay?" I set down the kittens and walk over to check her pulse and blood pressure. When old people have a sudden cognitive change, it's often because they're ill.

"I was fine until you brought this elaborate vengeance into my room." She yanks her hand away from me. "My pulse is fine. Take those creatures away and . . ." Her gaze shifts from me to the doorway and her lips compress into a thin line. "Speak of the devil and who shows up?"

Mason, cheeks flushed, tie off-kilter, leans against the doorjamb, as if he needs the support.

"Feeling guilty, Mother?" His words are not quite slurred, but the consonants run together, and the vowels are a little too relaxed.

"Go away," she says, but her voice lacks the energy of command.

"You," Mason says, looking at me. "Mother's been talking about the nurse with the dead rat. Would never have guessed."

"Always the charmer," Nancy says. "How many drinks was it tonight?"

"When I was ten," Mason says, entering the room carefully, as if the floor is quicksand and the placement of each step is important, "we had a mama cat. I called her Star. Such an imaginative name, wasn't it? I lacked the family flair for drama. Star had kittens. Mother was outraged that any cat of ours would dare to inflict such a burden upon her time and resources."

"Go away," Nancy says again. "I'm not well." She lies down on the bed and rolls away from us. "Take those kittens with you."

Mason lowers himself into the visitor's chair. "There was no shelter in Chicago that was interested in a whole family of cats. At least not the first shelter she called. So she killed them. Simple solution to a simple problem. I didn't know you worked here," he says again, shifting his attention to me.

"You're the son," I say. "The wonderful son who has just come to town."

Nancy makes a rude noise from the bed, and Mason's eyebrows go up like a theater curtain on opening night.

"She's been telling me all week how wonderful you are and how excited she is that you're here."

"Huh." He looks genuinely confused by this. Nancy's cheeks redden, and she pulls a pillow over her head.

"How's Kat?" Mason asks. "I went to visit, but she'd been discharged."

"Doing well, I believe." I'm not going to tell him where she is. The last thing in the world Kat needs is to have Mason come visiting. A dark worm of doubt twists inside me, insinuating that my reasons are not so clear, not so pure, but I squash it.

"These kittens," I say, tamping down my emotional reaction to this ugly little tale of kitten murder, "are very much alive and in need of feeding. I have work to do. Here's your chance to make restitution."

"Everybody killed kittens back then," Nancy protests, her back still to us. "It's not like I flattened them with a sledgehammer."

"No, just tied them into a sack and dropped them in the lake. On the way to dropping your son off for school."

The emotional weather in this room has progressed from squall to tornado warning and threatens to blow me away. Before either one of them can add to the storm, I pull out a kitten and hand him to Mason, along with a bottle and formula. "Feed this one first."

His eyes, imperfectly focused, come up to rest on my face. "You want me to feed it?"

"That would be why I'm giving you this bottle. Yes."

Despite Mason's intoxication and Nancy's protests, the staff is all busy, and these two are my best bets as kitten feeders. Mason has already proved his protective instincts, and Nancy is radiating curiosity at full-volume intensity, her dramatic posturing all an elaborate cover-up. At least that's what my instincts tell me, much as my brain balks in hesitation.

The kitten is not interested in waiting for me to make a decision. He smells milk and is already hunting the nipple. Mason makes a small sound of surprise as the kitten latches on. A short moment later, his free hand comes to rest on the kitten's back.

"Sit up," I say to the old sinner still curled on her side in the bed. "Since we're not killing these kitties, the only way to hush them is to get them fed." I set the carrier on the bed by her feet and wave the other bottle in front of her nose.

With a gusty, martyred sigh, she rolls over and uses the bed controls to bring herself up to sitting. She eyes the kitten I'm holding like it's a stick of dynamite about to blow up. Spreading a towel on her lap, I set the kitten down and get it started on the bottle.

A softness gentles the sharp lines of her face. "It's almost cute."

"Kittens have been called that, on occasion. When it's done eating, burp it."

"Like a *baby*? What if it spits up all over me?"

"One might wonder how I survived my childhood," Mason mutters.

"I was a good mother. You have no idea . . ."

My head has begun to ache, my body crawling with the complex web of love and guilt and anger that spins between the two of them. Fortunately I have work to do, and a valid excuse to leave them to their bickering.

But when I leave the room, I feel like I carry a contagion with me. I taste bitterness in my throat. There's a sensation in my chest that is simultaneously emptiness and a crushing weight. Restless irritability drives me, but at the same time I want only to lie down, right in the middle of the hallway, and rest.

Giving myself a brisk mental shake, like a dog coming in out of the rain, I knock on Elizabeth's door and push it open. She's sitting on the edge of the bed, waiting for me. Her cotton dress hangs off her bony shoulders like a coat hanger, her frail body collapsed in upon itself, spine hunched in a perpetual curve, fingers contracted into claws.

Unlike the rest of her body, which is all bones and skin, her lower legs and feet look like overfilled water balloons, about to burst. There's a spot on her right ankle that is open and weeping fluid, a result of the swelling and the venous insufficiency that causes it.

Elizabeth has always been nonresponsive. She follows simple commands for the most part, helping us get her dressed or out of bed, moving a spoon or fork to her mouth when a plate is set in front of her. But she's never spoken a word to me.

She doesn't speak now, but something has shifted, either in her or in me.

I feel her awareness as if it is a solid thing I could reach out and touch, something made out of misery and pain and a bleak despair. Mixed in with what I'm already carrying around with me from my encounter with Nancy and Mason, it's more than I can handle. The emotions foam up like baking soda in vinegar, and I can't keep them in.

Tears blur my vision. I've got gloves on to manage her sterile dressing, and I blot my eyes on my shoulders so I can see, so that tears don't fall on the wound. Otherwise, this seems a safe enough place to break down. Elizabeth isn't going to tell or even notice. The staff will never know.

But just as I finish smoothing a clear, breathable dressing over the wound, before I can take off my gloves, I feel a touch on my shoulder. Her hand feels like a leaf, dry and trembling and with so little weight that a breeze could blow it away. I look up from where I'm kneeling at her feet, and she wipes the tears from my cheeks with gnarled and bony fingers. Looking into her eyes, I see the essence of her looking back at me.

She nods, as if we've spoken words and come to some sort of agreement. Moved by impulse, I kiss her hand. The skin is cool and soft, lotion scented. Love and grief and feelings I have no name for fill me to the brim. I'm going to burst if I don't do something, and I can't afford a meltdown, so I start in nattering some sort of running patter about her foot and the unit and the kittens. I talk to her about Oscar and the Event, about dinner. About Kat. Words bleed off the energy, leaving me still intact but so weary I can barely get to my feet and drag myself out of the room.

Checking in on Nancy and the kittens, I find three of them asleep in the carrier, sprawled across each other for comfort and warmth. The last two are being fed. Mother and son are not talking, but they aren't sniping at each other either.

In the hallway, staff are herding residents toward the dining room for dinner.

Telling myself they can manage without me for once, I retreat to the office, collapse into a chair, and close my gritty eyes.

Just for a minute.

Tia's voice jolts me out of oblivion.

My neck hurts. My back hurts. The pillow is ridiculously hard. I can't think why Tia is in my room waking me up. Something about Nancy and kittens. I blink, twice, and the room comes into focus. Not my place, but the office. I'm sitting in a chair with my head down on the desk.

Tia's face blurs in front of my eyes, and she seems to have grown a third eye and two noses. "Sorry," she says, "you're obviously wiped out, but we need a skin check on Jack, and the insulins need to be given."

"Coming," I say, or mean to say, but all that comes out is a croak.

Tia vanishes from the doorway, and I let my eyes drift shut again, telling myself all the while to stand up and get moving. A touch on my shoulder, a joggling of my elbow, and the acrid aroma of burnt coffee interrupt a fragment of dream.

"Come on," Tia says. "Drink up. Did you take meds or something?"

My hands feel stiff and strange, but they obediently take a mug from Tia and manage to hold it without spilling. The first mouthful burns my tongue. This brew could serve as paint remover. Between that and my aching body, my brain begins to function.

"This is terrible coffee," I mutter.

"I know. They don't want residents drinking too much of it, probably. Are you awake now?"

"Yeah." I cling to the mug, shivering with a chill born of bone-deep fatigue.

"Good. I've got to go. We're trying to take up slack for you, but we can't sign off on skin checks, and Cindy doesn't have time to do all the meds plus insulin."

"I know, I know."

One more swallow of coffee that threatens to peel the skin off the roof of my mouth, and I'm able to get onto my feet. I know I'm not safe, so I triple- and quadruple-check all of the insulin doses to compensate, and it takes me forever. The evening crawls along, with me feeling like I'm running in slow motion to catch a bus that's moving in real time.

"God, woman, you have got to get some sleep," Andrea says when she comes on at eleven. "You can't function like this."

I'm not about to argue. I just don't know what to do.

It's not a long drive to my place, but the danger of nodding off is real. I drive with all the windows open and the stereo on, keeping myself awake by trying to figure out how to navigate the morning.

Kat has two appointments. Cole will be over to take a shift with the kittens. My parents are slated to hit Colville sometime tomorrow evening. When I see them Friday morning, my mother will go into full medical alert if she sees me looking like an extra for the *Walking Dead*, so I need to try to fit a nap in somewhere. The fragmented sleep I'll get between now and tomorrow morning's alarm is not going to cut it.

When I get home all of the desperate planning goes for nothing. There's a blue Prius parked in my driveway, a rental car with Washington plates, and that can only mean one thing—my parents have taken their new philosophy so thoroughly to heart they have showed up early. Which means they are at this very moment engaged in an unchaperoned encounter with my new roommate.

Chapter Ten

When I open the front door, Mom and Dad are ensconced on my couch. Kat sits across from them in my one and only armchair. My father, silver-haired but erect and distinguished in a dark suit and tie, holds my pillow on his knees. My mother, whose image could have been lifted straight off the cover of *AARP*, is engaged in folding my bedding into precise geometric squares I could never match if I worked at it for a lifetime.

A warm light from my floor lamp illuminates all three of them while leaving the corners of the small room in shadow. They look cozy and confidential, a picture-perfect family engaged in an intimate conversation.

"Hey," I say. "You're early!" This sounds better than *What the hell are you doing here?* and it's a good thing I thought of it, because in the time it takes me to set the kitten carrier next to an outlet and plug in the heating pad, I realize the full implications of *YOLO for Seniors* and understand that from now on, I can count on my parents to embrace the unexpected with the same fervor given to the scheduled days of my childhood and youth.

"Elizabeth," Dad says. "You look pale."

"It's Leila," Mom counters. "Have you been sick, dear? Come here and let me look at you."

"My name is Rae, and I'm fine. Just tired."

They look older than I remember. Close-up, Mother looks thin, the lines in her face visible despite a layer of flawless makeup. My father's salt-and-pepper hair has gone completely gray, and there's a bald spot on top of his head with a suspicious mole at center stage, waiting to be biopsied. I'm surprised my mother hasn't done it herself at home.

Neither one of them gets up to greet me. Grateful for the autopilot that tells my body what to do when my brain has given up and stalked off in exasperation, I cross the space between us and bend down to give them hugs.

Dad was tall, dark, and handsome when he met my mother fifty years ago. He's still tall, although the encroachments of age have stooped his shoulders despite a rigid resistance program involving exercise, diet, and positive thinking. His face has fallen into stern lines that make him formidable. Sharp eyes shadowed under a jutting brow, an aquiline nose turned blade sharp, lips thinned and pale.

When he hugs me he's all bone and sinew, no softness anywhere, but when I look into his face I'm surprised to see moisture in his eyes.

Age, I tell myself. *My father never cries. It's late. He's tired. Maybe there are allergens in Colville that are new to him.*

"It's been too long," he says. "How are you? You look exhausted."

"What a ridiculous shift you're working," Mom says. "You have enough seniority by now you should at least be able to get days."

"I like graveyard." When I stoop to put my arms around her shoulders and kiss her cheek, she smells of perfume and hair spray. Her hair is a perfect ruddy auburn without a thread of gray. A linen pantsuit drapes her in graceful folds that suggest she still has plenty of curves if she'd care to reveal them.

She holds my cheeks between her hands, talking while she looks me over. It's a distraction technique that works great on toddlers. Years of experience have taught me that she's taking the opportunity to screen the whites of my eyes for any trace of yellow, to check my lips for dehydration, to sniff my breath for indigestion or the ketones that might indicate I'm becoming diabetic.

"Days are where the opportunities are. Although, what would be wrong with a hospital job I don't see. Room for advancement. You'd make a capable charge nurse, I'm sure. Some hospitals have programs for further education and—"

"Mom."

"Get yourself a drink of water, honey. Your body is thirsty. We've been getting acquainted with your roommate."

Too tired to argue, I go to the sink and fill a glass, irritated to realize that Mom is right, as usual. My body sucks that water in like a plant in the desert, and I resist a second glass out of pure stubbornness.

I stay by the sink, using distance as both safety and support, leaning my butt against the counter and observing the three of them. Kat looks more animated and relaxed than I've ever seen her, and both Mom and Dad lean in toward her like sunflowers following the sun.

A shaft of jealousy thuds into my heart. I've never felt a close connection to my parents. They love me; I love them. I've never been neglected or abused. But I'm a misfit. Despite all of their careful plans, I have somehow gone awry.

They charted my birth from conception to delivery, beginning with the optimal time of the month, week, and day for the healthiest sperm to encounter the premium egg. Mom went to yoga classes and took special vitamins and perfected her Lamaze breathing. I was delivered by my father, not intimately at home, and not because they believed in some sort of super mother-baby bonding, but because of every extra IQ point that could be garnered by the healthiest pregnancy and the most natural delivery.

Their plans worked out all the way through the textbook-perfect birth, and then they were stuck with alien me. Mom diligently applied all of her best theories on structure and routine, but to no avail. I persisted in waking in the middle of the night, having meltdowns at the most inopportune moments, and draining the battery of every watch procured to help me keep track of elusive time.

When I was eight, I stumbled across a book about a changeling, and for the first time my world made sense. I carried that book with me. Slept with it under my pillow. My belief that fairies had slipped me into the Chatworth family as a mischievous joke lasted for nearly a year before my mother shattered it with a concise lecture on DNA and a photo album containing pictures of my grandmother.

Kat looks more like the child my parents should have had. Her hair and eyes, shades of cinnamon and amber, form a perfect link between Mom's auburn and Dad's dark. She's tall like them, and graceful. As for me, recessive genes played tricks with my construction, painting me in watercolors, with pale-blonde hair and eyes that shift from green to blue and back again, depending on the light.

"You could have told us," Mom says, drawing me back to the moment. Her voice sounds affectionate and almost light, as if there's a joke in the room that I'm missing. "We're perfectly fine with it."

"Good?"

I'm not sure why they wouldn't be fine with me having a roommate. Unless Kat told them how and why she came to be here. But that can't be right. My mother would never be fine with a suicide attempt, or with me sheltering an unstable stranger. Incompetence behind the steering wheel—especially of the kind that almost kills a bicyclist—would be even worse.

"I didn't want to talk about it," I say, buying time. "Besides, she's only just moved in—"

"Oh, honey," my mother says. "These things are not so uncommon. I think it's wonderful."

I look to Kat for enlightenment, but she shrugs and raises her eyebrows.

"It's a common trait," my father begins, in his lecturing voice. "Much more common than the general population realizes. Even in the animal kingdom there are multiple instances of same-sex relation-ships. I've been working on a hypothesis that we are seeing an increase in the human population due to overcrowding. Natural selection may be kicking in with the signal that we need to slow the birthrate . . ."

He's off on a tangent and I let him go, looking at Kat to signal my embarrassment and apology. She doesn't notice me. Her eyes are intent on my father's face, and she leans forward a little, listening.

"That's an interesting theory," she says. "I'd been thinking that peo-ple are just more open about it now, not that the incidence of same-sex attraction has increased. I mean, we know it's been present for thou-sands of years. The Greeks, the Romans, the biblical texts."

"Yes, yes, of course, this is partly what I'm saying. It is a normal and natural variant of human sexuality. But I believe it is increasing. Of course, there is no way to scientifically document this as we have no reliable numbers throughout history. We could begin now, though." He turns to me. "You never gave any indication in your teenage years, Elizabeth. I find this fascinating. When did you realize?"

"Richard," Mom protests. "Our Leila is tired. Look at her, about to drop on her feet." Mom moves over on the couch to make room for me, patting the open space beside her. I'm unable to resist what I know I'm going to regret. Zombielike, I cross the room and sink down between them.

My father bends his gaze on me, and any inner strength I have left wilts under his examination. I know this look. He feels deeply, but intellectual curiosity always wins out, and here I am, a perfect specimen to pick apart.

"I speculate that the energy required to hold on to this secret might contribute to your inertia," he says. "I understand the difficulty of self-analysis, and the Johari Window effect, but do you think it's possible that if you'd been able to come out sooner, you might have been freer to use your intellectual gifts?"

"I'm not out now." He won't hear me, but I say it anyway. My skin prickles like an oncoming heat rash.

Mother pats my hand again. "Coming out of the closet is an event, not a thesis, Richard. We should celebrate. How about tomorrow night? We could take you both out to dinner."

Something else is happening tomorrow night, but for the moment I can't think what. My brain, squashed between the two of them, spasms like an upside-down beetle, kicking its legs in a futile attempt to turn right side up. Again I glance at Kat, hoping for rescue, but she says nothing, and I can't even begin to read the expression on her face. As usual, I take refuge in evasion.

"This is such a surprise, seeing you tonight."

"We changed the plane tickets," Mom says. "We couldn't wait to see you! Plus, we thought this way we'd have more time to enjoy the drive to Seattle."

"But, the hotel." I'm still floundering in the cognitive dissonance created by the YOLO thing.

Dad beams at me. "The hotel was very accommodating. We got all settled in, and then we thought we'd take a drive—see Colville, and find your house. And then we saw the lights in the window and thought, *Why not?* You only live once, after all."

A vague resentment crawls into my belly. How dare they shake things up? I've spent most of my life rebelling against a bulwark of regimentation that apparently no longer exists, just because of some late-life existential crisis.

"So, maybe dinner tomorrow, instead of breakfast on Friday?" Mom is asking. "That way Leila and Katya can sleep in the morning."

I drop my head into my hands and rub my temples. "I have to work. As for breakfast on Friday, we couldn't be there before at least nine a.m. And you have a workshop. In Seattle. On Saturday. It's a long drive. You'll need to rest when you get there."

"We're not that old yet," Mom says, and she actually laughs. "Well, maybe your father is, but I can drive. All the time in the world."

"We only have one daughter," Dad adds. "Part of YOLO is never missing an opportunity to celebrate something wonderful."

I want to point out years of missed celebrations. Birthdays that didn't fit into the schedule. Inconvenient school concerts. The way my high school graduation party had to be held a week before the ceremony so Mom could start her summer lecture tour. I keep my mouth shut.

"I know what," Mom says. "We can come back through Colville on our way home—fly out of Spokane instead of Seattle, as we'd planned. We could have our celebratory dinner then. How does that sound? Can you get an evening off work, Leila?"

"Her name is Elizabeth," Dad protests, reflexively. "We agreed."

"I never agreed to anything." Mom's voice is adamant, a tone that signals the onset of an argument that is as old as I am and will never be resolved. Dad wanted to name me after Elizabeth Blackwell, the first woman obstetrician in the United States. Mom wanted to name me after Leila Denmark, the first woman pediatrician. The only reason Elizabeth precedes Leila on my birth certificate is because Dad snagged the form from the nursing staff and filled it out while Mom was busy breast-feeding their brand-new baby.

"She's just not a Leila," Dad says. "She doesn't even look like a Leila. What do you think, Kat?"

Before Kat can voice an opinion, I dive in. "Why don't we just go with Rumpelstiltskin and be done? Kat needs to rest. I still have to feed the kittens before I go to bed. And please, I'm begging you, don't reschedule your flight. I really won't be able to get any shifts off work."

My assigned role in our family dramas is to passively agree and try to make everybody happy, and this response befuddles them. Dad adjusts his glasses. Mom looks bewildered. I turn my back on them and start making formula for the kittens. My chest feels tight and heavy. There's a bitter taste in the back of my throat that I can't swallow down.

Name your emotions, Rae. Put labels on them.

I can't. There are too many, all mixed up with what belongs to my parents, to Kat. It must be sleep deprivation, but the boundaries of my self, the place where Rae begins and ends, are no longer well defined. It's like somebody has spilled water over a picture of the four of us, and all of the colors are bleeding into each other.

The only clarity I can find is with the kittens. They are hungry, have been hungry for a few minutes now, and are done with waiting. The mewling is increasing in intensity and making it difficult to concentrate on conversation. Since my parents are making no move toward getting up and vacating the premises, I hand each of them a kitten and a bottle of formula.

They stare at me like I've handed them something incomprehensible, like a cucumber and a chainsaw.

"They're just like babies. Nipple in the mouth. Burp them when they're done."

Dad, always the more maternal of my parents even though it's Mom who is the pediatrician, starts in feeding his kitten, or rather the kitten starts feeding herself, locating the nipple by sense of smell and latching on.

Mom sneezes. Her kitten startles and digs its claws in.

"Now look," she says. "It's ruined my blouse. Please. Richard, let's go. Clearly, Leila is tired and cranky." She detaches the kitten and holds it away from her body, pruning up her mouth in an expression echoing Bernie's when she first saw Oscar.

I rescue the crying baby and cuddle it under my chin, soothing it with endearments and milk.

"Interesting," Dad says, still feeding his kitten. "Rather rewarding, really. You should try it, Angela."

"No, thank you." She brushes her blouse and skirt as if they're plastered with cat fur, even though these kittens haven't begun shedding yet. "I've done my time with feeding human babies. I see no need to nurture abandoned kittens. The Darwin effect is the Darwin effect for a reason, Leila. There are more than enough cats on the planet."

She crosses the room and kisses me on the cheek, her lips barely making contact. I know her well enough to know she's angry but choosing not to show it.

"It was so lovely to have met you both," Kat says.

Dad's face warms into a smile. "Likewise. I think you'll be a wonderful addition to Elizabeth's life. Maybe even inspire her to take her fabulous brain to medical school."

"I'm not going to medical school. I've told you both how many times?"

Mom covers a yawn. "Look at the time. Come, Richard. Put that animal down. The girls need their rest."

In that moment she looks smaller than I remember. Fragile. Her lipstick is feathering into the tiny lines around her lips. When my father gets up from the couch, a small, involuntary sound escapes him. One hand still cradles the kitten, but the other braces his lower back. His spine uncurls one vertebra at a time.

My parents have been old since I can remember, but not this old. I have a sudden mental picture of both of them in shoeboxes, wrapped in cotton—tiny dead parents the size of a kitten or a rat. Sweat dampens my palms at the same time as goose bumps pop up on the skin of my arms.

Dad sets his kitten down on the couch, very gently, and pulls me to him in a hug that is warm and genuine. "I'm fond of kittens," he whispers in my ear. "Don't tell your mother."

A hint of liniment drifts into my nostrils, mixed in with soap and deodorant.

I hug him back, all of my outrage fading into loss as my hands encounter ribs beneath his suit coat and I recognize the decreasing muscle mass of an aging man. "Maybe you can come help us feed them in the morning," I whisper against his chest.

"I think we'll hit the road early and let you sleep in the morning. You're going to be ill if you don't get some sleep."

"I'm sorry breakfast won't work out." All at once I *am* sorry. I feel like maybe I would have liked having YOLO parents when I was a child.

Dad smiles and lets his hand rest on my hair. "We've already had our visit, yes? We hadn't realized how many plates you are spinning right now. We'll plan on seeing you for Christmas." He turns to Kat. "I do hope the driver who ran over you gets locked up for a long time."

"Drunk drivers should get the death penalty, I've always thought," Mom says.

"Was there indication of intoxication? Kat never said . . ."

The two of them move toward the door, gravitating toward each other and their usual form of communication as they leave me behind. By the time they reach the door their arms are around each other, even as their voices continue an argument that is based entirely on a faulty premise.

"Good night, girls," Mom says, as if we're sixteen and this is a slumber party. "Don't stay up too late."

I bite my tongue on the retort that it's already too late and they're the ones who made it that way, pasting a smile on my face and waving good-bye.

When I close the door behind them, I turn and lean against it. Kat sits in her chair, feeding the kitten, but it's me who has her full attention. All of the smiles and dimples have fled and her eyes smolder.

"I'm so sorry," I say, sliding down to sit on the floor, right where I am, letting my eyelids close over my gritty eyes. "They can't help themselves."

"Are you always rude like that, to your parents?"

My eyelids fly open again. "I'm sorry, what?"

"How can you talk to them like that? They are your *parents*." Her cheeks are flushed, her eyes lasered in on me like weapons of mass destruction.

My brain refuses to process. Kat is pissed. Not at my obtrusive, nosy, overbearing parents, but at me.

"I don't . . ."

"The whole time they were waiting for you to come home, they talked about you. How smart you are. How much they love you. How proud they are of you. How bewildered they are that you have chosen to live across the country where they can never see you. And then you come in and are rude and disrespectful—"

"Me?" I lever my protesting body upright. "I was rude! Look, I m too tired for this. I'm going to get your pills and finish feeding the kittens, and then I'm going to sleep for a couple of hours before I have to wake up again."

I fumble for the key to my lockbox and count out an oxycodone and a sedative. I run a glass of water from the sink. But Kat won't let it go.

"Is this what you do when somebody calls you on your shit? Evade?"

All of my suppressed anger flares, and I turn on her, my voice rising. "You don't know thing one about me or my parents."

"They want you to succeed. They would pay for you to go back to school."

"I don't want them to pay. I don't want to go to school."

"Well, aren't you a special snowflake princess."

"What the hell, Kat?"

"You want to know how many student loans I have? No. You don't. I put myself through college and graduate school. I have a freaking law degree. You know what my mother wants from me? Babies. Lots and lots of babies."

If one of the kittens morphed into a rabid dog and bit me, I couldn't feel more ambushed.

I feel myself about to explode. *The big bang, emotional version, life of Rae.* I can't let this happen. I can't say any of the things I suddenly want to say. Clenching my fists so tight I can feel my fingernails digging into my palms, I try to stop the apocalypse.

"Take your pills, Katya. Go to bed."

Kat shoves my outstretched hand away. "Who made you my mother?"

The glass slips from my fingers and shatters on the floor, water spilling everywhere.

I take a huge breath and try to count to ten, but I manage to breathe in spit and have to stop for a coughing fit that renders me incapable of defending myself while she rampages on.

"You're enjoying this whole thing. You get off on it. *Oh, look at Rae, the saintly martyr, taking in the emotional wreck—*"

"Right. It's been a barrel of monkeys and a ton of laughs."

Every one of my instincts is to escape, but I have nowhere to go. If I flee into the bedroom and slam the door, I'll be trapped in my own house. If I sit outside, the neighbors will be all full of questions. I can't go to a hotel, because I've made myself responsible for this woman. I'd thought we had some deep and mystical bond, but I was wrong.

"You want to know something? I chose you and your car. You had that same insufferable look on your face as you're wearing now—poor, misunderstood Rae. You have freaking everything and don't even know it."

"Oh, pardon me—I hadn't realized that all the sadness in the world belongs to you. You want to talk selfish? You couldn't even kill yourself without dragging somebody else in with you."

My words hit her like a mortar. I see the shock of contact in the way her face stills as her body tenses. She sets the kitten down, gently, on the arm of the chair. Hoists herself up with the walker. Pain pinches her lips tight together, and her breath hisses between her teeth.

"Kat . . ."

"You think you have some sort of market cornered on grief. You haven't got a clue."

My feet have grown roots. I don't follow her as she works her way into the bedroom, don't try to stop her. Only after the door closes behind her do I take a shuddering breath, and then another, sick with the realization of what I should have seen all along. I feel like I'm emerging from under a spell.

There is a strange woman in my house. Sharing my space, breathing my air, sleeping in my bed. No wonder Cole was against the idea of me bringing her home. I stand in the middle of what was once my exclusive living space, dazed and stupefied, grounding myself in small details.

Two water glasses and a teacup on the coffee table. Five kittens asleep in a pile. My blanket perfectly folded by my mother, my pillow on the floor. A shattered glass in a puddle of water.

Unfamiliar currents of energy swirl around me on the outside, unnamed emotions gurgle like swamp gas within. My brain wants to sort what happened here tonight, but I'm too exhausted and numb. I get a trash bag and a towel and start picking up the biggest shards of glass. The fragments are sharp-edged and dangerous, not the harmless pebbles of a safety glass. One of them slips in my hand and slices the pad of my finger. Blood wells up in a vivid crimson line.

Cursing myself for a clumsy idiot, I wash the cut at the bathroom sink, pour peroxide over it, and wrap it in a Band-Aid. It hurts, but I figure that serves me right for being careless. I sweep all the rest of the mess up with a broom and dustpan, water and all, and dump it into the kitchen trash.

When I finally collapse on the couch, my blanket smells like Kat, my pillow like Dad's liniment. As my eyes drift closed and my brain gives up the battle, my last conscious thought is that enough is enough. I'm taking Kat to the crisis house tomorrow.

~

A cool hand on my forehead. A whiff of soap and shampoo. Two soft-spoken words.

"I'm sorry."

The world blurs through sleep-graveled eyes. Kat stands beside my couch, leaning on her walker. Her hair is damp and loose on her shoulders.

Memories shift and slide, sorting themselves into waking and dreaming. My throat feels as dry as a two-day-old chicken bone.

I push myself up to sitting, scrub at my eyes, try to line up my thoughts. Dim morning light straggles in around the window shade. There should have been another kitten feeding last night, but I don't remember doing it. Panic that they've all died of neglect rises on a wave of adrenaline, but they are sound asleep.

"What time is it?"

"Don't worry, I fed them," she says, following my gaze. "I didn't want to wake you."

Kat sinks down onto the couch beside me, glances at me sideways, and then away. Her hands twist in her lap. "You'll probably want me to go away."

"I don't . . . I can't . . . I don't understand." My brain feels groggy and stupid. The only comprehensible thoughts it latches onto are *coffee* and *bathroom*. But I can't get myself coordinated enough to move in any one direction.

"Jealousy," she says. "Pure and simple. I wanted what you have, and I was ugly. I can't say how much I'm sorry."

"You were right." My words sound thick and heavy. I scrub my hands over my scalp. "Snowflake princess. That's me."

"I said I was sorry. I don't know what else to say."

"Me, either. Give me a minute."

I shove myself up off the couch. Load the coffeemaker. Go to the bathroom. Splash cold water over my face. My eyes in the mirror are bloodshot, and there are dark circles under them. I'm not sure I recognize myself.

Kat is still sitting on the couch when I come out, and the coffeepot is gurgling. I pour us each a cup. She accepts hers without making eye contact, blowing on it while I go ahead and start drinking. If it burns my tongue, maybe that will help me wake up from whatever dream I've slipped into.

"I wasn't being sarcastic," I say, after the caffeine starts connecting my synapses. "A lot of what you said was true. Probably. I'm still processing."

"Shades of truth," she murmurs. "I put a dark, dark spin on it. You're a good person. And you were right, too. I don't know anything about your childhood or why you are this way with your parents."

"Maybe we got swapped at birth. You and my parents seemed to hit it off better in one evening than the three of us have in thirty years."

And there it is, my own little ugly, jagged spear of jealousy.

"Swapped?" Kat's lips curve into a hint of a smile. "You wanted to have lots and lots of babies?"

"More than I want to be a doctor."

She sets down the coffee mug and digs something out of her pocket. "I wanted to show you. This is my mother. Education for girls wasn't high on her priority list." The photograph is old and bent. There's a white line down the center as if it's been folded. A strongly built woman with a hard face, a kerchief tied around her hair, stands at the center of a brood of five solemn children. Her hands rest on a heavily pregnant belly.

I survey the faces of the children—one girl, and four boys. The girl has a serious face, her long hair covered by a scarf. She doesn't look at all like Kat.

"Is that you?"

She taps the pregnant belly. "I'm the baby."

"Where's your father?"

"He died a month after she emigrated. Two months before I was born."

"I'm sorry."

She shrugs. "I never knew him. My oldest brother was more father than anything."

I try to place Kat in this family. Her precise English, her degrees, the tiny tattoo on her left ankle. And then I try to imagine growing up with a sister. Sharing a room. Girl talk at night, clothes, boys.

All of it is alien and foreign and strange.

"Do they know where you are? That you're okay?"

"I'm not up to them right now."

"Because of the baby expectations?"

"Because they disapprove of me. My husband. My education. My clothing. And yes, my inability to produce a living baby. When they hear about the . . . about what I tried to do, that will be the final straw for them. Russian women are strong. They have babies. Life is like that. God will condemn me to hell."

"You don't believe that."

She shrugs, takes a sip of coffee. "What I believe, what I don't believe. All a muddle, and does it really matter?"

"Of course it matters. It has to matter."

"And if it doesn't? That's what I keep coming back to. I'm no use to anybody, not like this. I want to believe in God, but I can't. When I try to pray, there's just a . . . an emptiness where God should be. If I believed there was a purpose or a plan, it would be different. But I don't. I can't. Life sucks and then you die."

I don't know what to say to this. Sitting here beside her, the world feels dark and gray and cold. What if she's right? What if there is no purpose, no point, no hope? Death, the sooner the better, seems like an obvious conclusion.

"There are always kittens," I whisper, more to myself than to her.

"You can't heal the world with kittens, Rae," she says. And for the first time in my life, I am afraid that I can't heal the world at all.

Chapter Eleven

Neither one of us is anywhere close to ready for the day when a knock comes at the door.

Kat is settled in the armchair with the TV tray in front of her, drinking tea and pretending to eat the oatmeal and fruit I made for her. I'm at the kitchen table with a bowl of cereal and milk. Both of us stare at the door like the grim reaper is on the other side.

I know damn well it's Cole, but I haven't told Kat about that yet. After last night's squabble, the peace between us feels tentative and precious, and I'm reluctant to do anything to break it. Maybe if I ignore him, he'll go away.

"Are we expecting company?" Kat asks. "Maybe your parents decided to hang around."

The knock comes again. It's a nice knock, polite but firm and determined.

"Reporting for kitten duty," Cole says, when I finally open the door. "Am I early?"

Kat flashes me a glance part shock, part betrayal.

"No, you're right on time. Sorry. We were up late. My parents came to visit."

"Change of plans? If your parents are here . . ."

I'm still blocking the door. Across the street, Thelma Willis is staring. Maybe she thinks I've suddenly come by a boyfriend. More likely, given the lack of men going in and out of my house, she knows Cole is a social worker and thinks I'm the one in trouble.

"They're gone. Or at least leaving. They stayed at Benny's." I step away from the door and wave him in.

Even after I close the door behind him, the room seems brighter. I feel my mood lifting, despite Kat's hostile silence.

"I love Benny's."

"I rather doubt my parents will be sharing your opinion. Their tastes are a little more—sophisticated." Even as I say this, I know it isn't true. I'm describing the parents I thought I knew, not the adventure-embracing seniors out to seize the day.

Cole gravitates directly to the box of kittens. "So these are the guilty culprits. Damn cute little sleep stealers, they are." He runs his hand over the tiny bodies before glancing at Kat. "You look better."

"I'm complying with everything. I didn't realize you'd be checking in personally."

"Completely unofficial capacity," he says, keeping his tone light. "I'm just the kitten babysitter while Rae takes you to your appointments."

"Well, then. I'll go get ready." Kat leans forward and lifts the TV tray to set it aside, freezing in the act with an audible gasp of pain.

"Let me help you." I start toward her, but she warns me off with a gesture.

"What do you think I do when you're not here? Or are you spying then, too? Watching on nanny cam, maybe?"

I flinch away from the impact of her resurrected anger, watching helplessly as she gets to her feet and shuffles into the bedroom, slamming the door behind her.

An awkward silence follows in her wake.

"Can I get you a cup of coffee or something?" My voice is too loud. My brain is split between Kat, angry and hurt, barricaded in the bedroom, and the fact that I'm wearing a giant T-shirt and baggy leggings and once again have failed to comb my hair.

"I'm here to help. No need to entertain me." Cole has donned the persona of Professional Kitten Wrangler, as if he's a paid professional like the plumber, or maybe the Orkin man, come to eliminate a plague of spiders.

It takes a lot of energy to refrain from explanations about how I'm a woman who usually showers and combs her hair, but I manage it, figuring there's no need to draw attention to the obvious. I focus on a short kitten tutorial instead.

We're standing side by side at the sink, me intent on filling a bottle with a funnel, when I feel his gaze on me. His face is close to mine, so close, his eyes focused on my lips. Heat rises from my toes to the top of my head and on up into the shafts of my hair. I'll be rocket woman if he keeps this up, flames shooting out of my feet and lifting me off the floor.

If I think there's a kiss in the works, though, I couldn't be more wrong.

His finger traces my upper lip. "You've got a milk mustache."

The bottle clatters into the sink, both of my hands flying up to cover my mouth. He catches them in midflight, traps them in his. His touch burns through me, more fuel to the fire. His face is solemn, but amusement lights his eyes. "Every girl should have one. You could start a fashion trend."

I don't know where to look. His lips are too close, his eyes too intent. A visible pulse beats at the hollow of his throat. My knees feel weak.

And then it occurs to me how this will look to Kat if she comes out of the bedroom.

"The kittens are hungry," I croak, pulling my hands away and turning back to the bottle.

They support my claim with a crescendo of meows. My hands are shaking, and I drop the bottle again, this time splashing formula all over the sink. If Cole thinks I'm an incompetent idiot, though, he doesn't show it. He fills the second bottle and follows me across the room. Steadfastly ignoring my couch bed, which seems suddenly far too intimate, I plunk down on the floor by the kittens. Cole follows suit, sitting easily cross-legged, yoga-style, and accepting the bit of fluff I place in his hands with great care.

"Have you named them yet?"

I shake my head. "They're so fragile. I get too attached. It's a little easier if I don't name them."

"Does that really work?"

"No. I just tell myself that it does."

He's a natural and really doesn't need much instruction. Doesn't even raise an eyebrow when I bring up the burping and the post-meal rubdown.

"Makes sense" is all he says.

We settle into quiet, each feeding a kitten, and when I reach for my embarrassment of a moment ago, it has evaporated into a peaceful stillness.

Until the doorknob rattles and Kat emerges. She's fully dressed, for the first time since I brought her home, in expensive blue jeans and a silky blouse. Her eyes are made up to give her an exotic Eastern look. Her hair is spiked up with gel. She doesn't smile or make eye contact, just heads for the door.

"You almost ready?" Her voice reminds me of my mother's, mornings when I lost track of time and was still dawdling around in pajamas when it was time for the school bus. Which is pretty much what I'm doing today, only I'm the driver, and I wouldn't be dawdling if Kat hadn't accepted the kittens.

"Give me a minute."

I hate to leave the two of them alone together, but there's nothing to be done about it. For that reason, and also because we're going to be late to Kat's first appointment, my grooming is minimal. Clean clothes. A splash of water on my face. A wet comb dragged through my hair.

When I come out of the bathroom, Cole is still feeding the kittens. Kat is nowhere to be seen.

"I presume she's waiting in the car," he says, in response to my unspoken question. "Either that, or she's walking to her appointment."

"Damn it, she'll hurt herself."

I grab my keys and head for the door.

"She's a grown woman," Cole says behind me. "She gets to make choices."

I'm already on my way out and pretend I didn't hear him. Kat sits in the passenger seat, door open. The walker waits on the pavement beside the car. Her face is tight around the lips, and I know she's hurting. She doesn't look at me while I fold up the walker and deposit it in the backseat.

"I should have warned you."

"You think?" She keeps her eyes fixed straight ahead.

"He said he'd help. I didn't know how else to get you to all of your appointments."

"Because of the appointments that *he* said I have to go to. He's like—the brain police. Or the parole officer for mental cases, and you just invited him over."

"It's not like that, Kat. He's trying to help."

"Is he? You really don't think he gets some big jolly out of making people do things?"

"He gets a little intense. But no, I don't think he gets off on control." I'm not entirely sure I believe what I'm saying. Cole doesn't fit into any box or category, and I don't know where to file him.

Kat doesn't answer, but she's thinking plenty. Fortunately it's not far to the clinic, because by the time we get there the silence in the car is so loud I can't think straight. Neither one of us says a word while I haul out the walker and Kat gets herself out of the car. I don't offer to help. When she checks in to reception she asks, "Do you think somebody might be able to run me over to physical therapy from here after my appointment? Rae has other commitments."

The receptionist smiles. "Of course. No problem."

I open my mouth to protest, but I'm not quick enough.

"Go home. Hang out with your boyfriend." Kat's voice carves through me.

There's no defense I can muster against her, and I stumble out of the waiting room, feeling like every eye in the clinic is following me, sure that all of the patients and staff are whispering behind my back.

Look at her run away, softhearted little fool. When is she ever going to learn?

Outside the air is heavy and hot, trapped beneath a leaden sky. It feels thick in my lungs, each breath a conscious effort. I can't sit in my car and wait, because now the tears are falling, and somebody will see me. The last thing in the world that I need right now is pity. And I certainly don't need to fuel whatever gossip is already circulating about me and my activities. Bernie is out of the question. Home is no longer a sanctuary.

I drive to the only other refuge I know.

But even my wishing beach looks different. The water reflects back a flat and tarnished sky. A dank, fishy smell of decaying vegetation rises up from slimy rocks at the edge of the water. The stones, usually a varied kaleidoscope of colors and textures, look uniform and gray. When I bend to pick one up, it feels gritty and wrong. I drop it with a little clatter, realizing that there is not a stone in the world that can wish away all that is wrong with Kat, or with me, for that matter.

Facts are facts.

Kat tried to kill herself. She chose me as her weapon, not completely randomly, but because of some expression on my face, something about me, Rae, that fueled her anger. All the time I've been believing we experienced this incredible moment of bonding over her almost death, she's been quietly hating me.

Snowflake princess.

Fragile. Precious. Selfish. Avoiding so much of life out of fear that it will break me.

Well, here's the news bulletin, princess. Life breaks everybody, long before death comes to sweep up the fragments.

I try to separate the barbs from my heart, but they've grown into the flesh, fused with the essence of me. Kat is right. It's time to grow up, accept the harsh realities, and stop wishing for things to be other than they are. I'm too tired. It's all too much.

What I ought to do, what I need to do, is move Kat out. Give back the kittens. Maybe even give notice at work and go do something entirely different. Fast food, secretarial. I'm a horrible cook, and I'm hell on electronics, but maybe I could still flip burgers.

The sky weighs on me, and I sink down onto a small boulder to rest.

My eyes drift half closed, and the world shifts back into magic. Colors appear where there were none, dancing on the water. Stones elongate into curious shapes. A tiny puff of wind brushes my cheek. A dragonfly alights on a stone, only inches from my right foot. Its wings are black lace, its body white.

As a child I had a dragonfly pendant with a prism at the center. I loved the way light refracted through that glass bauble, how it turned an ordinary world into rainbows. My heart swells with remembered magic. The dragonfly shimmers through a haze of sudden tears.

Something shifts inside me, a physical sensation, tentative and only half-realized.

Name your emotions, Rae.

There is heat, but it's not anger. A vein of sadness, but it isn't grief. It's elusive and fleeting and slips away before I can grasp it. The dragonfly flutters its wings and darts away over the surface of the water.

~

Kat is waiting outside when I get to the hospital. Neither one of us says anything while she navigates her way into the car and I stow her walker in the backseat.

We have thirty minutes before her counseling appointment, but I drive her directly there rather than suggesting that we swing through Taco Bell for lunch.

It's Kat who finally speaks.

"I thought maybe you wouldn't come back for me. Not that I'd blame you," she says, before I can apologize for the sin I didn't know I'd committed. "There I go again, being a bitch. Of course you'd pick me up. Even if you hated me, you'd never just leave me there. You're not like that."

My fingers tighten on the wheel while I digest all of this. I'm not sure if it's good or bad, what she's saying. Maybe it means I'm a good person. Maybe it means I'm a doormat, prepared to be trampled by a multitude of feet without standing up for myself.

"What was all that?" I ask, finally. "So much hate. Last night. This morning. The switch keeps flipping with you, and I can't figure out where I'm at."

"Honestly?"

"Probably lies would be more comfortable. But yes. Honestly."

"I don't know. Don't look at me like that. It's the truth, Rae. I open my mouth, and the words spill out and part of me is standing back in horror, wondering what the hell I'm doing."

"Maybe the parts of you need to start talking to each other."

"Maybe I need to see a counselor or something." A smile lights her face and vanishes again.

"Good thing I know exactly where to find one."

"Rae." Her hand settles on my arm. "Don't hate me."

"I don't hate you. I'm hurt. I'm confused. I don't know what I am, other than that I can't go on stepping on land mines every time I turn around." I pull into the lot outside the counseling building and park the car. "If you don't want to stay with me, you could ask your counselor about the crisis house they have here."

Her fingers, still resting on my arm, tighten. She shakes her head. "No. Please. I know I'm imposing on you and your kindness, but I can't. I won't."

"I thought we were friends," I say, very softly.

"We are! I told you, I don't know why I keep saying hateful things to you." Her fingers slide down my arm and intertwine with mine, still resting on the steering wheel. I don't know what to do with this. I want to pull my hand away. I want to hug her. I want to get out of the car and make a run for it.

What I do is sit perfectly still, staring at our interlaced fingers. My skin is brown, tanned by the sun. Hers is pale and lightly freckled. Her fingernails, once manicured, are chipped and broken. Mine are neatly cut and unvarnished. She's wearing long sleeves, but in my mind's eye X-ray vision I can see the thin white scars running up her wrists.

"Your parents," she says, her voice tentative.

"My parents are a force of nature. Like the tides."

"Have you ever thought about . . . well, about what they assumed. Us. As more than friends."

Heat rises to my cheeks, my eyes fall, grazing across the curves of her body on the way down. The soft swell of her breast, the narrowing at her waist, the flare of her hip.

Nope. Nothing. None of it moves me to anything but embarrassment. I remember Cole, and the way my knees wobbled when I thought he was going to kiss me. I shake my head. My throat is dry and tight. Her cool fingers touch my cheek, trace the line of my jaw, then fall to her lap when I refuse to look her in the eye. "Me, either. But I think sometimes it would be easier."

"Was it awful, with your husband?" I ask.

"Not awful—just complicated."

I do look up now, to catch an even deeper shadow in her eyes. "Did you ever press charges?"

"Me? For what?"

"Well, if he hit you, or—"

"Tom? Lay a hand on me? Where on earth did you get that idea?"

Reality shifts around us. "There were some things you said. And the way you left him."

"I was too weak to stick around and see how much I hurt him." Again that swift smile that never reaches her eyes. "I'm a coward. And as a coward, I'm going to ask you to please not make me do this counseling thing."

"It's not up to me."

Her face hardens. "Right. It's the mandate of your boyfriend. That Cole person."

"Actually, it's up to you. Nobody's holding a gun to your head."

"Did you just . . ." She laughs, a short, sharp burst of surprise. "I can't believe you said that. To a suicidal person."

"It's time. You going in there, or coming home with me?"

"If I come home with you, then Cole will know, and he'll start digging again, and maybe he'll pack me off to bedlam. I'm going. I'm going." She takes a deep breath, runs her fingers through her hair, and opens the door.

I fetch the walker.

"Don't forget to come back for me."

"I'll be here. Lunch and an oxycodone and express taxi service from Rae, all waiting for you."

"I love you, Rae. In the purely platonic BFF sort of a way."

"I'll remember that."

"Do."

I watch her shuffle into the building before driving away to find us both some lunch, feeling unexpectedly at peace with myself and the world.

Chapter Twelve

Saturday morning dawns clear and bright, calm, with no chance of rain. If the weatherman can be believed, the evening will be perfect for a bonfire and an Oscar Event. Not that he actually mentions the Oscar Event, but I wouldn't be surprised if he did. It's become big enough in my head that I wouldn't be surprised if the whole town of Colville and half the city of Spokane showed up.

The weather forecast elicits mixed emotions from me, ranging from anxiety through anger and avoidance to expectation and pleasure. Historically, parties have worked out about as well for me as shiny new electronic devices. Horrible weather would be too bad, so sad, but it would also offer me a graceful exit strategy.

I have one last hope of evasion.

Kat. The two of us have spent the last few days in a state of truce, both of us trying a little too hard. If there were a sitcom called *The Nice Sisters*, we'd be the stars, oozing politeness and consideration until I want to scream unfamiliar curse words at the top of my lungs. The emotional subtext, absorbed through my pores and processed by that internal receptor I'm supposed to have, is a dark mix of jealousy, love, hope, despair, and an indefinable restlessness.

All day I tell myself my uneasiness is a product of my overactive imagination, fed by sleep deprivation and the traumatic events of the last few days. But it persists, lurking in corners, stalking my every move.

An hour before it's time to go I can't stand it anymore. I pop out of the bathroom, an open mascara bottle in one hand, the wand in the other. "Seriously. You should come. I can pick up a wheelchair so you don't have to use the walker."

"I'm not crashing your party," Kat says, cuddling a lapful of kittens. "Besides, who would take care of these guys?"

"I could stay home."

"No. Not on account of me." There's a warning in her tone.

"You're still not strong. I can see how much you're hurting, even with the oxycodone. What if—"

"Rae. Stop. You need to have a life."

"But—"

"There are no buts. I'm not going. You are. End of story. You're getting mascara all over your pants."

Damn it, she's right. I'm not sure I even have another pair of jeans, and I am not wearing scrubs to my one social outing of the year. Back in the bathroom I blot at the black streak with a damp washcloth, managing only to smear it.

"It will be dark," Kat calls from the living room. "Nobody's going to notice."

I pop back out, careful to cap the mascara this time. "It won't be dark right away. Not during the drive." And then I blurt out what I've been avoiding telling her. "Cole is picking me up."

Her lips press together and fold in at the corners before she can duck her head to hide her face.

"I can call him and cancel. If you wanted to come. Or I could stay home. I don't think I even want to go."

"Be careful with a guy like that. Not that it's any of my business."

"I can meet him somewhere else. So you don't have to see him."

"That's ridiculous. This is your house. He's your friend. Do what you want."

Such a dangerous little phrase those four little words make. *Do what you want.* Nobody on the face of the planet ever says that line and means it. The tension in the room alone tells me that what Kat wants is certainly not what she thinks I want, but that she's hoping I'll change my mind. Not about the Oscar Event, but about Cole.

"A lot of fuss about a dead rat," Kat says. It's the sort of statement my mother would make. I picture Kat as a child of six, earnestly discussing science with my father and putting together anatomical models with my mother. All of them enjoying each other and speaking the same language. No bewildering meltdowns over imaginary friends. No tears and heartbreak over words never even spoken.

Kat is right, of course. It is a lot of fuss over a dead rat. The part of me that was excited about the party deflates, and I just stand there, limp and tired and trapped by forces beyond my control.

"Oh God. I'm sorry," Kat says, but it's too late. "I don't know what's wrong with me. You look great. Come hug me, and then I'm going to vanish."

Squashing unease, hurt, and a small, futile anger, I follow her directive, leaning down to hug her where she sits in the armchair. Her breath catches and she squeezes me tight. "Forgive me," she whispers in my ear.

"We're good. It's fine." I pull away and smile at her to demonstrate the truth of this.

"You're missing something," she says, tilting her head to one side and looking me over. "I know. Earrings."

"Nobody's going to notice. It will be dark."

She smiles at my joke. "Wait. I have the perfect ones for you. Let me get them."

"Kat, don't. It's not worth the effort."

"Let me. I want to give you something. Hang on."

I watch as she painfully hoists herself to her feet, using the walker as an anchor, and shuffles into the bedroom. She's gone long enough to make me fidget, worrying whether she's okay, wondering when Cole will arrive.

Finally, Kat returns. She hands me a small jewelry box. "Here. I want you to have them."

Inside the box, on a white satin lining, nestle two fire opals.

I touch them with a reverent finger, and rainbows shift across the surface.

"They're gorgeous."

"They're yours."

I shove the box back toward her. "I can't take these. It's too much."

"I owe you. Let me give you something. Please."

I shake my head.

"Just for tonight, then," she says. "I want to see them on you. Here, let me."

I still mean to say no, but instead I kneel in front of her chair and let her fasten them onto my earlobes.

"Perfect. They suit you. Go look."

When I look in the mirror I don't see my face at all, only those two shimmering stones and the way the color shifts and plays every time I move my head. I tell myself to take them off, to give them back, but Cole's knock at the door scatters all rational thought right out of my head.

~

Usually a silence is full of complex emotional noise, but when the initial small talk between me and Cole ebbs and leaves us with nothing to say, what lies between us is quiet and calm. I'm vividly aware of my own emotions, all of the colors and shadings of Rae, but Cole somehow keeps to himself.

He catches me staring at him, trying to figure this out, and his eyebrow lifts in a question. "What? Is there peanut butter on my face?"

He grins, and my heart does a weird little flip-flop. This unnerves me, and what I'm thinking pops right out of my mouth.

"I can't read you."

"Cole, the book of mysteries," he says, lightly, his eyes back on the road. "Is that a problem?"

"Yes. No. I don't know." I laugh. "Probably not?"

"Let me help. The predominant mood for tonight is worried. Note the furrow between my brows and the tension with which I grip the steering wheel."

I peruse him for both of these signs and shake my head. "Poker face. Relaxed hands. Why the worry?"

"When I said the Oscar thing had gotten out of hand—I meant really out of hand. Just so you know."

A cold twisting sensation threads its way through my belly. I don't have a poker face, and I can feel the furrow between my own brows. "I don't do crowds."

"This is—more than crowds. Your friend Corinne got a little carried away with the whole thing."

"Oh God. What did she do?"

"If I tell you, I'm afraid you won't come."

"Is that an option?"

"It is an option. I'm not sure it's a good one." His hand reaches out and covers mine. There's a diagonal scar running across the back. One fingernail is chipped. His touch feels warm, comforting, and isn't asking anything of me. Instead, it feels like an offer.

I curl my own fingers up between his, liking the texture of calluses, the way his hand is so much bigger than mine. We don't talk the rest of the way. When he turns off the highway onto an unmarked road that leads to the beach, I want to ask him to just keep driving, just the two of us like this, joined by the hands, driving into the stars.

But an Event is an Event, and there's no escape from this one.

The field next to the beach is already full of vehicles, and there's a bonfire alight down by the water. It's not dark yet, although the sun hangs low in the sky and the air is beginning to cool.

Cor's head and upper body are stuck inside the back of her SUV. She emerges when we park beside her and waves. "Hey, can you guys lend a hand?"

"Ready?" Cole asks, his fingers tightening around mine.

"You're sure we can't run away?"

"From an Event of this magnitude? If you run, it will continue to grow and follow you around. Come on. Let's do this thing."

"Are you a people person, Cole?" He doesn't strike me as an extrovert. But my people-reading sense has been off lately.

"Me? I abhor crowds. I was thinking a few friends, a campfire, some contemplative thought. Maybe a couple of imported fireflies for effect." He laughs. "Truth. But I started it. You're the honoree. So we are in this thing together."

"Don't you leave me here."

"Never." He looks at me as he says it, his eyes truly seeing me in that way he has, and I feel like my entire being is limned in fire.

"Help," Cor calls again. She's got a box in her arms, but it's slipping away from her, and Cole runs to catch it. I peer into the back of her SUV. There is more food here than my kitchen sees in a week.

"Holy smokes, Cor, you left the fridge and stove behind."

She laughs. "Once I get started, I can't stop. You know? I took a trip up to Costco. The hot dogs and fixings were on sale. And then I saw the pies, and I couldn't decide which one, so I bought five. And brownies. You've got to have brownies. The soda was a steal. And then I didn't know if anybody else would bring plates and cutlery . . ."

I load up while she chatters on. Cole, loaded down with whatever is in that box, is already staggering toward the beach. A couple of ice-filled coolers are stuffed with drinks. A balloon centerpiece hovers above a table laden with snacks. People cluster around in little groups of two and three, laughing and talking. I'm shocked to realize I know them all. They smile and wave, as if genuinely happy to see me. A few come over to offer condolences on the loss of Oscar.

It's a party, I tell myself. *People like parties. They do this on purpose, all the time.* But the familiar dread is working its way into my bones.

"What's your poison?" Cole asks. "Soda? Beer? Cider?"

I accept a cider. The bottle is icy cold, slick with condensation. A wind flows in across the lake. Cole steers me toward a log on the far side of the bonfire, his hand warm on the small of my back.

We're intercepted before we get there.

"Hey, Rae! Sorry about Oscar. He was a cute little guy."

"Raphael, hey. I didn't know you ever met him."

"Are you kidding? I used to smuggle him cheese when you weren't looking."

Raphael is the occupational therapist at Valley View. He's older than me. Stocky, graying, kind to the residents, and fabulous at lightly teasing them into complying with his exercise regimes. Despite his ready laugh and easy banter, as we walk past him I feel a heaviness trailing after me. Before I can begin to put thoughts to the unexpected emotion, I'm momentarily blinded by a flash of light.

"And the guest of honor arrives," a voice says. "You are Rae, correct? I'm Lorinda Thomas, reporter for the *Statesman Examiner*. Is it true this entire event is on behalf of a rat?"

"Not precisely, since the rat in question is deceased."

When my vision clears, I see a woman with a camera standing just inside my personal space bubble. Her appearance is mousy and unremarkable, but her energy feels fierce. I don't know how she knows me; I'm certain we've never met. My life is not fertile soil for reporters.

"Must be a quiet news day." Cole echoes my thought, steering me around her.

She lets us pass, but turns and walks on the other side of me. "Honestly, I'm not here about the rat. Although, may he rest in peace and all that. I've got nothing against rats. But what I really want to know is how that woman is doing? The one you ran over with your car."

My feet stop moving. The reporter looks bigger, all at once, as if she's towering over me, even though she's about the same height.

She flushes. "I can see you'd rather not talk about it. Can't say as I blame you. And I hate asking, only it is a story and sort of my job."

Officer Mendez materializes beside her, so suddenly I feel like I've conjured him out of sheer desperation. "It's a party, Rin. Come get a drink."

"Maybe later?" she calls over her shoulder as he tows her away. "I'll buy you lunch."

"She has no comment," Mendez says.

I'm grateful for Cole's steadying hand as I miss my footing and trip over my own feet.

"Hey, you okay?"

"Just nerves," I tell him, gripping the sweating, ice-cold bottle to keep me grounded.

"You don't have to do anything but sit here," he says as we settle down side by side on the rough bark of an old log. "I'll protect you from the ravening paparazzi."

My laughter in response is fleeting. There are emotions coming at me from all directions. Some direct and forceful as rockets. Some insidious and vague, snaking around my feet, worming their way into my belly. Everybody here is laughing on the outside. Inside, where they've hidden whatever is incongruent with the party spirit, is another story.

I shouldn't have come.

"How are we going to roast anything on that fire?" Corinne demands. "We'll all burn to cinders before we get close enough to roast anything besides ourselves."

She's right. This is not a campfire. This is a raging inferno. Good thing we've had plenty of rain this summer, or we'd be at risk of lighting the forest on fire.

Raphael grins at her. "Patience, patience, it will burn down. Have a drink. Did you put anything good in those brownies?"

"You're bad." But Cor is laughing as she pops the top on a can of Bud Light.

I want her to come sit beside me. She's easy. No subtext there, because whatever she's feeling comes right out of her mouth and you know where you're at. Since she pretty much loves everybody and is the most determined optimist I've ever met, where you're at is a pretty good thing.

But she's busy playing hostess and isn't likely to sit any time in the near future.

And then the little groups part to make way for a procession.

Nancy has dressed for the occasion, in a crimson evening gown that would probably pass muster at the real Oscars. Mason, always overdressed for Colville, looks working-class next to her extravagance.

He is also obviously drunk and using the wheelchair as a support. As he reaches the transition from gravel to sand, one of the wheels sticks. The chair lurches dangerously sideways.

Nancy shrieks, clinging to the arms.

A dozen hands rescue her from disaster, righting the chair, rolling her safely to a position on the other side of the fire. Nancy orders them around with all the aplomb of a queen on a throne. Cor brings her a beer. Raphael brings a brownie. Tia spreads a blanket over her lap to protect her from the breeze that has begun to blow.

Cole is laughing. "She's a piece of work."

"You can say that again." Mason settles heavily onto the log on my other side. "Nursing home hasn't changed her one bit."

"I can only imagine what she was like when she was young," I say.

"She was, as Cole says, a piece of work." Mason takes a long swig of beer, wiping his mouth with the back of his hand.

Cor saves us from any more conversation, approaching the crackling fire and clanging on a cowbell with a stick.

"Listen up, everybody."

The babble of voices hushes. Just for an instant the sound of lapping waves, a hint of wind, clears my head. But then Cor's voice goes on.

"As you all know, this is not just a party. This is a tribute to Oscar, the rat we all knew and loved."

"Seriously?" Mason slurs. "This whole thing is really about a rat?" His voice carries through Cor's dramatic pause.

Maybe he's thinking about sewer rats or plague rats. Maybe he shares Bernie's opinion about naked tails. Everybody stares at him, and at me by proxy, sitting next to him.

"I need a drink," Mason says, and proceeds to finish his beer without stopping to breathe.

Cor clears her throat. "As I was saying . . ."

"For real?" Mason whispers loudly to me, his breath enveloping my entire head in a miasma of beery fumes. "I mean, cats. Rats. They go together like, like, I got nothing. They don't go together."

Deciding to ignore the disruption, Corinne raises her voice a little louder. "This is a memorial. So we'll begin with a toast. Everybody got a drink?"

Mason shakes his can, which remains empty.

All around us, hands raise drinks up into the air.

"To Oscar!" Cor says.

"To Oscar!" voices echo in response.

The only toasts I've ever been part of were at weddings and were instantly followed by laughter and voices and more drinking. Here, the silence remains, winding through the group like an invisible thread weaving us all together, just for an instant, with an acknowledgment of loss for a small white animal who was in the world for such a short time.

I feel the tears encroaching, but the flavor of this silence gives me courage to hold my head up and let them do what they want. All around me, faces are serious, reflective.

"Amazing how many lives can be touched by a small creature who is only on this planet for about the blink of an eye," Corinne goes on. "Sorry. Just a minute." She digs in her pocket for a tissue and wipes her nose.

"Now, then. Due to a horrible accident, Rae didn't even get to bury him. We can't fix that now, but every grief needs something physical as a reminder. So, Rae, we all pitched in and got you this."

Cor bends over and reaches into a capacious beach bag, coming up with something white and fluffy, with a silvery satin tail. A plush rat, big enough to be mutant if it were real. She brings it over and presents it to me, ceremoniously.

"To remember Oscar by," she says. And then she envelops me in a hug, rat and all. My hands take on a life of their own, clinging to her, not letting her go, my face squashed into her shoulder, the rat a soft lump between our chests. She drops a kiss on the top of my head when I finally release her. There are tears on her cheeks.

She clears her throat.

"All right. Who wants to say something about Oscar?"

"I never had the chance to know him," Cole says. "I wish I had."

Raphael stands up, raises a glass, and takes a swallow. "When you first brought him to work, I thought you were crazy."

A ripple of laughter travels through the group. My cheeks start to heat, but he goes on.

"In all honesty, I thought he should have been done away with. They sell baby rats in the pet store as snake food. You know? But then his cage ended up in my therapy room one afternoon. And I saw people take interest. This one lady who had refused to do any exercises, who would just sit staring at the wall, actually asked to hold him." He smiles at me. "A little rat. And look how he changed the world."

The warmth of his emotion flows through me, and I return his smile.

Above us, the sky arches, twilight blue, with Venus hanging on the horizon over the water.

"Oscar was the first and only rat I ever knew," declaims a polished stage voice. I know who it belongs to without looking and feel my smile growing. Also without looking, I know Cole is grinning beside me.

"Oh Lord," Mason mutters, a little too loud. "Make way for the prima donna. I need another drink." He sways on his feet, and it takes a minute for him to round up his legs and get them both going in the right direction.

Firelight sparks off Nancy's diamonds as she waves her hands in the air, dramatically. "A rat. Can you imagine? I very nearly called the health department to make a complaint. How can such a thing be sanitary? It was the midnight hour of a sleepless night. I had tossed and turned. Slumber refused to come to me, and so I called for aid. Rae appeared in my doorway, framed by the hall light, a small white creature in her arms. A kitten, I thought. I abhor kittens."

"God have mercy." Mason settles back down beside me, fresh drink open in one hand, an extra in the other.

He catches my expression. "Sue me," he says. "I'm a drunk."

Nancy's voice cuts across his words.

"But a rat? Within the sterile environs of a nursing home? I was intrigued. I was captivated. I'd never met a rat before. Rae brought him over to say hello, and he climbed up onto my shoulder and snuggled there. Adorable creature. I, like all of you gathered here, am deeply saddened by the loss."

She raises her plastic cup high. "To Oscar. May he live long in a land where rats eat cats and there is an endless supply of cheese."

Despite her obvious love for the stage, a warmth fills my chest at Nancy's words. My senses open, taking in the acrid scent of woodsmoke, a whiff of pine drifting in on the breeze. Water splashing against the shore. Cole's self-contained presence on one side, Mason on the other.

"A rat, huh?" Mason slurs. "Go figure. I was always a fan of Templeton, though, in that book about the spider. What was her name again?"

"Charlotte."

"It was also about a pig," Cole chimes in. He rolls his eyes at me, and I stifle a rising giggle with the back of my hand.

"Book was named after the spider," Mason says, with dignity. "Anyway, I didn't like the pig. Too naïve, too needy. Templeton now—self-sufficient and smart."

"Shhhh, somebody's talking."

He shushes, but only to take another swig.

Tia stands up, clutching a can of Coke in both hands and shuffling her feet nervously. "I never knew a rat before. I was scared of him. Rae showed me how gentle he was. I bought a rat for my kids, after. They love him. So—I guess Oscar taught me to love a whole new kind of animal." She sits down, head bent and hidden by her hair.

"Forgive me yet?" Cole bends over to whisper the question in my ear. His breath is warm on my cheek. A star hangs over his left shoulder.

"Possibly," I whisper back. "Night's still young."

He laughs and drapes his arm around me, pulling me in tight. I fit perfectly beneath his arm, my body molding to his at chest and hips, the warm weight of him an anchor that keeps me together and grounded as other people talk about how Oscar touched their lives.

By the time Corinne gets back up to speak, the sky is black. The fire has died down enough to make me snuggle closer to Cole for warmth. All of my insides feel relaxed, the tight knot of pain and anxiety and guilt I've been carrying around replaced by a comfortable warm glow.

"One more thing before we eat," Corinne says. "Although we can't bury Oscar, we need some sort of symbol of letting him go. So, Rae, if you would do the honors, we have these balloons. And we thought maybe you'd like to release them. Sort of like the movie *Up*, you know, only in this case the balloons won't be carrying you or the house any-where. Just our memories of Oscar."

I look from her to the balloons—once just a bit of festive décor, now a grand, theatric gesture likely to contribute to the demise of birds. Or possibly light aircraft. All eyes are on me, and about to be on me carrying a bunch of balloons and letting them go.

A flash goes off.

Perfect photo opportunity. No reporter, even a nice and unassum-ing one, is going to pass that moment up. And then I, along with my balloons, my rat, and everything, will be in the newspaper for all the world to see.

My scripted move is to get up and go get those balloons from her, but I can't do it. Last time I had a full-on anxiety attack was in college. That time, too, was at a party. My heart is going to break right through my rib cage. Cold sweat soaks my shirt. My breathing is getting away from me and my hands are tingling and *Oh my God, I'm going to die.*

Somewhere my logical brain is trying to tell me things.

You're not going to die.

Anxiety attacks are self-limiting.

Anchor yourself. Focus on your feet on the ground.

Get control of your breath.

But I can't even feel the ground anymore. The firelight and the faces around it are a blur. My breath is about as amenable to my control as a herd of wild mustangs thundering across the plains. The only physical sensation outside my body's wildly erratic insanity is Cole's arm around me. So strong, so steady, so warm. A link to reality and sanity.

Corinne looms over me, holding out the balloons. Well-meaning, kindly, wonderful Cor, but she might as well be Stephen King's *It* given my reaction. Her hand looks swollen and distorted.

But then another hand is there next to hers, grasping the strings, taking over the responsibility.

Cole, I think, for a minute, but the hand isn't his. "We'll all three go," Mason whispers. "Down to the river. The camera can have our backs. Ready?"

He lurches onto his feet, almost as if the balloons have lifted him, then reaches down for me. Cole takes my other hand, and the two of them drag me upright. Linked together, Cole serving as ballast for my uncertain feet and Mason's inebriated ones, we weave across the beach to the water's edge. It's blissfully dark away from the fire and easier to breathe.

In the distance, I hear Corinne introduce Ben, the chaplain from Valley View. He clears his throat. "Shall we pray? Father, we know that not even a sparrow falls without your knowledge. Oscar was but a rat, and yet we know you cared for him . . ."

The breeze coming off the water cools my burning face.

"All three of us, then?" Cole's free hand grabs the strings, right below Mason's. I reach up and there are three fists, instead of just one.

"Extra drama for the camera."

"On the count of three," Mason says. "You know, I loved that movie, *Up.*"

I loved it, too, although I cried inordinately.

"Rae?" Cole asks.

I nod my head. *Ready.*

"On my count. One. Two. Three."

I let go. The balloons stay where they are. Mason's reflexes, delayed by alcohol, slow his fingers so that in the end, he's the one who releases the balloons. They catch an updraft almost at once, soaring upward faster than I expected, vanishing into the dark.

What remains is a complex sense of loss, release, community, and the last vestiges of a tsunami-level panic attack. I'm aware of voices behind us, distant, cheering and laughing, as the Event moves from memorial to party. The three of us stay where we are, linked by the hands, gazing across the dark water with our feet firmly planted in the sand.

A choked sound comes from Mason. A shudder runs through him and into me, as though I'm a conduction wire and he's electricity. The wall of grief hits me, naked as I am from the panic attack, and nearly drops me to my feet.

"Sorry," he says, jerking his hand away. "Need another drink."

"No, you don't." Cole's voice is low and urgent. "What you need is to feel that, whatever it is."

"You're a sadist."

"I'm a counselor."

"Same difference." This from me. It surprises all three of us. Cole laughs. Mason takes a minute to process.

"Haven't tried that," he says, finally. "The feeling thing."

"Not what it's cracked up to be," I tell him. "I've been considering trying the drinking approach."

"What about you, counselor?" Mason asks. "What's your secret?"

"Overwork and adrenaline."

All three of us turn back to the lake.

"I used to think it was kittens," I whisper.

Neither of them laughs. "You sure it's not?" Mason asks.

"Katya says not."

"Would this be the Katya who is currently alive and feeding kittens?" Cole's hand tightens around mine. In this moment, I feel grounded and, weirdly, home.

"What *are* you guys looking at?" Cor's voice cuts into the moment. Stones rattle as she crosses the beach toward us. "Are you coming back or what? Aren't you freezing? This wind is enough to chill the bones. Feels like September down here already. Come back to the fire. Have a drink. Mendez got a smaller fire going to actually roast hot dogs."

"What are we doing, Rae?" It's Cole who asks, but Mason looks to me, too, both of them respecting my mood, waiting for my lead.

"We could swim for it." I'm joking, but the moon path on the water is a definite lure. I love the caress of the wind, the plash of the waves, the companionship of these two very different men.

"Long swim," Mason says wistfully. "Up through the stars to eternity. Oh, don't look at me like that. I'm too chicken to die. Let's go find the beer."

With that, the mood is broken. We straggle back to the fire as three separate people, that moment of unity blown away like smoke from the campfire. Our log has been commandeered by a group of hospital workers, all laughing uproariously over an inside story. Mason stops to talk to Nancy, leaning down to kiss her cheek. She makes some remark I can't hear, and he stiffens, flings his hands up in a gesture of frustration, and heads for the beer cooler.

I can't fit back into the group and feel like an outsider all over again. "Maybe I should be getting back. I hate leaving Kat alone at night."

"She's probably sleeping. Or feeding kittens."

"Probably." But an unease creeps through me, not connected to any one thing, just a generalized worry I have no name for.

"Tell you what," Cole says. "You should eat. Grab us some chips and a perfectly boring and safe brownie. I'll fix us a couple of hot dogs. And then I'll take you home. Plan?"

"Plan."

I find myself wanting to go with him. Holding on to his hand, letting him shield me. Not going to happen. All of my very good reasons for keeping people at a distance come trooping back into my head. *Stand on your own two feet, little girl. The only person who is going to take care of you is you.*

I manage to load up a plate with sides and a couple of brownies without having to talk to anybody. Absorbed in my thoughts, I very nearly trip over Nancy's wheelchair.

"You wouldn't think I'd be invisible, what with this shiny chair and all of my diamonds. Are you drinking, Nurse Rae?"

"I had one drink. Just thinking about other things."

"Which is more than can be said for my good-for-nothing son."

I track her gaze to where Mason is regaling Officer Mendez with some long saga about a hunting expedition gone awry. My lips twitch upward despite my sense of foreboding. Mason might be a drunk, but he's a charming drunk.

"I'll ask Raphael to drive you back."

"Mason is right, you know. I was shit as a mother. The role wasn't in my repertoire." Before I can respond to this uncharacteristic remark, she's already shifted gears. "My dear girl, where did a backwoods nurse come by those earrings?"

"They were a gift."

I clap my free hand to my ear, broadsided by guilt. Kat is home alone while I'm out having fun. It's well past time for her pain medication. She'll be hurting and tired, and the kittens need attention.

"They suit you," Cole says, showing up with a plate full of hot dogs and buns. "Hope you like mustard and ketchup."

Nancy glances slyly up at him. "You must have a job on the side if you can afford stones like these. Those are quality opals, those are."

"The extent of my gift giving is limited to a cold drink and a hot dog," Cole says. His tone is light, but I feel the emotional undertow. "That, and a burned finger. Let's go eat so my burnt offering is not in vain."

We beat a retreat, but I know Nancy is burning holes in my back with her curiosity. "Can we just go eat in the truck?"

"Had enough peopling for one night?"

"Probably for a week. I'm sorry. Not the best company."

"I like your company. You're an introvert. People are draining, and this night was emotional."

"It's more than that."

"People are vampires, and they've sucked the life out of you?"

He's teasing, but he's come so close to the mark my feet stop of their own accord, my belly tight with dread. It's time to tell him about me and my super sensors.

"Rae?"

I've stopped in the darkest part of a shadow where he can't see my face. His hand reaches out for mine, though, and I cling to him, afraid that this will be the end of us before we've fairly begun.

"Tell me," he says.

"You're not far off about vampires, only people don't suck me dry so much as overload me. I feel—everything. Everybody's emotions. I mean, really feel them, as if they were mine. It's physical, just waves and waves, and I can't sort them all, and they drown me. I'm not even sure if that panic attack was mine, or if I was channeling Mason."

"You're an empath," Cole says.

"I am?" I'm not sure exactly what he means, but I like the sound of the word in his mouth, and the matter-of-fact way he says it, as if I've just mentioned that I have skinny feet or blue-green eyes.

"Yup. Come on, the hot dogs are getting cold." He tugs me out of the shadows and over to the truck, and we settle into our seats without turning on the lights. The moon provides just enough illumination so we can see to eat.

All at once I'm starving. I bite into my hot dog. The crunchy, smoky skin pops between my teeth, mingling with mustard and ketchup. A hum of pleasure escapes me before I can stifle it.

"Glad you approve." Cole licks mustard off his upper lip and grins at me.

"I've never had a hot dog like this before."

"You've never—tell me you're joking."

I shake my head and take another bite. "My folks weren't into camping. I grew up in a city. And after I moved here, I just never went to any events."

"This must be remedied. You need the full experience of roasting your own. I'm sorry I took that away from you."

"I couldn't wait to get away from the people. I would have probably burnt it or dropped it in the fire or made it explode or something."

"Camping," he says. "We need to go camping."

My heart flutters a little at the thought of the two of us in the wilderness somewhere. Sitting around a campfire. Eating hot dogs. Sleeping in the same tent.

"Oh shit." I've squeezed too hard. The rest of my hot dog squirts out of the bun and into my lap, staining my jeans with mustard and ketchup.

"Have a napkin." He hands me one, then another, seeing the extent of the disaster. "Don't look so tragic. Poke it back into the bun and eat up."

"I . . ." My parents' germ lectures swarm like mosquitoes. But that tempting little morsel taunts my taste buds and I do as he says. It tastes even better for its little excursion.

"See?" he says. "Nothing to worry about."

"Cole?"

"Mmmm?"

"About the empath thing. That doesn't bother you?"

"Should it?" He swallows his last bite of hot dog and licks his fingers. "It's not like you've got three heads or something. I'll go tell Corinne that we're bailing, okay? And make sure Nancy has a safe ride. Not sure what to do about Mason . . ."

I dangle the keys I swiped from his pocket while we were communing on the beach. "Good job, chickadee. What shall we do with them?"

"I'll keep them. Let him think about it a little."

"Are we going to let him sleep on the beach?"

"We're going to let him catch a ride when he realizes he must have dropped them somewhere. Corinne won't leave him stranded."

"Never took you for a tough-love type." He says it with approval, but the words ruffle the smooth edges of my momentary peace. For all of his surface acceptance, he doesn't know me any better than I know Kat. By the time he comes back I've rebuilt the wall between us, stone upon stone. If he notices, he doesn't comment.

But this time, he doesn't hold my hand.

Chapter Thirteen

Cole walks me to the front door. I tell him this isn't necessary, there are no monsters living on my street. He says sometimes there are visiting monsters. Electricity buzzes between us. I can feel it, like having a balloon that wants to stick to your hair, only warmer, better, and rife with promise. I'm intensely aware of him, of the now-cool night and how he is a manifestation of warmth. Walls and all, I won't stop him if he tries to kiss me good night.

Not such a good idea, with Kat waiting and the way she feels about him.

I don't think I care.

But when we get to the door he just stands there, hands in his pockets, while I dig out my key and turn it in the lock. I don't open the door yet. When I turn to him his eyes are in shadow, his face serious. Unreadable.

"Thanks for taking me. I had no idea that so many people cared about Oscar."

"Did you ever consider that it might not be Oscar they care about?" His voice sounds roughened, husky, and maybe he's the one who needs a dimmer switch, because that full-on intensity is lighting up every nerve cell in my body.

"That whole Event business, you mean?"

"It's not what I mean at all."

His gaze is locked with mine. Looking away would be an impossibility. I can't move, can barely catch my breath. When his head bends down over mine I quiver, a small tree in a big wind.

But the moment passes, and there is no kiss.

"Good night, Rae. Get some sleep," he says in a strangled voice. My stomach follows him when he walks away, as if it's attached to a rubber band. I feel boneless and limp, relieved and a little lost. Maybe I am too much of a freak for him after all. But no, he wants to go camping with me. If I stand out here much longer staring at the door, he *will* think I'm a freak for sure, so I turn the key and go inside.

All of the kittens are meowing. They are not in the carrier. Two of them huddle together in the middle of the floor. Feeding equipment and formula sit out on the counter. One bottle is full of formula; the others are empty and clean, precisely where I put them.

Kat lies on the couch, eyes closed, apparently asleep. Unless she cleaned everything up and put it exactly where I left it, the kittens haven't been fed since I left. Their box is soiled.

I switch on the overhead lights to see better.

"Kat! Are you sleeping?"

Her eyelids flicker open, but I'm not sure if she sees me. Her eyes are glassy, dazed. In the bright overhead light she looks washed out and faded.

"Sorry," she murmurs, and then her eyelids drift shut again.

"Where are the rest of the kittens? Have you fed them?"

"It's—I can't . . ."

Her lips barely move. Maybe she's drugged. I do a quick mental check. Did I lock up all the medications? Yes. I have a clear memory of that. Just to be sure, I check the lockbox. Still locked. I open it. Everything there and accounted for. On the way I retrieve another kitten, making the count in my head.

Three.

When I look at Kat again, I see that her breathing is rapid, not slowed way down like it would be with too many pain pills. "Are you all right? What's the matter?"

"Jus' tired." She's slurring as badly as Mason, but there's no alcohol in the house. Kneeling beside the couch, I reach for her wrist to check her pulse. She pulls it away from me, but her movements are weak, uncoordinated.

"Rae . . . please . . ."

I peel back the blanket that covers her and stand there, frozen with shock. The blanket is wet with blood. Her shirt is soaked with crimson. I grab her hand and rotate her arm, staring stupidly at the stain, at my own bloody fingers.

"What did you do?"

She doesn't answer, and I peel back the sleeve.

Her forearm is swathed in blood-soaked bandages. "It's nothing," she croaks. "Just a little cut. Fine."

"You're in shock. How long have you been bleeding?"

Her eyelids drift shut again, and she doesn't answer.

"Kat! Don't you dare go to sleep."

I squeeze her arm, tight; she gasps with the pain and her eyes open. "Don't be mad, Rae. I just . . ."

"I don't want to hear it. You can tell me later."

She needs an ambulance, but I don't want to let go long enough to call one. The kittens are mewling piteously, and three of them are still unaccounted for, and it's hard to think. If only I'd brought Cole in, if he'd wanted to come in, I'd have an extra pair of hands, an extra brain.

But he's not here, and it's up to me.

Keeping a tight grip on Kat's wrist with one hand, elevating it above her heart, I use the other hand to dial 911. When dispatch comes on, I'm surprised to hear my own steady voice giving clear details.

Severe laceration. Shock. Possible suicide attempt. My address.

When I end the call, Kat's eyes are open and looking at me. Tears roll down her cheeks. She turns her face away toward the back of the couch, and we stay there like that, not talking, me squeezing her wrist so hard my hands start to cramp. Still, blood seeps through my fingers and runs down my arm, and hers.

It's the accident scene all over again, with the difference that this time I'm not sure she'll thank me for saving her life.

The woman on the ambulance crew is the same one who responded when I hit Kat with my car. She shakes her head, sadly, as if reading everything between the lines, and then gets directly to work.

"Life is good here," she says to Kat. "Don't be in such a hurry to move on."

Her hands are busy, purposeful. Her actions measured. How many times has she acted her part in scenes just like this one? Her partner gets an IV going and radios in to the hospital, reporting low blood pressure, rapid pulse, shock.

My role switches from active participant to audience member, hoping the screenwriter believes in happy endings, but with a sick feeling that I've become involved in a tragedy and there's no way to change it.

"Please," Kat says as they lift her onto the gurney and wrap her in blankets.

"Please," she says again, as they strap her in and wheel her away.

I'm not sure what she's asking.

The door closes behind them, leaving me alone in a room so empty it echoes, despite the pitiful clamor of the kittens. There is blood on the sofa cushions. Blood on the floor. I follow a trail of crimson drops to the bathroom, where I can't take in the extent of the carnage.

I'm a nurse, but I don't work trauma, and I've never seen this much blood in one place. This is not Snow White pricking her finger and shedding three perfect drops. This is *Game of Thrones* and the Red Wedding. Blood on the floor, in the sink, on the mirror. Drops of blood, pools of blood, smears of blood. Blood-soaked towels, a splash of bright color in the corner. I register all of this with my eyes, but my brain refuses to take it in.

My stomach grasps the reality just fine and rejects it. I make a dive for the toilet as my body rids itself of half-digested hot dog and, seemingly, my toenails. My body shudders and shakes. I can't bring myself to touch the knobs on the sink, one of which bears a perfect, bloody fingerprint. The soles of my shoes make sucking noises with every step, and I stop at the bathroom door and slip out of them.

The kitchen sink is pristine, and I run cold water over my hands for a long time before splashing it repeatedly over my face and finally bending down to drink directly from the faucet. Emptying my stomach has cleared my head, and I shift out of shock and into action.

Jenny is on speed dial. It's late, but she sleeps with the phone by her bed.

"Rae? What on earth?"

"I need you. Here. Now. It's an emergency." I don't wait for her questions. Curiosity will bring her faster.

I mix up formula and start in with the weakest kitten while hunting for the missing. One is in the kitchen, bumped up in the corner. Another has made it into the bedroom and crawled under the dresser. The tiny gray tabby is still missing.

Jenny arrives when I'm feeding number three.

"Oh my God. What happened?"

"Kat cut her wrist. She was on kitten duty, and I don't know when they were last fed. I need to go to the ER."

"Wow," she says, still stuck in the entryway. "Your couch."

"Sit in the chair. Do not go in the bathroom. I'll clean it up. Can you help? These little guys are starving."

The kittens prod her into action.

"Right. Sure." Jenny sinks down in the middle of the floor, takes the bottle I hand her, and starts feeding.

"You'll need to take them with you." I look down at my ruined clothing, thinking I can't keep throwing clothes away every time Kat tries to kill herself. And then realizing there is something wrong with this line of thought.

Jenny's head jerks up like it's been yanked by a string. "For how long?"

"Maybe until they're ready to adopt. Sorry. I can't do this right now."

I've been waiting for her to notice the still-missing kitten. It's taken longer than I would have thought, but all of the blood is a little distracting, I'll give her that.

"Did the little one die, then?" she asks. "I was afraid for him, but I thought if anybody could save him . . ."

"Anybody who wasn't already trying to save a suicidal human." My tone is sharper than I mean it to be.

"If you had too much on your plate, you should have told me. Pick up the phone."

I want to scream at her, but she has a point. I should have called her the night she left the kittens. I knew it was too much. Why didn't I?

Kat.

Kat was engaged by them. I thought they might help her, heal her.

You can't heal the world with kittens, Rae.

Or with wishing.

"They were out when I got here. I don't know where the little one is. I've looked. I can't find him." My voice quavers, and I give myself a brisk, mental shake. I don't have time for a meltdown over kittens. Later. When Kat's all right.

"I'm sorry. I shouldn't have left them here. I thought—I thought maybe they'd help you get over Oscar. I hadn't realized what you were up against with that woman."

Her tone on the final words is a clue to what she feels about Kat, but she's a good person, and she still asks, "Will she be okay?"

"She was in shock, but she should be fine."

"You don't have to go up there. You didn't have to take her in. I know it's not my business to tell you, but somebody has to."

I let her words sink in.

She's right. Probably. Except that I feel responsible. If it hadn't been for Oscar and me and my car . . . But that line of thinking brings me full circle to tonight. The blood in the bathroom, the untended kittens, the way my careful little world is spinning away from me so fast I can't even snatch at the wreckage before it is whirled away out of my reach.

"She has nobody. Nowhere to go."

"And maybe there's a reason for that. I'm sorry. None of my business. I'm going to take the kitties home with me, okay?"

I just nod, not capable of speech, and start looking for the little missing baby. Jenny cleans out the carrier and loads up the now-sleeping kittens and helps me look. We both know it's probably too late, that he's likely crawled into a tight spot somewhere to die. We search the house, not that there's much to search, and come up empty.

"I'm sorry," she says again, and gives me a swift hug.

My phone rings. Call display tells me it's the hospital before I even answer. The voice is unfamiliar, the crisis worker on call. Could I please come up to the hospital to answer some questions and help make a safety plan?

Somehow I'd been expecting Cole, but of course it wouldn't be. He's off tonight. He doesn't even know. This should be an obvious fact, but it makes me feel breathless and frightened. I don't want to deal with a stranger.

"Go," Jenny says. "I'll look one more time."

I just nod, and then give her a hug, hoping all of the things I don't know how to say will translate through the action. The lost kitten is probably already dead, but I still hate to leave him. Human lives come first, I remind myself, although a tiny voice in the back of my head demands an explanation why.

Chapter Fourteen

A nurse directs me to Bay Six.

Kat lies on the exam table, eyes closed, still far too pale. Her left arm rests on top of a white blanket, neatly bandaged. An IV drips into her right. Her blood pressure, heart rate, and oxygen readings display on a screen above her head.

The woman sitting beside the stretcher is fiftyish and plump and so obviously wakened from sleep, there's still a faint crease down one cheek.

Sadness fills the room, a deep, dark lake of misery that will drown me if I fall into it. I stay by the door.

The woman nods at me but doesn't smile. "Are you Rae?"

"That would be me."

At the sound of my voice Kat's eyes open. Neither of us says anything. There are no words big enough to carry what needs to be said. In my memory, in my soul, I hear again the word *please*.

Please what? Please save me? Please let me die?

"Can we talk for a moment?" The strange woman gets to her feet and pushes past me out into the hallway. Out here it's all bright lights and action. An ambulance crew rolls a stretcher into the trauma room, nurse and doctor in its wake. A call light is on above Bay Two. In Bay Four somebody coughs, then moans.

Pain and fear snake around my feet, immobilizing me while I try to process, to find that dimmer switch Bernie preaches about. For years I've had this emotional sensor switched off, but it's full-on now.

Warning. System overload. Crash imminent.

"I'm Marci," the woman is saying. "I'm the designated mental health professional on call, and I'm here to evaluate your friend. Do you understand what that means?"

"Yes." My voice sounds far away, as if it belongs to some other Rae in some other universe.

"I've already read Katya her rights. She said you would explain everything."

I blink. "Everything? That's a lot of explaining."

Marci sighs, as if I'm being deliberately obdurate and stupid. "About her cutting behaviors. She says she's not really suicidal. That she only meant to cut but accidentally went too deep."

Please lie for me. Don't let them lock me up.

My lips feel like I've been to the dentist, so much so that I reach up to touch them, assure myself I can still feel, that these lips belong to me.

"I don't know anything about cutting. We never talked about that. How could she do this? I locked up all the sharps."

"Are you sure?" Disappointment and fatigue are written all over the woman's face. She's hoping for an easy resolution to this call, that she can wrap things up and go home to bed. In this we have shared desires, but I'm learning that when it comes to Kat, nothing will ever be easy.

"Lots of women cut," Marci says, still hopeful. "As a way to dull pain. Or sometimes the opposite, if they're numb. It's different than suicide. No intent to die."

"Right. And how often do they manage to open an artery in the process?"

My own words push me over the edge into emotional territory I've never entered before. I want to scream. Throw things. Stomp my feet on the floor like a child having a tantrum. Before Marci can answer

173

that, I push past her back into the room. Kat's eyes are closed as if she's sleeping, but I know she's awake. Listening. Waiting.

"Talk to me." I'm back in control of my body, full enough of my own emotions to shove back against hers.

"Don't be mad, I—"

"I trusted you. You said you wouldn't kill yourself. You said you'd be okay home alone. Now you're here, and one of the kittens is dead, and it could have been all of them. How could you?"

Marci makes a disapproving clucking sound. "I'm not sure this is helpful. Could we—"

"Stay out of it. Well, Katya? Answer me."

When Kat's eyes well up with the inevitable tears and she reaches her hand out for mine, it doesn't move me.

She sniffles, pitifully, but I refuse to bend.

Her hand falls back onto the stretcher and she closes her eyes. "It was the kittens," she says finally. "I let them out of the box, and I was going to feed them, truly I was. Only I was so tired and my hip hurt and I told myself I would lie down, just for a minute. I must have fallen asleep. I'm so, so sorry. I can't tell you how sorry I am. When I woke up they were all starving, and the little one was dead, and I couldn't . . . I wasn't trying to kill myself, Rae. Honest to God. I wouldn't have done that, not in your house. Not when you'd be the one to come home and find me. What kind of a person would do that?"

"Maybe the same kind of person who would throw themselves in front of a stranger's car."

My eyes are prickling with tears now, too. My throat feels thick and hot. But I won't believe her. I can't. "Where did you get the blade?"

Her head moves restlessly on the pillow. "The truth?"

"That would be nice."

"Hidden in my backpack. You were right about that."

"Oh my God! What else did you lie about?"

"Really." Marci puts a hand on my shoulder. "This is not the time for this conversation. I was thinking maybe Katya could go home with you with a crisis plan in place, but clearly—"

"We had a crisis plan. It's been violated. What reason would there possibly be to make another one?"

Kat is weeping now, harsh, wrenching sobs, but for some reason they fail to touch me. I can't remember ever being so angry. It feels good. Strong, powerful. I don't care that I'm hurting her, I don't care that I'm inconveniencing this excuse for a crisis worker. Cole would have this situation figured out by now. He'd know Kat was lying. He'd know what has suddenly gone wrong with me.

Marci is apparently not one to give up. "As I explained," she says patiently, "cutting is not necessarily a desire to die. She only cut one wrist. She wrapped it and tried to stop the bleeding." Her voice softens. "I understand. You're hurt and you're scared and so you're angry."

"Actually, I'm pretty sure I'm just angry." She's right, though. Part of me knows it, but I shut that part down and refuse to acknowledge it. The anger feels too good. It blocks out Kat's despair and Marci's frustration. I have no intention of letting it go. Not yet.

A doctor comes in, glancing from me, to Marci, to Katya weeping on the bed.

I know her, slightly. She's a recent graduate, working ER exclusively for now. Dr. Merrit or Merril or some such. She avoids entanglement in our controversy by crossing the room to check the IV, the monitors. Ignoring the extraneous factors, she talks directly to Kat.

"I want to admit you overnight for observation. Your hemoglobin is quite low, but I don't think we need to transfuse you. I do want to monitor your vital signs and keep the IV running. All right?"

"That would be fabulous," Marci says, even though nobody has asked her. "There aren't any psych beds available, and our less restrictive alternative has fallen through." She shoots a glare at me that holds me responsible for everything that has gone wrong with her night.

Deep down beneath the anger, guilt stirs and bubbles, but it's too far away to motivate me.

"What if I don't want to stay?" Kat asks.

"You don't have a choice." Marci sounds more like the exasperated parent of a toddler than a professional, crabby and overwhelmed. "You're here under mental health evaluation."

"I don't think you can do that. Can you?" Kat ignores Marci and asks the doctor. "Don't you need a single bed certification or something? This isn't a psych hospital."

Marci's night has clearly gone from bad to worse. She pinches the bridge of her nose between thumb and forefinger. "I have twelve hours to complete my evaluation," she says, in a martyred tone. "If you try to leave before that time is up, I call the police and they keep you here. I also amp up my search for an acceptable psych bed to put you in, as you're clearly not cooperative."

"I don't think you have enough to hold me."

Kat sounds like the lawyer she is. A stab of panic pierces my comfortable anger at the thought that she might talk her way out of this.

The doctor's face remains compassionate and grave. "Medically, no, I can't hold you. I do think it's in your best interests to stay. If you leave, I would ask you to sign a document saying you left against medical advice. No, we don't do single bed certs at this hospital. Now, I have other patients waiting for me. Let me know what you decide."

"It's up to Rae," Kat says.

I turn on her. "No, it's not up to Rae. Don't you try to put that on me."

She flinches as if I've slapped her. One hand rises to her cheek and stays there. The naked hurt in her eyes unravels my anger at the edges, making room for shades of grief and love and guilt.

"I didn't ask to be rescued," she says, quietly and with dignity.

All eyes in the room turn on me, the heartless monster, and I feel the heat mounting into my cheeks as my heart picks up its tempo. My emotions, my thoughts, are a tangled mess. I can't even guess at what choices would be right or wrong, smart or stupid. I need time to put the pieces together.

"Just stay here tonight, okay? Rest, get better. Listen to the doctor. Tomorrow I'll come back and we'll talk."

"Are you going to shout again?"

An involuntary smile dissolves the last of my anger. "I hope not. Can't promise anything."

"I bet it felt good."

That I can't argue.

"Are we all agreed, then?" The doctor twirls her stethoscope in her hands, impatient to be moving on.

"Katya?" Marci asks. "Are you willing to stay? And can you promise to be safe?"

"I think we've established that my promises are not good currency. But yes. I'll stay. I'll be safe. If Rae promises to come in and talk tomorrow."

"I'll be here." The words feel suffocating as I speak them, a binding promise I don't want to make.

Driving home, deserted by my anger, I'm nothing more than an empty shell. Thank God I've sent the kittens away with Jenny. I will crash and sleep for a million years. Or, at least, until tomorrow when I'll have to go back in and face Kat.

When I open the door and enter my house, though, I just stand there. I'd forgotten. Blood on the couch and on the carpet. Carnage in the bathroom. Tears of exhaustion threaten, but I'm tired of tears. Tired of emotions. I want my house back. I want my life back.

I want to just hit "Rewind" and go back to the day before Oscar died. Closing my eyes, I picture him in his cage waiting for me. My room, my bed. My parents on the other side of the country following a predictable routine. Bernie still a part of my Mondays.

No Katya.

And then I realize this also means no Cole. No Oscar Event. No moment of epiphany where I understand that I have friends, despite my best efforts to push them away.

"Just do the next thing," I tell myself out loud. "No need to think it all out tonight."

This gets me across the threshold and closes the door behind me. It might be only my imagination, but the house smells of blood and loss. I go around and open the windows, letting the cool night air flow in. And then I start cleaning.

I clean the bedroom first. All the while I'm packing Kat's belongings into her backpack, stripping the bed and throwing the sheets into the washing machine, I'm braced to find the body of the kitten. It doesn't show up in the bedroom, and when every trace of Kat has been removed, I go to the living room and survey the couch. It's a lost cause. I have enough money put away to get a new one. Maybe this time I'll get one that is truly new, and not Goodwill new. For now I just throw an old blanket over it.

Hydrogen peroxide takes care of the carpet, although it leaves weird bleached-out spots my landlord isn't going to like. Probably he'd find them preferable to bloodstains, but either way, this isn't going to be pretty.

With the lesser tasks done, there's no more excuse to avoid the bathroom.

It occurs to me, a little late, that I know nothing about Kat's health prior to the accident. What if she has AIDS, or hepatitis C? I've got gloves stashed away with my first aid supplies, and I glove up and put on an old shirt I can throw away when I'm done.

The towels will never be clean again. I pick them up by the edges and reach for the trash can, but just as I start to shove them in something glints in the light, and I freeze. Half-obscured by a piece of tissue is a shard of glass. One end, dagger sharp, is stained with blood.

I look down at the bandaged cut on my finger, remembering how easily the broken glass sliced into my flesh. I remember Kat, bent nearly double in the chair as she leaned forward and then rocked onto her feet. And I wonder if the night of our fight was the night she planned a second attempt.

Careful of blood and sharp edges, I retrieve the glass and set it out on the side of the sink. Evidence.

Then I get the mop and scrub the floor, dumping the wash water twice, and then get down on my hands and knees to get at the cracks and crevices. Blood pooled on the floor beneath the sink has spread into a narrow space between the floor and the vanity. I'm trying to reach in there with my rag when my gloved hand brushes against something soft and inert.

All I can see is shadows, but even before I strip off my gloves to get a better grasp on the object, I know I've found my missing kitten. He doesn't move when I pull him out into the light. He's cold to the touch. Dried blood crusts the fur on his back and the top of his head.

"I'm so sorry, little one." I pick up his tiny, limp body and cradle it in my hands.

And then I feel it, a faint, rhythmic movement of his ribs. He's still breathing. His tiny heart is beating. I run through the differential diagnoses in my head.

Hypothermia. Dehydration. Low blood sugar. His tongue and gums are pale but not yet blue, which means there's a chance to still save him.

I tuck him up under my shirt for warmth and run for my phone.

The first call is to the veterinarian emergency line. This is a small town, and there is no twenty-four-hour animal hospital. I leave a message and my callback number, knowing that by the time somebody responds it's going to be too late. Besides, the truth is, anything a vet could do for a cold, hungry kitten, I can do myself.

And then I dial another number, delete it, and dial it again before I finally let it ring through. I lecture myself about standing on my own two feet and being my own woman. I remind myself that help always comes with strings attached. But I don't want to be alone, not tonight.

What I want is Cole. His quiet strength, his support, his companionship.

He answers on the first ring, sounding muffled and sleepy, and I'm afraid I've made a mistake.

"Sorry to wake you."

"I was dreaming about giant winged snakes. So thank you. What's up?"

"Can you come over?"

My voice trembles, but he doesn't ask questions. "I'll be right there" is all he says.

While I'm waiting for the vet to call me back, for Cole to show up, for some sort of miracle to fall out of the sky and make my world okay, I do everything I can for the kitten.

The first priority is getting him warm.

Jenny has my heating pad, so I wrap the little scrap of bedraggled fur in a towel warmed in the dryer, leaving only his mouth and nose exposed. An empty jar filled with warm water and wrapped in a towel substitutes for the heating pad.

I inject some warmed IV fluid under the loose skin at the back of his neck to rehydrate him and replace electrolytes and then start in making an emergency glucose formula.

When Cole shows up, he takes in the situation with the kitten, the sheet-covered couch, the open door to the empty bedroom, but his first question is "What can I do?"

"I don't know. I shouldn't have called. It just . . . all got too big for me."

"How about if I just hang out, then? Where are the rest of them? Where's Katya?"

"The kittens are with another rescuer. Katya is in the hospital." My hands move as if they have a life and intelligence apart from my own scrambled brain. Sure and steady, I insert a tube into the kitten's stomach and slowly push glucose solution through it with a syringe.

"Why not formula?" Cole asks, leaving the more difficult questions alone.

"He can't digest it until he warms up. Sugar water every thirty minutes for now."

"Will he live?"

"Doubtful."

The kitten doesn't move when I insert the tube, or when I pull it out. I check his temperature. He's warming, but any inanimate object will warm with radiant heat. It doesn't mean his body is working.

I lean back against the sofa and let my eyelids fall closed over my burning eyes.

"Come here," Cole says, settling beside me. He puts an arm around me and draws me over beside him, nestling my head on his shoulder. I breathe him in and allow my body to relax against him. Even in the dark, exhausted as I am, he smells like a summer day. My mind drifts along mountain trails, bright with flowers. A lake, water limpid and clear, reflecting diamonds back to a blue sky. Nighttime, with a crackling campfire beside a tent, a velvet sky studded with stars. Cole is part and parcel of it all.

"Thirty minutes," he says.

"What?"

"Time to feed the kitten. I'd do it, but I can't do that tube thing."

My eyes feel glued shut. I scrub at my face with my hands and manage to unstick my eyelids.

"What were you thinking of just now?" My body weighs about a million pounds, and I can't make myself move.

"My favorite place in the Colville forest. Where I want to take you camping."

That wakes me. He blurs in and out of focus through my sleep-clouded vision. "A mountain trail," I say. "A lake. There's a loon calling."

"How did you know?"

"Better question. How did you do that? Put the pictures in my head?" I feel like I should be spooked. I'm not. A quiet hum of energy runs through me. I'm alert. Calm. Able to get up and prepare another infusion of glucose for the kitten.

"I didn't do anything," Cole says. "Other than wish you could be there. With me."

This time the kitten's eyes open when I insert the tube. His legs push back against my restraining hand. When I check his temperature it's closer to normal. At my direction, Cole refills the bottles with hot water before I lay the little one back in his nest.

"Where did you learn to do all this?" Cole asks. "Seems like it goes a little above and beyond the average pet owner."

"I worked for a vet part-time while I was in college."

"I'm pretty sure all vet assistants don't have your ninja skills."

"Probably they weren't all pushy and demanding to be taught. You want coffee?" Much as I want to snuggle up against him again and drift off to sleep, the waking up is too hard. It will be easier to just stay awake.

"Coffee sounds awesome. Are you going to tell me about Kat?"

Please. Don't let them lock me up. Loyalty binds my tongue, but only for a minute. The whole thing spills out of me. Everything. The very first promise I made to her. The visit with my parents. The reason I took on the kittens in the first place. The blood, the glass, the kitten under the vanity. His coworker's take on the situation.

He sighs. "Marci's a fill-in. Good therapist, I think, but crisis isn't her thing. I'm back on duty tomorrow."

"Oh God." I stare at him, stricken. "And I'm keeping you up all night when you have to work. Go home. Get some sleep."

"Not on your life." He settles back against the blanket-draped couch. "I'm part of the kitten vigil now."

"It will probably die."

"And yet, here we are." He gives me an inexpressibly sweet smile. "What I do. What you do. Maybe it's the trying that matters more than the saving."

"How could that be true? If the kitten dies, all of this is a useless expenditure of energy."

"Or not. Maybe it's like the butterfly effect. Just the act of love shifts something in the balance of light against dark." He flushes under my scrutiny and shrugs. "Or I'm just playing head games with myself to make what I do make sense."

"It's a beautiful idea." I find myself wanting it to be true but knowing that an idea is nothing compared with an actual life. The kitten's. Or Katya's.

Twice more I tube-feed the kitten glucose solution. Each time it struggles a little harder. By three in the morning Cole has collapsed on the floor and is snoring slightly. Both of us have been avoiding the couch. I fetch a blanket and cover him.

The kitten wakes on its own, yawns, and opens its eyes. Its tongue is pink again. Its temperature is back in the safe zone. It's still very weak, but it licks my hand when I caress its fuzzy head. This time I mix up a little formula, keeping it at half-strength. Using a syringe, I squirt a few drops into the kitten's mouth.

He swallows.

It's a miracle. A small one, maybe, important to nobody but me, but a miracle all the same. And then it dawns on me that maybe the kitten is important to somebody else as well.

I put my hand on Cole's shoulder, call his name.

His eyes pop open, and he bolts upright as if I'd lit a cannon next to his ear instead of whispering. "I'm awake, I'm awake. What?"

"Easy." I can't help laughing. He's so serious, so intense, so ready for some sort of disaster when there's nothing bigger going on than a kitten with an appetite. His hair stands straight up on top of his head, and the look—half man, half boy—turns my heart upside down and shakes it for lunch money.

"Watch."

Again, I give the kitten a few drops of milk. Again, he swallows.

Cole scoots over beside me. Ever so gently, he strokes the top of the kitten's head with a single finger.

"Have you named him?"

"It's too early. I mean, this is a good sign, but—"

"He should have a name. Even if he's only here for a minute, he should still be named. Don't you think?"

His face is very close to mine, both of us bent over the kitten. The intensity in his eyes makes my head swim. My breath flutters in my throat, my heart sets off tap-dancing to a rhythm I don't know and can't follow.

"All right," I whisper. "He's such a little bit of a thing. Not much more than a wish and a prayer."

"Call him Wish, then," Cole says.

There's no way he can know all of the ways this name is not a good idea for me. "I'm not sure about that" is all I say.

"Did you want to call him Prayer?" He grins, that mischievous, crooked, little-boy grin, and I can't catch my breath.

"Wish it is." I give the kitten a few more drops of formula.

"Rae."

Cole's voice is low and husky. I can't look up. I can't move. His hands cup my face, strong and oh-so-gentle, and tilt it up toward his. Our eyes lock. I don't think I'm breathing anymore, but that doesn't seem to matter. He leans forward and rests his forehead against mine.

For a long minute he holds me there, an intimacy between us that goes beyond a kiss.

My heart slows and steadies into a strong surge, my breathing eases. The energy between us finds a steady state, heightened, but not erratic and wild. I'm exquisitely aware of my own boundaries, That Which Is Rae, and his, That Which Is Cole, and the place where the two intertwine to make That Which Is Us.

"Thank you," he whispers.

"For what?"

"You are a light in the dark." He draws a deep breath and releases me, leaning back on his heels and breaking the moment. "If I was an artist, I'd paint you and that kitten. The Madonna of Cats."

"You're a funny guy. Here, hold Wish for a minute."

I hand him the kitten and dampen a cotton ball at the sink. As I take the kitten back from Cole and massage him with the cotton ball to stimulate elimination, Cole laughs, a low, throaty sound halfway between amusement and desire.

"Who knew rubbing a kitten's butt could be romantic?"

This sets me to giggling so hard I can barely keep on, and when the kitten rewards my efforts with a few drops of urine, I giggle even harder.

"His kidneys are working," Cole says, when I settle down. "That's good, right?"

"Very good."

He yawns. "God, I'm tired."

"You and me both."

"You more than me, I suspect. Go sleep for a bit." He tucks a strand of hair behind my ear.

"The kitten will need feeding again. If it lives."

"I'll wake you."

I'm caught in a backwater of drowsiness too strong for me to resist. It's all I can do to keep from lying down right there in the middle of the floor and letting my eyes close. *Cole has work in the morning,* I remind myself. *I should . . .*

He presses a finger over my lips. "Shhh. Don't argue." He scoops me up into his arms. My head rests comfortably against his chest, his heartbeat a steady, soothing rhythm in my ear. He carries me into the bedroom and deposits me on the bed. The mattress is bare, but it doesn't matter. A fog of exhaustion and love and desire holds me silent as he picks up a blanket from the floor and tucks me in. His lips touch my forehead, gentle and warm. My hands reach up to clasp his neck, pulling his face down toward mine.

Our lips touch, cling, and part, a butterfly kiss, no more.

"Later," he murmurs. "You can count on it. I'll wake you in two hours."

My eyes close into oblivion before he makes it to the bedroom door.

Chapter Fifteen

The vet calls back in the morning, and I take Wish over and get him settled while Cole goes home to shower and change. He's the on-call crisis worker today, and Katya is his first order of business. She's also my business, although my emotions in her regard are so tangled, I don't even try to sort them.

Cole comes back for me so we can go see her together. He has shifted into his official crisis worker mode, and I feel stiff and awkward and shy. But then he glances at me and asks, "You're sure Wish is okay at the vet's?"

He reaches for my hand, his warm fingers twining around my cold ones. My heart swells too big to fit in my chest. "Better there than at home. They've got an incubator for constant heat. Maybe they can even find a queen to foster him."

"A what?" His startled tone triggers a laugh from me. "As in 'pussycat, pussycat, where have you been?'"

"Nope. Mama cats are called queens. Don't worry, I didn't know, either, before my first rescue litter."

"Figures. Always knew cats thought they were royalty, anyway."

He pulls the car into the parking lot but doesn't turn it off, leaving the engine running. "You sure you're okay with this?"

"I'm not sure at all, but I'm coming with you anyway."

There are so many ways this interaction could get ugly, and part of the reason is my emotional entanglement with Kat.

"Discord," I tell him. "Even in music."

"I'm sorry, what?"

I hadn't meant to say it out loud, but now that it's out there I might as well carry on. So far he seems to like me despite my weirdness.

"If I get upset, or she gets upset, it's like discord in music. It resolves back into harmony and everything is okay."

"Sometimes," he says. "In the good songs."

"Help me, here." I feel all the ways my smile is ragged at the edges.

"No false pretenses between us," he says. "My job is to get to the truth, and then decide what to do with that once we find it. Maybe it would be better . . ."

"If I'm not there?"

It's an enticing thought. I could wait out here, or in the cafeteria over bad coffee, and let Cole do his job. I wouldn't ever need to see Katya again. No need to confront her with the lies she's told me, or to face the betrayal she's sure to feel that I've shared all of her secrets with Cole.

"I'm not a coward." I cringe internally at the sound of my own voice. Small, childlike, not calm and confident as I'd intended.

"No," Cole agrees. "Coward is not on your playlist. I believe you'd face down an angry elephant if it meant salvation for some small creature. I'm not entirely sure that your instincts for self-preservation are quite so strong."

"I need to do this. It is necessary."

"All right, then. Don't hate me." He smiles, but the skin around his eyes looks tight and the corners of his lips are tucked in.

At the door to the hospital he grabs my hand and squeezes it, then lets me go. I feel the shift to objective detachment, but we're still a team as we walk through the door of Kat's room together, and this time I don't pretend otherwise.

She looks from one of us to the other. "Should I have an attorney?" Her tone is biting sarcasm, but Cole responds directly to the words.

"You can call one if you like. This is an official evaluation, Katya. I don't want there to be any false pretenses. Anything you say this morning can be used as cause to send you to a psychiatric facility for treatment against your will. Do you understand this?"

"Spare me," she says. "I know the law." Her eyes look bruised. Her color is a little better, but she's far too pale. The IV still drips into her arm; she's still hooked up to monitors.

"Could you sign this for me, then?" He hands over paper and a pen. She looks at it, but doesn't sign.

"We already went through this last night. Marci and I."

"Humor me."

"I'd rather not."

"All right." Cole crosses to the door and vanishes, leaving the two of us alone together. I stare after him in dismay, feeling abandoned in enemy territory.

"I thought we were friends," Katya says.

"We are."

"Then help me. He's trying to lock me up."

"Maybe that's what needs to happen."

Katya gasps. "How could you? You promised."

"All promises were neutralized when you broke yours." Detaching the opals from my ears, I hold them out to her. "I don't want to keep these."

She turns both hands over, palms down, and shakes her head. "Those are a gift."

"That is one of the classic signs of impending suicide, the giving of gifts," Cole says, walking back into the room with a nurse behind him.

The opals, once so beautiful, make me think of blood now. I drop them onto the sheet between Kat's hands. "I refuse the gift."

"Rae," she says.

"Don't." She's going to say *please* again. I don't want to hear it.

"Since you're not willing to sign that you've received your rights, I've brought in a witness," Cole says, not getting sucked into our little drama.

Katya glares at the three of us, then shrugs. "Fine. I'll sign it."

The nurse gives Cole a questioning look. He nods, and she slips out of the room. Cole pulls up a chair for me, and one for himself on the other side of the bed.

"All right, let's talk about what happened. I don't want to put you in a psych ward, Katya, but I will if I need to."

She rolls her eyes. "Save your breath. As I explained last night to Maria—"

"Marci."

"Whoever. I was cutting. I didn't mean to go so deep—"

"Don't do this," Cole interrupts. "You're an intelligent woman. I've been around this particular block more than once. Let's have the truth."

"I don't know what you mean."

"Let me see your arms."

"They're perfectly visible."

"You know what I mean." He touches the back of her bandaged wrist lightly. "Turn them both over. Let's see."

Still, she doesn't move.

"Anybody who cuts habitually enough to keep a special blade hidden for the purpose knows better than to cut lengthwise along a vein. And they are always scarred. I asked the nurse just now, and she doesn't remember seeing any marks on your arms in addition to the suicide scars."

"Do we have to use that word?" Katya asks.

"*Suicide*, you mean?"

"It's such a judgmental word."

"Fair enough. We can just talk about you trying to kill yourself instead."

"God, you're a terrible person. That's not better. And maybe I do my cutting somewhere besides my arms. Maybe I'm smarter than that."

I can't figure out why she keeps lying. Obviously he's not buying the story, and it's easy enough to prove. "There aren't any scars on your legs," I say. "Or your belly or your breasts. You don't have a razor blade hidden away; you used a piece of broken glass."

Her mouth opens and then snaps shut.

"Probably you weren't thinking," Cole says, gently, "or you might have realized Rae would find it in the trash."

"So I'm an opportunist."

"That glass broke two days ago. You picked up a piece the night my parents were here and kept it. You practically pushed me out the door to the party. You gave me a gift."

"No," she says, shaking her head. "No. Rae, you have to believe me even if he doesn't. It was on impulse. The kitten died, and I—"

"But the kitten's not dead," Cole says, very gently now.

"What?" Katya's eyes flicker from him to me and back again. She has the desperate look of a trapped animal. "Rae said, last night . . ."

My throat feels clogged with dust. "I thought it was. I couldn't find it. You know where it was, Kat? In the bathroom. Under the vanity. It had your blood all over it. You knew where it was the whole time and you didn't tell me. Last night, you said you cut yourself because it died."

Maybe my throat is dry, but my eyes aren't. I can't stem the rush of tears. Kat's hand twists the edge of the sheet into a little knot and clamps tight around it. She turns her face away from me. "You don't understand. You'll never understand." Her voice sounds flat, hopeless.

"I understand that you lied to me. Took advantage of my friendship. Maybe you even planned some sort of murder-suicide thing with the kitten."

"No!"

"How can I believe anything you say?"

Unlike Marci, Cole doesn't try to stop us from ripping open each other's wounds. He sits. Quiet. Watchful. Waiting for something.

"You want the truth?" Katya flares. "Because I don't think you can handle it."

"Try me."

"Fine. Yes. I want to die. I can't think of one single thing worth living for. I tried. I meant it when I promised you I would be safe if I stayed at your house. I swear it. You're a good person, Rae. Naïve. Full of all sorts of magical ideas about how life should be, but good. So I figured I owed it to you to at least wait until I got away from your house to finish the job I botched. Because I'm truly sorry I dragged you into this.

"But that tiny runt kitten . . . he's going to die. Despite anything you do, or try to do, and all your dedication, he's not going to make it. He wouldn't eat. He was crying and I tried to feed him, but he wouldn't eat."

"You should have called Rae. If there was a problem with the kitten, you know she would have come straight home." From the way Cole glances at me, I see he's trying to protect me, but there is no shelter from what Kat is saying.

She laughs, a horrible, twisted sound. "Don't you see? That's the point. She would have come home. And she would have tried and tried to save the kitten, but it would have died anyway. And then I thought maybe it would be better, kinder, to just end things now instead of stretching them out. Let Rae get on with her life. End the charade of my own."

Her eyes are dry, but her breathing sounds like she's been running, ragged, tortured. "Is that twisted thinking? Probably. Maybe. I don't know. How can I tell? I didn't have a plan when I picked up the piece of glass. I just felt better, safer, not so trapped, knowing I had the means if the pain got too much . . ."

She pauses, one clenched fist resting over her heart. "Oh God, it hurts."

I make a move toward her, but Cole gestures me back.

"Why did you stop?" he asks.

Kat gasps, a sound half sob, half moan. "That thrice-damned kitten. I couldn't—couldn't cut him with a blade. So I thought maybe I'd drown him in the sink, but I couldn't do that, either, and then he crawled under the vanity. I was desperate by then; I'd come this far, I wasn't going to stop because of a kitten. So I did the first cut, and after I was already bleeding out, before I could do the second, I heard myself promising Rae everything would be fine. And the crying kittens just became deafening, and I couldn't—I couldn't make the second cut. So I tried to bandage it. And I tried to get him out from under the vanity, Rae, truly, only I was too dizzy and weak, and I couldn't . . ."

"Why?" Cole asks.

Katya stares at him but doesn't answer. Her face goes quiet and remote. She holds her breath.

His voice is as inexorable as a slow-moving glacier. "Why do you want to die? Not this time with the kitten. Not the bike. Tell me about the first time."

The room falls into silence, broken only by the rapid beeping that records Kat's heart rate, and the whir-click of the IV pump. It seems to me that all three of us are in suspended animation.

"I don't want to talk about it," Kat says, in a strangled voice. "Go ahead. Lock me up. Just leave me alone."

"I think there's something you're holding back. Something bigger than kittens or an unhappy marriage. What is it, Katya? Tell me."

All of the darkness I've sensed in Kat is in the room with us now, growing and swelling and expanding. It's going to suck us all under. The air is thick with grief and rage.

Cole is pushing too hard. "She can't have babies now," I blurt out, trying to ward him off. "Since the accident. There was damage—"

"Shut up!" Kat shouts at me. "Just shut up. Don't—" Her voice breaks. The corners of her mouth turn square. She sucks in a great gout of air and begins to weep—ugly, racking sobs that make her splint her rib cage with both hands.

"It—hurts—too—much," she gasps, and I feel the first brush of panic.

Cole doesn't move from his chair. His face is focused, calm, his eyes looking into Kat with such a single-minded intensity I could probably dance around the room singing clown songs and he wouldn't even notice.

When the weeping eases, she says, "Tom told you, didn't he? About the babies. Six miscarriages in three years. Pain and blood and failure. Every single time Tom locked himself in the bathroom to weep, I know he did. He tried to hide it from me, but it hurt him so. And my mother, every time, 'A woman has babies, Katya. That is what she does in this world. What is wrong with you? Do you take the vitamins? Maybe if you stop this working and bicycle riding, you can hold on to a child. Stay home and cook for your husband. All I ask in this world is grandchildren. Is that so much?'"

She pauses, breathing hard, both hands pressed against her eyes as if to block out memories or hold back tears. I remember the picture of her family, the little girl wearing a scarf, her face oh-so-serious. The older brothers looking older than their years.

"But your sister," I say. "Your brothers."

"My sister died when we were kids. And my brothers married American women and moved away. I'm her last hope for a house filled with children. Tom's family is just as bad. Always polite to me, always reserved. He wouldn't tell me what they said, but I knew. 'What kind of woman did you marry, that she can't produce a child?' I couldn't even blame it on him, since clearly he was capable of getting me pregnant. I just couldn't carry them.

"And then . . . after those six lost pregnancies, we had one that seemed to stick. I didn't tell anybody for the first three months, not even Tom. I couldn't bear to see the disappointment. But then my doctor said I was past the highest risk. I had a special doctor, and he said everything looked good. We bought baby clothes. Tom fixed up a room. He built the crib himself, a beautiful thing. Four weeks before my due date we went to see the doctor. He came in smiling, and then he listened for the baby . . ."

She puts both hands over her mouth, and the keening sound she makes is one I'll never forget as long as I live. It's a sound torn up from the bottom of her soul. I want to tell her to stop, that it's okay—she doesn't have to talk about it. But I've been in counseling long enough to know that she probably does.

Still, I wish I wasn't here.

I wish I could do something to ease her suffering.

As usual, my wishes count for nothing.

Kat catches her breath. "He sent us for an ultrasound, to be sure, but I knew. I wanted him to take the baby, then and there. I demanded a C-section, an induction, threatened to cut it out myself with a carving knife. The doctor said no to everything, that I had to wait. He gave me something to soften my cervix, and I walked around for a week with a dead baby inside me. It was—I couldn't . . .

"Tom tried to help. He tried to hold me, comfort me, tell me it would be okay, but I wouldn't let him. And then there was the labor and the pain, for what? They gave me sedatives, opiates, an epidural. But I still had to push. It took forever for my body to rid itself of the—thing—inside me. And when it came out, the nurse wrapped it in a blanket. They wanted me to hold it, said that it would be good for me. I refused.

"So they gave it to Tom.

"And he stood there, in the middle of the delivery room . . . He was wearing jeans and a flannel shirt, his comfort clothes. He hadn't shaved in a week, so grief-stricken, so worried about me, and he looked rough and ragged. And the image of him, his head bent over that bundle in his arms, tears falling, him sobbing . . .

"Oh my God. I can't. I can't. I can't."

It's too much. I don't care anymore what Cole thinks, or that Kat lied to me. All that matters is easing her agony, or sharing it if I can't. I climb into the bed beside her. "Hold on to me."

I put my arms around her, careful of her ribs, and start murmuring stupid things about how everything will be all right.

She rolls toward me onto her good hip, her hands knotted into my shirt, twisting it tight. Her whole body shakes with her weeping. Hot tears, hers and mine, mingle together.

After a long time, the sobbing begins to quiet and slow. Her breathing grows easier. The tears ebb.

"Everything got twisted after that," she says, very softly. "Tom and I couldn't seem to talk about anything without getting into a fight. He started staying late at work. I accused him of having another woman. And then it occurred to me that he should have another woman. He should have children and be happy."

"I can tell you from experience," Cole says, "that your death is going to cause him pain and misery that is never going to end. Believing otherwise makes killing yourself easier, but that thinking is a lie."

She doesn't answer, but she's listening. I can feel her listening, drinking in every one of his words.

"If you kill yourself, he will always feel the pain of that, and guilt for it. As will Rae. And me," he adds, after a pause. "I will always feel that I failed you."

"That's not fair," Katya says. "It's my life. I'm not asking for any of you to feel guilty."

"Life's not fair," Cole counters. "Like it or not, that's the way it works."

"But then Tom's as trapped as I am. Tied to me forever. That can't be right."

"Divorce is a slightly less drastic solution than suicide," Cole says.

"He's Catholic. Divorce is . . . don't say it. I know." She sighs. "This is weird, but I never even thought about divorce as an option."

"Depression and despair twist up your thinking. If your reason for dying is truly so that he can be happy and have children, you're much more likely to achieve that purpose by ending the relationship. Which, of course, doesn't solve the problem of what does Katya do about Katya."

"You're a scary guy," she says. "You see too much."

He doesn't answer that.

Now that the weeping is over and her pain has eased, I suddenly feel self-conscious and out of place in Kat's bed. I roll over and sit up, mopping my damp face with my sleeve.

"Now what?" Kat asks.

"No," I say, before anybody can ask. "You can't come home with me."

All three of us are surprised by my words, probably me more than the others.

"Agreed," Cole says, after a small silence. "I was thinking the crisis house, if you're willing. It's voluntary."

"Sounds more like the involuntary voluntary option to me." A hint of her usual sarcasm creeps into her voice.

"Agreed. Either you come voluntarily to the crisis house, or you go involuntarily to the hospital. Choice is yours."

"I thought there weren't any beds."

"That was then; this is now. Pretty sure I can get you in somewhere in the state if I'm persistent and persuasive."

"All right," Kat says. "Crisis house it is. Rae—"

"I don't hate you," I say, before she can ask. "I just can't . . ."

"What, fix me?"

"Make you happy."

"Nobody's asking you to," she says.

Chapter Sixteen

Back home in an empty, kitten-free house, I drop into bed and sleep for twenty-four hours, waking up a couple of times to go to the bathroom, drink water, and eat a bowl of cereal before crashing again.

When my eyes flutter open to daylight and I know I'm awake and going to stay that way, I don't know where I am in time and space. And I don't care. I just lie there, drifting a little. No heavy weight of responsibility or expectation. No dark shadows. No lurking anything. As long as I can keep my brain from thinking, everything is light and wonderful.

The landline rings, and it all goes to hell in a handbasket. Where is the phone? Where am I? What day is it, what time is it, am I late for work, what's happening with the kitten? My body feels stiff once I start trying to move it, my knees and elbows don't want to bend, and my head feels full of cotton wool.

I find the phone under the couch. It's already stopped ringing, and the battery warning flashes at me when I try to see who called. About two minutes later I realize I'm still staring at it stupidly, and I get up and put it back in the cradle to charge. As I start the coffeepot I realize I'm starving. Not cereal-and-milk starving, but steak-and-potatoes-and-bread starving.

There's not much in the fridge, but I find a couple of eggs and some bread and settle for a fried-egg sandwich. Salt and flavor explode in my mouth, and I wolf the whole thing down and make another. By the time I've consumed two egg sandwiches and four cups of coffee, reality has settled in, and I'm able to make some basic decisions about what to do.

I call in sick to work. This is not a good trend, but I can't imagine, no matter how hard I try, managing the pace and the thousand and one little decisions I have to make during a single shift. If I am able to pick out clothes to wear today, I figure I'll be doing great.

I call the vet. Wish is doing well, they tell me. Much better than expected. He's able to suckle from a bottle again. Plus, there's a mama cat who has lost some kittens who might take him. Can I leave him for a little while longer?

With Katya at the crisis house, the kitten at the vet, and no job to go to, I expect to feel footloose and fancy-free. Instead, I'm beset by a restless, unsettled meaninglessness. My skin feels itchy on the inside, and I catch myself pacing like a caged creature, door to window, into the bedroom and back again.

Maybe I should go out. I could go to the grocery store, take a walk. Maybe even do something for myself like a haircut or a shopping trip in Spokane. But even a simple decision like whether or not to take a shower is too much for me.

Every time I walk into the bathroom I see blood. It's not really there, and the bathroom smells like bleach, not copper and salt, but my brain insists on holding on to what was, instead of what is. I also keep thinking I'm hearing kittens crying, enough to get me down on my knees looking under couch and chair, even under the vanity in the bathroom, when I know good and well there's no living thing in this house with me, except for a couple of spiders.

By noon, I'm wishing I had gone in to work. I feel like I've already been through a week of time, and I'm going to scream if I stay here another minute. When someone knocks at the door, I open it without even checking to see who's there. At this point, I'd welcome a discussion of the LDS religion or even a solicitor. Anything to get me out of my own head.

Cole is an infinite improvement on all of the above.

"Hey," he says, looking me over, from the top of my uncombed head down to my slippered feet. "I'm not even going to ask how you're doing."

I don't ask him to come in. Don't do anything or say anything, just stand there, looking at him like he's a well in the middle of the Sahara. He puts his hands on my shoulders and maneuvers me backward so he can close the door.

His eyes rove over the house. The dishes in the sink, the pan still on the stove.

"What you need," he says, "is some fresh air and a change of perspective. Let me take you for a drive."

"Now?"

"Maybe after a shower."

My hand wanders to my tangled hair. It feels tacky to the touch, and I'm suddenly aware that I'm wearing an oversized T-shirt and a pair of yoga pants that should have gone in the laundry days ago. "I'm sorry, I—" There aren't any other words to follow this.

"Let me guess," he says. "You feel like your skin is about three sizes too small, and every time you try to think an anthill kicks over in your brain. There's absolutely nothing in the world that you want to do, and you feel empty in the middle. About sum it up?"

"How did you know?"

"Standard response to a series of traumatic events, emotional overload, and not enough sleep. It's normal."

"I keep seeing blood where there isn't any."

"Also normal. Come on. Day's a-wastin'."

"How's Katya? Is she okay?"

"Alive and in the crisis house. And that is the only thing I'm saying about her today." He takes me by the shoulders from behind and starts walking me through the living room and toward the bathroom. A faint glimmer of an idea emerges through the fog. Both of us in the shower. Together.

Water pouring over the contours of his muscular chest, down over his belly, running off his . . .

I stumble over my own feet.

"You are tired," he says, shoving me through the door and closing it between us.

I am also an idiot. I strip out of my wilted clothes and stand under the hot water, indulging in fantasies about Cole that might be dangerous but also make me feel alive.

When I emerge from the shower into a bathroom full of steam, I am caught on the horns of a dilemma. My discarded clothes lie on the floor like a molted skin. I don't want to touch them, let alone put them back on. My clean clothes are in the bedroom.

And there is a man in my living room. Not just any man. Cole. A man with eyes that light up every nerve ending of my body. A man who can get his mind around my love for a rat, who would stay up all night to help me save a kitten.

A man who has repeatedly turned down any opportunity to have his way with me.

In which case, there should be no problem with me walking across the living room wrapped in a towel. Women in movies do it all the time. Sometimes it turns into something. Sometimes it doesn't. It's not like my life is some glamorous romance novel with a hero who is waiting outside the door to sweep me off my feet and pleasure me five times over before he even thinks about his own manly needs.

My only alternative to the towel walk is asking him to bring me clothes. The idea of him in my bedroom, rooting through my drawers, my underwear, maybe finding my vibrator, is worse than the idea of me in a towel.

I take a deep breath, wrap myself up well, and step out into the living room.

Cole is at the kitchen sink, washing dishes. Good. Maybe he won't even see me. I take a step toward the bedroom.

He turns at the sound of the opening door, a sudsy bowl in his hands.

"Oh God." He says it like a prayer—whether of gratitude or deliver-me-from-evil or a plea for salvation, I can't tell. His eyes burn, even from across the room. The bowl drips water onto the floor, but he doesn't move. Doesn't turn around to put it away.

The muscles in his throat contract as he swallows.

"God, Rae, go put some clothes on. You're killing me."

His words and the tone of his voice say two different things. I can feel the electricity between us. It's cosmic, incandescent. The whole room lights up with it.

"Or you could take yours off." I smile and drop the towel.

He closes his eyes. Swallows. Opens them again. Heat follows his gaze as it moves over my body like a physical caress, but he stays firmly planted by the sink.

"That thing about not knowing what I want to do and feeling itchy in my skin? I figured out something I want." If what I'm thinking keeps coming out of my mouth like this, I'm going to need to buy myself a muzzle.

Cole shakes his head. "Sex comes in two varieties for me." His voice is pitched low, almost a growl in his throat. "Casual and strings attached. It's too late for casual with you."

"So I'm strings attached?"

"So many strings. This is not a good idea, Rae."

"And you're what—protecting me from myself? I'm a grown-up. Just because I'm a woman doesn't mean I need you to preserve me from my own sexual cravings." Frustration gives my voice an edge.

"It's my strings I'm worried about. Just because I'm a man doesn't mean I can indulge my desires without emotional fallout. I can't . . ."

Clearly, *can't* is not the word he really means. I can see the bulge in his jeans now. There's a spot of color in each cheek, and his breathing is harsh.

"Not yet. Not today. Please."

It's the first time he's ever asked anything of me. Another long moment we stand there, eyes locked. I'm shivering with cold, desire, and something far beyond either. Finally, I turn without another word and walk into the bedroom to get dressed. My hands won't stop shaking. I have no clue what I'm feeling.

Embarrassment? I ask myself. *Shame? Rejection?*

To my surprise, none of these labels resonates. I've just offered myself to a man. Stood there naked and asked him for sex, and he's turned me down. These would be the reasonable emotions. But as I pull on a pair of clean jeans and a T-shirt, I realize that what I feel is cleansed. Exhilarated. Energized.

Alive.

~

The back of Cole's truck is loaded with supplies. A cooler. Blankets. A backpack.

"Are we going on an expedition?"

"I always carry this stuff with me. You never know when disaster will strike."

"Oh my God, you're a prepper."

He laughs, the tension easing from his jaw, the atmosphere downgrading from dynamite charge to a pleasant buzz of electricity.

"Nah, I'm kidding. The cooler would be useless during the zombie apocalypse. I have a favor."

"What's that?"

"Mind if we stop by the vet's and check in on Wish?"

Since he's already pulling into the parking lot, my approval is only a formality.

Mel, the receptionist, lights up at the sight of me. "He's so cute," she gushes, all smiles.

I assume she's talking about the kitten with the cute comment, although the way she eyes Cole gives her words a double meaning.

"And he's doing awesome. Perfect timing. Come see."

She disappears through the back of the reception area, and I grab Cole's hand and lead him through the door, past the treatment rooms, and into the boarding area. In a comfortable kennel a mother cat lies on her side, nursing a row of five kittens. She's a Himalayan, a big, long-haired seal point. Four of the kittens are miniature versions of the mother. The fifth is a small gray tabby.

"Owner brought mama and all the kittens in this morning for boarding," Mel says. "Family emergency. We told him about Wish, and he said, 'Sure, why not?' Mama cat took right to him, and so far the other kittens are accepting him fine."

"What happens when the cats all go home?" Cole asks.

Mel shoots him a mischievous grin. "One bridge at a time."

"What she means," I say, "is that the man loves his cat, and by the time he gets back from vacation, mama cat will be very offended at the idea of leaving one of her kittens behind. Wish will be a permanent addition to the litter."

"Even if he pitches a fit—and he won't—a week of mama cat attention will do wonders for the little guy." Mel pats the top of the kennel affectionately. A buzzer sounds in the background.

"Customers," she says. "Guess I'd better get that."

Cole curves his hand around mine as we walk, linking us together, Cole-and-Rae. It's companionable and warm and new. It's not that I haven't dated or had sexual liaisons and even, once, a friend with benefits. I've just never progressed to this level of comfortable intimacy.

Trust, maybe, would be the word I'm after.

In the truck, Cole puts the keys in the ignition, but then just sits there, staring straight ahead.

"Thank you," he says.

"For what?" I'm genuinely bewildered. He brought me here. Came to check on me. Stayed up all night taking care of a tiny, unwanted feline.

"I see people at their worst. Hurt, angry. Hopeless. Sometimes I start to see the world that way. And then you come along, with your wishes and kittens . . ."

"Small, inconsequential things in the grand scheme. I can't wrap my mind around bigger issues."

"Maybe the small things aren't so inconsequential after all," he says. "Has it occurred to you that maybe that's what matters? If everybody was dialed in to caring for small lives, maybe the bigger things would take care of themselves."

The moment is too serious. My heart is tap-dancing in my chest again. "Hobbits," I tell him.

He blinks. "Pardon?"

"Like Gandalf said. What matters, really, is the hobbits. That's what all of the big important people are fighting for."

Cole snort-laughs, then leans over, out of the blue, and kisses me. This time it's no light brush of lips. It's not a reassuring kiss or a goodnight kiss or even an exploratory one. His lips mold to mine as if we are each one of a pair, designed to fit together. He tastes a little bit like coffee but mostly just like Cole. All of me rises to meet his lips, my insides and my outsides and the secret, reserved Rae self that never shows itself to anybody.

A dog barks, and then a terrible screeching sound breaks us apart.

My eyes open on a dog nose pressed against the driver's-side window. Frenzied barking, nails scratching the paint, his frantic owner pulling on the leash.

"Sorry," she calls, tugging at the dog. "Bandit, get down. Come *here.*"

She's just a kid, thin and wiry. Probably traumatized for life by the sight of old people kissing and then having her dog go berserk in the parking lot. A scowling man rounds the front of the pickup truck parked next to us. He takes the leash from the girl's hands, utters a harsh rebuke to the dog, who immediately responds to the voice of authority, and the three of them disappear into the clinic.

Cole starts laughing, a big, booming laugh that throws him back against his seat, turns his face red, and brings tears into his eyes.

It takes about ten seconds before I'm laughing, too, both of us hysterical.

"See what you're doing to me?" He sobers up and wipes his eyes. "Last time I kissed a girl in a public place I was sixteen."

He starts the engine and backs out of the parking lot.

"Where are we going?"

"That, my little hobbit, is a bit of a surprise."

"Hobbits have hairy toes."

"I've never seen your toes. You might well be a hobbit, for all I know."

My hands fly to my mouth to stifle a giggle. I've never been a giggly sort of a girl. Not that I don't have a sense of humor, it just tends to be on the dry side. My mood has shifted to flighty and exuberant.

"I am fond of snacks. And presents. Seriously. Where are we going?"

"To visit somebody."

"Is there a wizard involved?" I keep my tone light, but inside I'm more than half-serious. *Visit* is a wet blanket of a word. Exhilaration gives way to apprehension. How many mood shifts is this for one day? I'm like a north country spring, changing weather every fifteen minutes.

"Don't jump out of the window just yet," he says, as if he really can read my mind. "I wouldn't take you there if I wasn't sure you'll be fine."

"Me and strangers don't have a huge compatibility rating, in general."

"She'll love you, and you'll love her. Trust me."

"She who?" Now I'm picturing an ex-girlfriend. One of those maybe-she's-born-with-it types who spend hours putting on a face that men think is natural. One of those sweet-as-pie-to-your-face-but-rip-you-to-shreds-behind-your-back women. I trust Cole as much as I trust anybody, but in my limited experience men can be incredibly stupid when a beautiful woman is involved.

"My grandmother. And I'm 99.2 percent sure that you will still love me after. I reserve a small margin of error."

His tone is light, casual. Is the use of the word *love* intentional? Does he mean love in the way of chocolate or the way I felt while we were kissing? For some reason this question of usage seems much more pressing than the fact that he is taking me to meet a family member.

She lives out of town, way out of town, which could be either a point in her favor or a point against her. People who live out here either like their solitude (point for) or are avoiding law enforcement for one reason or another (point against). Since Cole obviously loves her, and he seems to be an upstanding citizen, I'm hoping for a pleasantly introverted old lady.

When we turn off the road onto a rutted driveway, the house is still screened from view. I'm not sure what to expect out here. Manufactured home, single-wide trailer, cabin, hovel, or beautifully constructed house. We've seen variations of all of the above along the way. My imagination fails to prepare me for what meets the eye as Cole parks in a graveled yard.

We just sit there for a minute. My brain can't process what I'm seeing, but my soul takes to it like a duck to water. The war between the two parts of me makes me dizzy.

"Is she . . ." I stop before finishing the question, unable to find a word that will encompass the riot of flowers, the naked gnome peeking out from a patch of raspberry canes, the open door in the middle of a small field of clover, leading from nowhere to nowhere. The house itself has been pulled out of a storybook world, a cozy little cottage painted daffodil yellow with lilac trim.

Cole laughs, clearly enjoying my reaction. "Clear as a bell, sharp as a tack."

"That wasn't what I meant."

"I know. It's impossible to mean anything when it comes to Gram. I do assure you that her oven is used only for baking cookies and that she abhors gingerbread. Come on."

A dreamlike daze moves with me out of the truck and up the paving stone path that leads to a neat front porch topped by a rose-covered trellis. Wind chimes, seashells, and crystals dangle from among the leaves and scarlet blossoms.

I stop in the shade of an apple tree, heavy with more than fruit.

"What's with the bottles?"

They are tied to the branches with bits of twine wrapped around their necks. Some are old and weathered. A few are new and shiny. Beer bottles, coke bottles, green glass bottles that might have once held olive oil or even perfume.

"That's the prayer tree."

"But why are there bottles on it?"

"To keep the prayers in." He keeps moving, and I follow him, although I could stand in the shadow of that tree for hours, immersed in a sensory heaven made up of rose perfume, humming bees, and ever-shifting rainbows from the prisms hanging overhead.

Cole knocks, then pushes the unlocked door open and calls, "Gram?"

"She knows we're coming, right?" I whisper.

"Probably," he replies, not an answer that inspires confidence. He reaches back for my hand and gives a comforting squeeze, but I realize, suddenly, that it's only my mind that's frightened, and only because it thinks it should be. My emotions are merely hushed, waiting.

The inside of the house is as unlike the outside of the house as it could possibly be. I'm primed for knickknacks and fussiness—doilies on antique tables, a collection of figurines. What I don't expect is a whole lot of nothing.

The room we enter has a split bamboo floor without a throw rug in sight. No antique tables, no chairs, just a couple of oversized floor pillows and a yoga mat. The far wall is all windows, opening onto a green space bounded by a closely woven hedge. A doorway on the left opens into a dim hallway, to the right into a small but efficient and spotless kitchen.

The only wall décor is a photograph of a naked tree in winter, a blue jay making a bold splash of color in its branches. All around the tree, tangled in its branches, floating above the grass, are small, glowing spheres. Some are white, others colored; no two are the same. The picture draws me in, even more than the fountain burbling in the corner and the view from the window. *Bubbles,* I think. *Soap bubbles,* only these look more substantial. On closer look, some seem to have mandalas inside. Maybe it's a painting, not a photo, but the details are so pristine, so perfect.

"What is this?" I breathe. "How was it done?"

"It's a photograph, taken with an ordinary camera." The voice reminds me of the clear tones of a bell. "You can see the tree through the window."

Spinning around, I see a small woman emerge from the shadows of the hallway. Silver hair hangs over her shoulder in a braid. Her spine is ramrod straight, and there's nothing of age in her movements or her voice.

"Cole," she says, "I thought you might come today."

He crosses the room and bends to enclose her in a hug. She kisses his cheek and then turns to me. Her eyes are darker than Cole's, almost black, but she has that same intensity of focus that narrows the world down to the two of us; everything else, even Cole, fades into the periphery.

"This is Rae," I hear his voice saying, but my name doesn't matter.

"And I am Tana." She reaches for my hand. As my palm nears hers, a light in the ceiling fixture above us flares and burns out with a little pop. The fountain in the corner stills. Cole's phone makes a garbled ringing sound that dies without completion.

Before I can snatch my hand back, Tana grips it strongly in hers, her eyes looking into me all the while. "Oh dear," she says, a slight smile tugging at the corners of her lips. "There goes the electricity again."

"Does this happen often?" I ask. There are a lot of burnt-out light bulbs in my past, along with the dead watch and cell phone batteries. I try not to think about this. It's certainly not something I talk about.

"Not so much anymore. I'm glad Cole brought you."

Not the slightest whisper of annoyance about the light bulb or the electricity. No commentary on the strangeness of it all.

"Damn. My phone's dead," Cole says. He also doesn't sound surprised, although there is unmistakable irritation in his voice.

"Good. You young people are entirely too attached to those objects. It won't hurt you to be without it for a while. Shall we sit outside? I've made tea."

"I'm on call. The phone is necessary." Cole pokes at a button as if the thing is going to magically come back to life. "I don't suppose you have a charger?"

"You still locking people up, then?" She releases me from her searching with a smile and turns her attention to her grandson.

"I don't lock them up." There's an edge to his voice I haven't heard before.

"No, you leave that part to other people."

"What do you want me to do? Let them die? Not everybody can come sit in your garden and have a cup of tea."

"Then maybe we should be building more gardens and making more tea," she says, her tone very gentle. "You can use the landline. Call your dispatch and let them know where you are."

Cole excuses himself to go into the kitchen. He says nothing, but the line of his jaw is tight.

"Come, dear." Tana reaches for my hand, but I jerk away, thinking enough damage has been done to her electrical circuits. "It will be fine," she says, in the tone of voice I use to calm a frightened animal. Hesitant, I reach out, and our hands connect. This time there are no fireworks.

"You see?" she says, leading me across the room and out the door into her garden. I don't see at all.

"Wait here. I'll get the tea and the boy and we'll talk."

Standing dead center in Tana's beautiful backyard, an incredible peace flows through me. A stream burbles across one corner, entering and exiting through the hedge. Hummingbirds chase each other around a feeder hanging from the branches of a maple. And then a wild, sweet music springs up out of nowhere, a haunting song without melody thrumming through my entire being.

The sound seems to come from the tree. It draws me, step by slow step, until I'm standing under the branches, looking up at a canopy of green. Little balls of light dance at the edges of my vision.

"Amazing, isn't it?" Cole's voice is quiet.

"What is it?"

"Aeolian harp. It's actually on the other side of the hedge; it just sounds like it's coming from the tree."

"That photograph . . ."

211

"Orbs," Tana calls, from over by a wooden picnic table. Once again I haven't heard her coming, this time because of the wind music.

I look to Cole for an explanation.

"Weird photographic phenomenon," he explains. "Little balls of light showing up in digital pictures all over the world. Nobody knows for sure what they are."

"Spirits," Tana says. "Or energy, maybe. Sit with me a little. I'm not as young as some."

"You can't know that," Cole says, leading me over to the table. "It could be dust flecks or a trick of the light."

She wrinkles her nose at him and lowers her voice to a theatrical whisper. "Or ghosts of the dead."

"You've been on the Internet again."

"I love the Internet. Portal to alternate realities."

"They are beautiful, whatever they are," I say.

Tana smiles approvingly, as if I've said something wise, rather than admitting that I have no idea what we're talking about. "Just so."

"And your yard . . ." I wave my arms and then shrug. "*Beautiful* isn't the right word."

"Sacred space," Cole says.

But that isn't right, either. Sacred space makes me think of religion and solemnity and ritual. What I feel here in this garden is free. A weight I didn't even know I was carrying has been lifted off my shoulders by the music of the wind, and scattered far and wide as lightly as dandelion seed.

Tana hands me a tall glass filled with ice and a clear amber liquid. "It's the harp music that does it, I think. The orbs love music as well."

"They're not static? They come and go?"

"Oh, absolutely. How about I show you how it's done? So much easier than telling."

"I'd love that."

"Perfect." She beams at me.

Cole, on the other hand, slumps backward in his chair and makes a gesture with his hands that clearly means *Here we go again.*

"You and Cole go stand under the tree, and I'll take pictures of you."

I stare at her, my glass halfway to my mouth. This was not at all what I'd been expecting. I've never liked myself in pictures.

"Again?" Cole protests. "I've posed five times for you and never yet seen anything besides myself and the tree."

"That's because you're posing, dear."

Tana pulls a digital camera out of her pocket and stands up, waiting. Feeling like an actor who hasn't been given any lines, I grab Cole's hand and pull him out of his chair. He slouches over to the tree with all the enthusiasm of a teenager being coerced into kitchen chores. Self-conscious, I look toward Tana, who has already begun snapping nonstop pictures.

"What are we supposed to do?"

"Forget about me and think about the orbs," she says. "Invite them."

"Out loud?" I've been willing to go along with this, but standing under the tree and openly invoking some invisible magic bubbles isn't in the same universe as my comfort zone.

"Like making a wish," she says. "It doesn't need to be out loud."

Make a wish. It's a common enough phrase. She can't possibly know about my wishing stones. And surely it's not possible to call in little glowing spheres of light. But then the wind picks up and the harp vibration shakes all of the doubts out of my head. I look up through the green leaves above me, focusing on light and shadow, letting the sound flow over and through me like water. Turning my back to the camera, I let my arms drift upward to touch a leaf, then spin toward Cole, suddenly laughing like a child.

He sweeps me off my feet and twirls me around and around until I'm dizzy and out of breath. When he sets me down I lean into him for balance, the world still moving around me, the music inside and outside and everywhere.

And then the wind dies away.

Everything goes silent.

My breath, Cole's breath. My forehead resting against his chest, his hands on the small of my back, the rich scent of earth and grass and leaves intertwined with the fragrance of roses. He kisses the top of my head.

We're not alone.

It takes me a minute to remember that. There is an old woman and a camera. A world of realities demanding my attention. With a sigh, I stand up straight and look out of the tree shadow into the sunlight.

Tana sits at the table, the camera nowhere in sight.

"Your tea is getting warm," she says, "better drink up."

My tea is not warm. It is icy cold and perfect, with just a hint of sweetness.

"Thank you for humoring me," Tana says to Cole, who has the grace to flush and drop his eyes. "And now maybe you'll tell me why you brought Rae to see me."

"I can't bring a girl over just because?"

"Rae's not just any girl. And I can tell when you want something."

"Rae's an empath."

That word again, said this time like it explains everything, when I'm still not even sure what he means. I feel myself go tense, my breath catching in my throat.

But Tana wears the same warm, curious expression she did when talking about orbs. "Empaths come in all different shapes and sizes," she says. "What particular stripe are you, Rae?"

I don't have an answer. In all my years of counseling, nobody has ever talked about empaths. Empathy, sure. Highly Sensitive People, definitely. But this is unfamiliar territory, and I don't have an answer.

Tana rests a hand lightly on my forearm. "I call it the Empath Continuum. There are empaths like Cole, who build their lives around helping others because they feel things deeply. And there are empaths who are blown to kingdom come by other people's emotions and end up as cat ladies in isolated houses. I suspect once upon a time they were burned as witches."

Given this analogy, it's pretty clear where I belong on her continuum. "Cat lady," I tell her. "Definitely."

Tana graces me with an approving smile. A warm rush of energy runs through me.

"I thought you could tell her what you do to shield yourself. The things you taught me."

"Please." I focus on the coolness of the sweating glass in my hand to keep from reaching for hers. "This empath thing—I think it's what I call the dimmer switch. That's what I'm looking for."

Both of them regard this request with raised eyebrows. The identical expression on two very different faces almost makes me laugh. I don't want to explain in front of Cole. But they are both quiet, waiting, so I keep talking. "People. Relationships. I have two modes, my counselor says. Full-on, or off."

"What's so bad about full-on?" Tana asks.

I laugh. "You're kidding, right? That thing that happened with the light bulb? That's what full-on does to my life. What if I don't want to be a crazy cat lady?" What I really mean is that I don't want to spend my life alone. Much as I love my animals, I want to have people in my world.

I want Cole in my world.

"Nobody says you have to be crazy." Tana drains her glass and refills it from the pitcher, then pours more for both Cole and me before going on.

"To be clear, I'd guess the problem is that other people's emotions get all tangled up with your own, and it all keeps amplifying until it explodes. This makes casual friendships rather difficult and large groups pretty much impossible. Does that sound right?"

When she puts it that way, it sounds so simple, and my heart beats with hope that the answer will be as simple. That I can walk out of this charmed space and into the world as a normally functioning human being.

But she pats my hand and shakes her head. "I'm sorry to say there's no magic trick that makes an empath not an empath, which is really what you're saying you're looking for when you talk about this dimmer switch."

Cole sets down his glass, leans forward in his chair. Tana waves him back with one hand.

"You're not broken, Rae, dear, and therefore not in need of fixing. You are designed to be *more*. You weren't meant to be what we call normal, not that normal really exists."

She goes on as if she's still talking to me, but her gaze zeroes in on Cole. "The number one thing I would tell you is this. You can't fix people. You can't change people. So the trick, if there is one, is to differentiate. Your emotion. Their emotion. Your responsibility. Their responsibility. Oh, you can offer your friendship, your support, even your help. But what somebody does with that is entirely up to them."

"That's it?" Cole asks. "All of that stuff you taught me, about shielding, about imagery, about toning down the energy . . ."

"That was you. This is Rae." Again she smiles at me, but this time it's tinged with sadness. "You are welcome anytime, to come sit in my garden. To talk, or not to talk. And I can tell you tricks and tools and teach you what I know. But if you can understand and grasp what I've just told you, that's the balancing point. The first step."

A trilling sound from the house startles all three of us, so out of place is the ringing of a phone. It rings twice before I even know what it is.

"That will be for you," Tana says to Cole. "Nobody calls me here."

The phone rings again, and Cole dashes across the yard to answer.

"Be patient with him; he means well." Tana pats my hand, then starts loading the glasses onto the tray.

"You really don't think I'm broken?"

She turns back, already moving toward the house with the tray. "I think you're Rae. Balance is the quest of a lifetime."

I want to believe her, but my belief in my own brokenness is stronger than her words. What does she know of me? We've just met. Rae isn't even my legal name.

My feet weigh about fifty pounds each as I plod out of enchantment, through the transitional zone of the house, and out into the blazing heat of the front yard. The door handle on Cole's truck burns me; the seat is hot enough to scorch my butt and the backs of my thighs.

Cole gives his grandmother a quick hug and gets in without a word. He opens the windows, instead of turning on the AC, and the road noise is sufficient to prevent casual conversation.

The silence that grows between us is more complex than the silence on the way out. When I glance at Cole, he is intent on driving, his forehead creased, seemingly unaware that I am here beside him. Maybe it's the crisis call, or maybe it's something from the visit.

Maybe it's me. I'm becoming entirely too outspoken lately, blurting out what's in my head instead of keeping it to myself.

"You think I need fixing."

He jerks at the sound of my voice, as if I've wakened him from sleep.

"What? No. I think you're wonderful. You may have noticed that." He smiles, but it's a half smile, distracted, and the first tentacles of returning anxiety start probing my belly.

I should stop. This conversation isn't going anywhere I want to go, but my mouth has a life of its own. "I also noticed that you took me to your grandmother so she could fix what ails me."

"I thought she might help you manage. I watch you floundering under the weight of everybody else's emotions, and I hoped she could spare you that."

"Floundering. That's a flattering image."

"Drowning, then. You have to admit, you got in way over your head with Katya."

"She tried to kill herself with my car! What do you expect to happen?"

"So you don't think you have a little problem with codependency?"

"I think since you're the one who likes to go around playing rescuing hero, maybe the pot is calling the kettle black."

As soon as the words are out of my mouth I want to call them back, but they're already expanding into squat black blobs of ugliness. I should say I'm sorry, but I'm afraid that what I've done is release a truth that should never have been spoken. I can't apologize for saying what's true.

It's not the first time I've blurted out things that live in the realm of the unconscious and should stay there. Cole's hero complex makes him a good man. He helps people. He's been good to me. Any other woman would accept that at face value.

Not me. Nope. As usual, I'm ruining everything.

Already I feel him withdrawing into a protective shell. He might accept this truth about himself, embrace it. But he'll always resent me for calling it out. I see what is meant to be hidden, know what I'm not supposed to know. This is the place where every close human relationship has ended for me. Sooner or later.

Please, let me be wrong.

I realize I'm squeezing my hands together until they're bloodless, and I unlock them, one slow finger at a time. The light hurts my eyes. I almost hold my breath with waiting for him to say something, anything, but mile after mile unfolds and he remains silent.

"I'm sorry it ended up like this," he says, when he pulls up in my driveway. "Not what I had in mind, at all."

"Can we talk about it?"

"I've got a crisis to deal with. I'm sorry."

"Right. I almost forgot." I scramble out of the truck, the world blurring through a haze of tears I don't intend to let him see. Nice brush-off. Convenient. He's just being responsible. *Don't call me; I'll call you.*

I've got my key in the lock, the door already opening, when he calls after me, "Don't forget about the camping thing. I'll call you."

I spin around at that. He waves as he backs out of the driveway, and then I'm standing on my porch, alone, letting all of the heat into the house.

Chapter Seventeen

My not-so-bright idea hits me at work, in the middle of my shift.

I've been in a state of betwixt and between all day. I miss Katya; I miss the kittens. I miss Cole. All day yesterday, all day today, I've caught myself listening for my phone to ring, which it steadfastly refuses to do. At the same time, it's good to be alone in my own space with time to think and let all of the emotional trajectories settle out.

Everybody at work is still buzzing with friendly gossip about the Oscar Event. More than one person got a little extra plastered and needed a ride home, from the sounds of things. I'm included in their casual conversation, their laughter. Instead of recoiling from the camaraderie, I find myself on the inside of a few jokes. It feels unusually pleasant and easy until I walk into Nancy's room, where the whole illusion of normalcy blows up in smoke.

She sits in her bedside chair, all bedecked in her sparkly evening gown, her hair perfectly styled, makeup in place. From the expression on her face, however, she is not amused.

"What's up?" I ask her, getting ready to prick her finger and test her blood sugar. "You look like the queen of a country in the midst of a revolution." I smile at her. She does not smile back, and she snatches her hand away from me. I don't need super sensors to know she's angry.

"I don't want my blood sugar tested."

"Oh, come on, Nance. Don't be difficult."

"If I don't want my blood sugar tested, I shouldn't have to have my blood sugar tested. My body, last time I checked. Free will."

"And what brought on this attack of free will, if I might ask? I notice you have also chosen to not eat your dinner."

"I'm not hungry. I don't want my blood tested. Go away and leave me be." Her tone is imperious and haughty as she waves me off with a beringed hand.

I know well enough what her problem is, but decide to give her privacy. Corinne told me all about it in report, how Nancy was put out with Mason for getting so drunk at the Oscar Event he couldn't drive her home, how he'd promised to make it up to her by taking her out for dinner. And now here she is, all dressed up with no place to go.

I'm debating whether calling Mason and telling him to get his sorry ass up here would fall under codependent behavior, when Tia pages me to the phone. Maybe it's Mason calling me. Maybe he's had an accident, and I'll have to feel guilty for my uncharitable thoughts. Maybe he didn't have an extra set of keys and needs the ones I lifted on the night of the Event.

I pick up the phone. "Hello?"

"Rae, you've got to get me out of here."

"Kat?"

"I'm not kidding. I'll do anything. You can put me in a straitjacket. Keep me in handcuffs."

"I can't—"

"There's a psychotic guy here. He thinks the radio is talking to him, directly. The voice from the mother ship. And there's this manic woman who can't sit still or stop talking for like two seconds at a time. You have got to help me."

I feel the emotional pull, inexorable as the tide. She doesn't belong there, doesn't belong in a hospital. What if she tries to kill herself again? My fault. Can I live with that?

And there's that hated *codependent* word again. I poke at it to see if it will bite me. It growls a little. Cole's probably right. Bernie's probably right. Tana's theory that I'm fine as I am is insane. I'm not high up on some empath continuum; I'm a codependent, dysfunctional mess. Maybe I should embrace all of that and just go with it. Some people are born to be wild. I'm born to be codependent.

"Rae?" Kat's voice demands over the phone. "Are you even listening?"

"I'm listening. I'm thinking."

"They'll let me out if I have a place to go. I know I've already taken way too much advantage of you, but I thought maybe—"

"No."

Such a strong word. I like the round, solid shape of it in my mouth. I resist the urge to dilute it with excuses or rationale and just let it be its unembellished self.

"No? You mean I haven't taken too much advantage of you?"

"I mean no, you can't come and stay with me."

"Just like that?"

"Just like that." But the guilt is creeping in now, insidious and slippery. Maybe I'm being selfish. Kat's life at stake. I could help her.

She's safe where she's at.

"When did you get to be such a hard-ass? You've been hanging out with Cole. I can tell."

"Look, if you want out of there, maybe you should call Tom."

A small hesitation. "I can't." Her voice sounds uncertain, though, and I push the issue.

"He's your husband."

"And he knows where I am and hasn't come to see me. In case you hadn't noticed that."

I close my eyes and breathe. Somewhere, in that indeterminate instant between inhalation and exhalation, I get my bright idea.

Codependent? Probably.

Meddling? Oh, hell yes.

222

"What level are you on?" I ask her.

"What are you talking about?"

"You know—locked up with no escape, or they'll let you go out for a bit if you're with a friend."

"That last one. Only I don't have any friends. Apparently."

"This non-friend will try to arrange an outing. All right? Maybe we can just go sit in the sun or something."

"Please. Anything. It's not like I'm a huge flight risk." Her tone is bitter. I hold my silence, rather than remind her that killing herself is flight of the permanent variety, and she's proven herself at huge risk for that.

When I don't answer, she sighs, heavily. "When?"

"I'll get back to you. I have to go, Kat."

I feel the familiar bubble of grief and guilt when I hang up, but with a little something new, a bright thread of anticipation.

The rest of the night passes at the usual rapid-fire pace. Dressing changes on pressure sores, skin checks, medication problems. One of the residents takes a bad fall requiring an ambulance and a trip to the hospital. I'm in the office trying to get charts updated before my shift ends, when Tia walks in.

"Crazy night, eh?" she asks.

"You might say that."

"Sorry to bother you, but Nancy is still sitting up. I've had no luck with budging her. Want to try your charm?"

Sure enough, our resident drama queen is still sitting in her chair, clad in her sparkly dress. Her chin droops on her chest. She's snoring. A tiny rivulet of drool runs down the crease from the corner of her lip to her chin. She looks old, and sad, like a cast-off toy. I put my hand on her shoulder and give it a gentle shake.

"Nance. Come on. Time to go to bed."

She startles awake, wild-eyed, clearly not recognizing me for a few seconds. Her hand smoothes the dress over her knee. Her forehead wrinkles in confusion and concentration.

"It's ten o'clock here at Valley View, and time to be getting out of your party frock and into bed." I try to restate the facts to give her clues without insulting that sharp intelligence that is going to kick back in at any minute.

"I am tired. What am I doing in my chair? And I'm hungry. I didn't eat, did I?" And then the full realization kicks in. "He didn't come," she whispers. "He promised, but he didn't come."

Her sadness floods into me, a dark river that wants to sweep me away. I thrash about for something solid to hold on to, and find the tree in Tana's garden. With that, I also find the demarcation line between my own emotions and Nancy's. I feel sadness for her, anger at Mason. It's not overwhelming or all-consuming. I can handle it.

Nancy's feelings do not belong to me.

This is a novelty. I want to test it, play with it, but Nancy interrupts.

"So, are you going to stand there all night, or are you going to help me get into bed?"

"I'm going to help you get into bed. Let's start with that dress."

She shakes her head. "I'm not taking it off."

"Come on, Nance. It's a beautiful dress, but it won't make a comfortable nightgown."

"I am wearing this dress until Mason comes to take me for dinner. Don't argue."

"Far be it from me to argue with you. I would never win. All right, then. That's a fancy new nightdress you've got there. You're a trendsetter. All of the ladies down the hall will be wanting one, too."

Nancy laughs at that. We get her to the bathroom and then into bed. I fetch her some toast and peanut butter from the kitchen, which she practically inhales, mindless of the crumbs falling onto her dress and into her bed.

"If I could go back in time," she says as I'm turning to go, "I would be a better mother."

"Maybe you should tell him that."

She gasps, theatrically, back to her usual self. "Me? Admit guilt? Say I'm sorry? Surely not."

"Good night, Nancy."

On the way out to my car I spot Mason in the parking lot. He leans against his car, smoking a cigarette.

"You're a little late."

"I was here on time. I just didn't come in."

"She waited for you. In her evening dress. She's sleeping in it."

He drops the cigarette and grinds it out with his heel. "Truth is, I was plastered. Couldn't bring myself to take my scolding. I'm not a good son, Rae."

"Be better, then." There's too much entanglement here, too many layers of hurt and anger and betrayal between the two of them. Mason's emotions, and Nancy's, are still all tangled up in my heartstrings when I get into my car. I sit for a minute, open windows letting in the cool air along with a cloud of mosquitoes.

I try an experiment, breathing in fresh air, breathing out whatever isn't mine, feeling along all of the jagged edges of guilt and hurt and anger for the places where my reality intersects with Mason's, with Nancy's, with Katya's.

Not mine. Mine. Not mine.

It's possible to trace the lines, but just seeing where they fall is not enough. Maybe these emotions don't belong to me, but that doesn't make me feel them any less. I'm tired, and the mess is too complicated. Tomorrow, maybe, it will be easier.

~

In the morning, fortified by sleep and coffee, my reality buffered by a night of absurd dreaming, I lay out my thoughts in black and white on a notepad. Written down that way, it's easier to put things in perspective.

Katya is not my responsibility. Despite the way it feels, my brain acknowledges this as reality. Cole would say she's responsible for herself. But I have this crazy idea that maybe the marriage vows give her husband some responsibility in all this. All of that for-better-or-worse, for-richer-or-poorer jargon has to mean something. Tom needs to step up to the plate.

And I need a phone number.

I could ask Cole, but he won't give it to me. In fact, I'm pretty sure it would reinforce his belief in my severe codependency issue. Which I don't really have, outside of Katya.

Google is my friend. Searching for Tom is pointless; every male Manares in the world seems to be named Tom or Tomas. Katya Manares, now, that's a different story. *Bingo.* Only no phone number or address pops up. She's unlisted. Unless, of course, I want to pay for the premium report.

Maybe I do. I click the "Preliminary Report" button. Maybe I'll pay, maybe I won't.

Whitepages tells me what I'm about to see. Any criminal history, including speeding tickets. Family members. Job history. Addresses. Phone numbers.

I feel like a stalker. Much as I want to talk to Tom, I'm not sure I can live with myself if I engage in this level of snooping behind Katya's back. Fingers drumming on the table, I stare at the computer, and then push back my chair and look around my room.

There are more productive things I could be doing. Like figuring out how to get rid of my ruined couch, for one. Katya's sadness still lingers here. Everywhere I look there is a memory of her pain. This Tom person contributed to that, pushing her to have babies, feeding her guilt when she couldn't. He needs to answer for what he's done, if not to her, then to me.

Stalker or not, I am going to have a conversation with this man.

The wiser part of me rebels when I'm inputting my credit card information and I get the numbers transposed. I see this as an opportunity to think better of my behavior. To stop now, turn around, let this go.

But I input the number again, and this time it takes. The web page spins for a minute, then presents me with a full report on Katya Manares, born Katya Nikolaevskaya. I've trespassed far enough and restrain myself from looking at anything other than her address and home phone number. She lives in Richland, or at least she used to live there, and I hope Tom still does. There is a landline listed; I'd feared maybe she only had a cell phone. I figure if Tom has a job, he's probably already gone to work, but I dial anyway, just to see if the number works.

When a man answers, I very nearly hang up on him.

"Hello? Can I help you?" His voice is a warm baritone.

"You don't sound like I expected."

"Pardon me? Are you sure you have the right number?"

"Is this Tom Manares?"

"This is *a* Tom Manares," he says, cautiously. "Manares Electric."

"If you're Katya's husband, then you are definitely the right Tom Manares."

"Who is this?" His tone shifts to suspicion and no longer sounds friendly.

"Please don't hang up. I need to talk to you."

"Katya doesn't live here anymore."

"That's why I'm calling. Oh, look, I've got this all balled up already. My name is Rae. I'm friends with Katya. At least, I ran over her and then she lived with me and I think we're friends."

His silence on the other end of the line is not surprising, given what I've just spewed at him. I can hear the shift in his breathing.

"It's bad, isn't it?" he asks. "That's why you're calling. God. Just tell me."

"It's not that bad," I blurt out. "I mean, it's not good. She made a second attempt, but she's okay. She's in the crisis house, but—"

"Why?" His voice is pain incarnate. "Why are you telling me this?"

My resolve wobbles, but I press on. "Because you're her husband and she needs you."

His breathing is ragged now. "She has a different opinion of that. I'm sure you mean well, whoever you are—"

"Rae."

"Right. I'm assuming you mean well, but I'd appreciate it if you don't call here again."

I can feel him making the decision to hang up. I need to hold him, and it's my anger that rises to the rescue. "I'm trying hard to understand how this works. You marry a woman and make all of those promises of sticking with her through good and bad, and then beat her up when she can't have a baby—"

"Is that what she told you?"

"Not—"

"That I beat her?"

"What? No. I meant beat her up in a metaphorical sense." Guilt colors my voice, as if I'd whispered my secret earlier suspicions down along the gossip chain.

"You mean emotional abuse, then. Look, lady, I don't know you. I don't know what my wife has said or implied, but I . . . oh shit." His voice breaks, and now he's going to hang up for sure. Desperation drives me. I have to find a better end for this conversation.

"She's asking for you," I lie. "She wonders why you don't come to see her. She thinks it's because she's not good enough, because she couldn't give you a son . . ."

"I don't care about the babies. I told her that. Over and over I told her, but she couldn't hear me. Shit," he says, again. "I can't do this. There's a limit on what a man can take."

Slow tears roll down my own cheeks as his pain flows through the phone line and into me. My own fault. I opened this door that was better left shut. In my head I still had him down as maybe an abuser, a self-centered jerk at best.

"I'm sorry. I'm so sorry. I shouldn't have called. It's just—she's so sad. And I know she loves you, and there's nothing I can do to help her."

"Maybe there's nothing anybody can do to help her. That's a truth I rolled around to. It's like trying to fill a black hole. Everything you give her gets sucked up and is gone."

He ends the call so gently it takes a minute before I realize the line is dead. Tremors of reaction shake me from head to toe, and I wrap up in a blanket, even though my brain tells me it's nearly eighty degrees in my house.

What have I done?

Wandered in where angels fear to tread, that's what.

It occurs to me, a bolt from the blue that should have been apparent to me from moment number one, that my call to Tom has more to do with my own emotional well-being than with any true love for Kat. I want to stop worrying. I want to stop hurting. I want my life back. So what do I do? Try to drag somebody else in to fill the gap. Somebody else who is hurting every bit as much as Katya, and certainly a great deal more than me.

Crazy cat lady, here I come. I'm not fit to be around people.

This house once felt like a sanctuary, but now the walls press in so tight I can't breathe. I can't think, can't feel—I only know that I have to get out. Without stopping to check what I'm wearing or to fix my hair, I grab my keys and bolt.

Nowhere to go on foot, so I get in the car and drive to the only place I can think of, all the way telling myself I'm crazy and there's no guarantee of my welcome.

Tana opens up at my first knock. Instead of sympathy or shock or worry or annoyance or any of the other emotions I'd anticipated, all I see on her face is joy. She doesn't say a word, just opens the door wide.

I open my mouth to let out a stream of excuses and explanations, but she shakes her head and holds up a hand for silence.

"Hush," she says. "It's all right."

The yoga mat is in the middle of the floor now, along with blocks and a strap and a folded blanket. I've interrupted her practice, but the only emotion I pick up is a genuine delight at my presence.

She leads me through the house and out into the backyard, and only then does she speak.

"Tell me," she says, gesturing toward the picnic table.

And I do. I sit down and tell her everything. All about Kat this time, from the minute I saw her on the road to my call to Tom. The way I screwed things up with Cole. My parents and my failure to meet even their smallest expectations for me. And finally, worst of all, with tears pouring down my cheeks, I tell her about my recent revelation about my own deep and abiding selfishness. She doesn't interrupt, doesn't ask questions, doesn't even make little sounds of either sympathy or dismay.

When I exhaust my supply of words, I sit in a wide stillness, awaiting judgment.

The garden is quiet today, with not so much as a breeze to ruffle the leaves of the tree or set the wind harp singing. All of the sounds are background noises. A low hum of bees, busy in the clover. A burbling of water from the stream. An occasional birdsong and the buzz of hummingbird wings. Not a single one of the small creatures in this garden is worried about me or Kat or the mess that seemed so all-consuming to me when I fled from my house.

Tana isn't worried, either.

"The great revelation of selfishness is harder for those who care," she finally says, smiling at me. "Here's the paradox. If you were completely self-centered, you wouldn't be worrying about being self-centered."

"That hurts my brain."

She laughs, with delight, not sympathy. "It's meant to. Try this. If you didn't care deeply about the feelings of others, you wouldn't be faced with a selfish need to make them better. You're self-centered, as you say, because you feel things so deeply."

"You're saying being selfish is good?"

"I'm saying it's not really selfish. Consider adopting the term *self-care.*"

"No." I shake my head to clear it. "That can't be right. Look what I've just done."

"You think this Tom person didn't have all of those feelings before you called him? All you did was open the door and let them out for a minute. You didn't miscarry babies or run away from a relationship. You didn't leave without a note or try to kill yourself. Neither did you stay at home instead of riding to the rescue. That marriage began without you, struggled for years without you, and will end or struggle on without you. All you've done is put yourself into the middle of an emotional storm that doesn't belong to you. Not such a great sin, my dear, in the grand scheme of things."

"But see—even there. I want to be able to fix it. I want to make the pain go away, soothe it back to sleep. God, Cole's right. I am hopelessly codependent."

"You care about people, even this Tom whom you have never met. Let me ask you this question. Why are Katya's emotions, Tom's, even Cole's, so very important, but Rae's don't matter at all?"

"Because . . ." I try to verbalize a reason but come up empty. There has to be one. The certainty of the fact that my emotions don't matter sits in my belly like a stone.

"Keep trying," Tana says. "I'll wait."

I breathe in the smell of tree leaves and grass and roses. An ant wanders across the picnic table by my hand and is rewarded by the discovery of a tiny seed, which it picks up and carries away. Losing the train of thought, I glance up to see Tana's keen eyes focused on me.

"What was the question again?" A trickle of laughter flows out of me, and the stone in my belly shifts, ever so slightly.

"The question, slightly reframed, is why do other people matter more than Rae?"

"The answer comes back to selfishness. Right where we started."

"Step outside your head for a minute. Pretend you're holding a camera. Adjust the focus back and away. Let's put five people in front of the lens. Katya. Tom. Cole. Me. And Rae. Can you see it?"

I see it all right. In my mind we're all lined up like suspects in front of a two-way mirror. An invisible accusatory finger points in my direction. *That one. She's the fraud.*

"Now. Of all these people," Tana says, "is one less human than the others? Less deserving? And if your answer is Rae, be prepared to explain to me why."

That's when I see it. Just for a flash, an instant caught out of time, I see that all of us are equal, that my weird self has just as much right to life, liberty, and the pursuit of happiness as anybody else in the lineup.

A glimpse, and then the insight is gone. An impression remains, the footprint of a thought that came in the night and vanished again.

"So we're all equally important in the grand scheme of things. I can see that. But how does that give me the right to pursue my own happiness at the cost of others'?"

Her lined face breaks into a grin. "Ah, that's the catch, isn't it? Everybody is important; everybody is responsible for their own path, their own happiness. But we are still responsible to each other. *To* each other, mind. Not *for* each other."

For her sake, more than my own, because she is so patient about explaining, I do my best to wrap my head around this concept. No dice.

Tana sees it in my face, but instead of reacting with disappointment, she just smiles again. "There is no easy answer, Rae. It's a lifelong puzzle, that's what it is. Personally, I've made peace with the problem by focusing on what I am meant to do on this planet, rather than on happiness. There is some justification there, I find."

"So—the fact that I've refused to go to medical school all these years, even though that is the one thing that would apparently make my parents happy, means I'm not selfish. Is that the concept?"

"Probably."

"Probably? I thought maybe I finally had it." With a heavy sigh, I sag back into my chair.

"Should you be a doctor?" Tana asks. "Would you be a good doctor?"

"Me? Hell no."

"There you go, then. Not what you're meant to do here."

"What if what I'm meant to do is be a codependent doormat who gives away all of her possessions and dies in the service of the homeless?"

"Then be that. Nobody accuses Mother Teresa of codependence, a fact which I find at least of interest."

"You're kidding. Mother Teresa was a saint."

"Did you meet her? Do you know what drove her?"

"No, but—"

"Then how are you qualified to decide that?"

While I'm trying to think of an answer, she gets up from her chair. "I need to go, shortly. I have an appointment."

Before I have time to draw an apology-laden breath for my disruption of her day, she goes on. "I have something for you. Two things, actually. Wait a sec."

I watch her cross the yard with her light, quick step, so fluid and full of grace for a woman of her years, and then let my eyes drift closed, rolling around the emotions this conversation has stirred, trying not to think too much.

Her voice startles my eyes open, as once again I fail to hear her coming.

"You walk like a ninja," I tell her.

"Thank God I have not yet resorted to shuffling." She hands me a framed picture, and I stare at it for a long time before I truly realize what I'm seeing.

It's me, standing under the tree in Tana's backyard. Cole is blurred out of focus beside me. I'm spinning, my arms reaching up toward the tree, my face tilted back, laughing. And hovering just above my upturned face hangs a golden orb.

Maybe it's just a water drop or a bit of dust, or a trick of the light. Maybe it's not. Whatever it is, it's beautiful. I'm beautiful.

Wordless, I press my fingertip to the picture glass, absorbing what I am seeing.

"It's yours," Tana say. "Maybe it will help get your world figured out."

I take the picture, but I don't think it will help with the figuring-out process. If anything, it adds a new layer of complexity to a reality so textured I'm far from understanding half of it.

"There's much more to the world than we can process with our limited senses," Tana says. "Just like there's more to people. You see more than most do, or maybe *feel* more would be the right word. It gives you extra perception, and that makes it harder to keep boundaries."

"Thank you." I clasp the picture to my chest. "I know I sort of barged right into your day."

"You are welcome anytime. Here's the other thing I have for you. You might give this a try."

She hands me a piece of paper, a printout from the Internet, with the heading "Loving-Kindness Meditation."

"Do you meditate?" she asks.

"Sort of." Bernie has taught me a basic breathing meditation. She's had me visualize my emotional self as a chalkboard, talked me through observing thoughts and feelings floating down a river. Not exactly any-thing transcendental.

"Give this a try," Tana says. "If I didn't have to go, we could do it together."

I'm torn by the idea of that. It sounds wonderful, but also frighten-ing, a new kind of intimacy I'm not sure I'm ready for.

"Thank you. For everything. And I have to go to work anyway." I follow her through the peace of her house. On the front porch, when we stop to say good-bye, my eyes are drawn again to the bottles in the tree.

"Would you like to leave a prayer?" Tana asks. "There's just time for that."

"How does it work?"

"You write your request on a slip of paper, tuck it in a bottle, and leave it hanging on the tree."

"It's like wishing." I reach up to touch an old green bottle and set it swinging. As its arc swings out of shadow, it seems to fill with light. "Do you believe in a God that answers prayers, then, Tana?"

"As it happens, I do. But whether you believe or not, I think prayer is an act of love, a conscious desire for good. It also helps to create a separate space for what you feel regarding the well-being of others."

I picture my wishing stones, skimming the surface of the water. Maybe making wishes is not foolishness after all.

"I'd love to leave a prayer on your tree. Can it be more than one?"

"What you put into the bottles is your business. There's no limit on prayers, last I heard. Hang on a second." She vanishes into the house, returning a moment later with strips of paper, a pen, and an empty bottle with a length of twine tied around its neck.

"I'm going to go inside and get ready. You take whatever time you need and hang that bottle when you're done. You can use the stepladder to help you reach." Her hand waves toward a wooden ladder leaning against the side of the house. Her smile, so clean and uncomplicated, warms me from the inside out, and then she's gone, leaving me to my own devices.

In the end, I put four slips in the bottle. One for Katya, one for Tom, one for Mason, and, after a moment, one for me.

Instead of going home, it seems like a natural transition to stop at my wishing beach. If a prayer is good, a wish and a prayer should be even better. It doesn't take a counseling degree to know that I need all the help I can get.

Instead of skipping rocks, though, I head straight for the boulder I sat on last time I was here, thinking dark thoughts and trying to grasp hold of that strange, elusive emotion. I think maybe I know what it is now. And there's something here I feel the need to do.

The stone isn't really a boulder, after all, just a big old rock. Flecks of mica flash and sparkle in the sunlight. A vein of quartz crystals runs up the side and into its heart. It's solid. Heavy.

But not all that heavy.

Bending my knees and using my weight as leverage, I heave it up and over toward the water. The underside is cool and damp, coated with sand. My thighs and lower back protest and thrum as I roll it over again. It topples onto the smaller stones with a rattle and thud. Again and again I lift and roll that rock across the beach toward the water, until it splashes into the shallows. Cold water sprays up into my face and soaks the front of my shirt.

Muscles aching, heart thudding, I brace myself on my thighs to catch my breath, then step into the water, shoes and all, to give the rock one more rotation. Submerged underwater, all of its colors come to life. Patterns of vivid red and green appear where before it was only gray.

Straightening my protesting back, I lift both of my arms toward the sky and breathe in deep, deep, the scent of river and stone. I wonder if there's a golden orb above my head, invisible to me but there all the same.

My body feels so light I could almost drift up above the earth and across the water, like the dragonflies. Or like the Oscar Event balloons. Just for this one moment in time, there is nothing but sun and water and the experience of what I think I might call joy.

~

My uplifted mood lasts about an hour into my shift. Usually I can make it through an evening just fine without getting torpedoed by other people's feelings. Emotions in general are more muted here, mostly to low-level despair and resignation, and I'm usually able to fend them off, to get through my shifts without feeling much at all. Now, I'm not only lacking a dimmer switch, my "Off" button seems to be broken as well.

I go through my tasks, playing a sorting game in my head with every interaction.

Rae.

Not Rae.

Rae.

Not Rae.

Depression and hopelessness stick to me like gum to the bottom of a shoe. So many of these residents are just waiting to die. Visits from busy family members, even the attentive ones, are too infrequent to allay the boredom of meaningless days. They've lost the satisfaction of doing useful work, and the arts and crafts, the endless loud TV, even the occasional programs put on by schools and church groups can't give back the sense of being a valued and important part of society.

Somehow, working here, I've managed to shut out all of that.

Nancy is the one who crystallizes it all for me. She's still wearing her party dress, rumpled now, stained by dinner spills and nighttime sweat. She's obstinate as ever, but her resolve is wearing thin, and she allows me to check her blood sugar without putting up a fight. She's only nibbled at her dinner.

"I take it Mason hasn't showed up yet."

She turns her head away, and there's an unmistakable quaver in her voice. "Maybe he moved back to Chicago."

I know better than to comment on that quaver, or on the sadness and guilt and loneliness I'm picking up like radio static.

"He was here last night," I tell her, sitting down on the edge of the bed. "Outside. He was late and didn't want to come in."

"Coward," she says, but there's no corrosive energy behind the judgment. "Let me guess. He started drinking and lost track of time."

"Maybe you should call him."

She glares at me. "He owes me an apology. And dinner. Why would I do that?"

"Because you're his mother, that's why. It's your job to be the grown-up."

"He's thirty-eight years old. It's his job to take care of me by now." But the absurdity gets to her, as I'd hoped it would, and she laughs. "I could apologize for being a shitty mother. Maybe that cancels out a dinner date."

Nancy is one of the few residents who uses a cell phone. I pick hers up from the bedside table and hand it to her.

"Now?"

"Yes, now."

"You are a martinet."

"And you are a diva. Call your son. And then buzz me, and we'll get you out of that dress."

I've already taken a step down the hall when she calls me back.

"What now? Did you forget his phone number?"

She waves that away. "You might, maybe, bring the kittens back in sometime. I could do penance by helping to feed them."

"You're allergic."

"Or not."

I open my mouth to tell her the kittens are no longer living with me, and then change my mind. "Maybe I will. Call. Now."

All of my intentions to get back to her are swept away as the evening devolves into chaos. A fall. An ambulance and all of the paperwork that goes into that. One of the residents taking a serious turn toward death and the need to notify the family. It's like everything and everybody is on a mission to show me the dark side of life tonight.

By the time I get back to check in on Nancy, she's asleep, still wearing that damned dress, the phone on top of the covers right beside her hand.

~

I don't see the blinking red light on my answering machine until I'm into my second cup of coffee. Tired as I was, and deeply as I slept, I'm pretty sure if the phone had rung during the night I would have heard it, which means that light has been blinking since sometime yesterday evening.

Generally nobody calls me, except for my parents during the regularly scheduled Sunday-afternoon obligation chat. Maybe they're switching things up again. Or not. I can't make up my mind whether this is an ominous red glow, or a happy surprise, or maybe nothing at all.

As long as I don't push "Play" or look at caller ID, it's a sort of Schrödinger blink, signaling neither good nor bad. Clearly, I need more coffee. I pour another cup and add in cream until it's the perfect tawny shade. Fortified and shielded by my favorite mug and a fair bit of caffeine, I finally push the button.

The voice on the other end isn't any of those that have played through my imagination.

It's Katya's Tom.

"Hey, Rae. I did some thinking about what you said. I figure if Katya wants to see me, I owe it to her—to us—to do that. I was hoping to talk to you before I headed that direction, but what the hell. I'm driving up to Colville from Richland tonight. Please call me in the morning and let me know where I can find my wife."

He leaves a cell number and the call clicks off.

I can't move. I can't breathe.

Tom is *here*. In Colville. Because I told him to come. *What kind of idiot does something like that?*

Denial rushes to my defense.

Maybe he didn't come. He might have changed his mind. There could have been road closures. A massive wildfire, a multicar pileup, an unprecedented visit from the president to rural Washington. I wasn't fully awake when I listened to the message; maybe I heard it wrong.

I poke at the machine and press "Replay."

Tom's voice fills my kitchen again, calmly expressing his intent to head up to Colville.

With a little groan I slump into one of my chairs and set my cup down on the table, before leaning over and giving my forehead one swift whack against the wood. Hard enough to sting, not hard enough to bruise.

If I go through with this stunt, I'm pretty sure Cole will never speak to me again. It's a little difficult to deny codependent tendencies when you're caught in the middle of this kind of machination.

Maybe it's not codependency, a little voice whispers. *It's not like you're trying to make Katya dependent on you. It's sort of the same thing as finding the kitten a surrogate mother. Tom is her person. Maybe this will be a good thing.*

Doubtful. Very doubtful. But the thought rallies me enough to finish my coffee and then return Tom's call.

"Oh good," he says, sounding entirely too bright-eyed and hopeful. "I was worried I'd driven all the way up here for nothing."

"Sorry about that. I was at work and got in late."

"No worries. If you'll just tell me where I can find her, I'll let you get back to your day."

I swallow hard, picturing Tom showing up unannounced and unexpected at the crisis house. As tempting as it is to stay out of what I've started, sending him to her while she's locked up is like sending a toddler to dismantle a bomb. I'm already up to my ears in alligators, and I might as well stay the course.

"I'm not sure about visiting hours at the crisis house."

"Give me the number, and I'll call and find out."

The best lies are mixed with a little bit of truth, so I go for the gold.

"Here's the thing. She doesn't want to talk to you there. No privacy, with all the prying eyes. I've got permission to take her out, so let me set up a time, and maybe you guys can talk in the park? It's going to be a beautiful day, and she hates being cooped up."

"Sounds fair. Listen, could I have your cell phone number? Just in case we need you later."

"Sure. But I should warn you that my battery always dies, so if you can't reach me, that'll be why. I'll call you when everything's set up, okay?"

He agrees, although I can almost hear him wondering what sort of person his wife has gotten hooked up with. And then I surprise myself with laughter at the absurdity of my own thoughts. I'm worrying about what he'll think of me. Like that even matters.

I'm not the one who has tried to kill herself repeatedly, or the one who came up to visit the wife he planned never to see again, because of the lies of a stranger. Maybe I'm messed up, a little, but I'm not the only one.

Still, when I call the crisis house my heart races with apprehension. If they don't let me talk to her, then what?

I need not have worried. Kat has listed me as a person with whom it's okay to share information. The pleasant woman who answers hooks us up before the second hand ticks all the way around the clock.

Kat's voice is subdued.

"I didn't think you'd call me back."

"I said I would. You ready to get out of there? Just for a couple of hours," I add hastily, before she can misinterpret my words. "I was thinking you need a little sunlight."

"I have become a vampire," she says. "Truly. It's dark in here. I'm avoiding mirrors."

"Then an outing in the sunshine will be perfect. Eleven a.m.? I'll pack lunch."

"Make it a cake with a file in it. Yes. Great. Eleven a.m."

We hang up, and I call Tom back and give him directions to where we plan to meet. "Can you keep your phone charged? This has so much potential to go wrong. What if I get lost?"

"This is Colville. You won't get lost. Trust me."

I hang up with a sinking feeling in my stomach. Only an idiot would trust me. But the wheels are in motion, and I'm going with the flow. I promise myself that after this I'm going back to animals. Human relationships are way too complicated.

～

Kat is waiting for me outside the crisis house. She's still pale and washed-out looking, but her hair is clean and shiny and she's wearing makeup. This is good. Whatever her response to the surprise I'm about to spring on her, she wouldn't want Tom to see her looking disheveled and unkempt. She's also wearing a long-sleeved sweater that covers both arms.

We hug, lightly, and only for an instant before awkwardness sweeps us away from the house and into the car.

"You make vampires look sparkly," I tell her, trying to ease the tension.

"I make vampires look healthy and vibrant. You, on the other hand, look fabulous. Let me guess—you have slept since I last saw you."

"Yeah, I shipped the kittens over to Jenny. Except for Wish. That's the little gray one. He has been adopted by a pretentious mama cat and is learning a lifestyle above his station."

We're both trying too hard, and I can feel that bringing up Wish was a bad idea.

I'm grateful that I've chosen a location about two minutes away by car, because our repertoire of safe conversational topics doesn't last even that long.

"That's it?" Kat asks, as I park. "That's the extent of our excursion?"

"Is it my fault they built the crisis house beside the park? The excursion is sitting in the sunshine, not driving miles to get there."

"You and sunshine. You're trying to kill me off."

"I left the stake at home. Come on."

Already her sadness is a heaviness that weighs me down. Even the light seems dimmer as I get out her walker and watch her struggle to get out of the car. In the brighter light I can make out a greenish-yellow stain that marks the bruise on her cheek, even under her makeup.

I almost tell her right then about Tom. This is a horrible mistake. I don't want to witness any more of her pain. I don't want to watch the crash of a surprise encounter with her husband. If I fess up right this minute, she'll blow up at me, insist I take her back to the crisis house, and probably never speak to me again.

Of all the possible endings, this seems the easiest, but it's too late for that. I've already stirred the pot.

I match my pace to hers over the short distance to a picnic table and help her get settled with her back to the road, positioning myself across from her where I can watch for Tom. I charged my cell before leaving home, but as expected it's already signaling the one-bar battery warning.

We pick at the sandwiches and nibble on baby carrots, mostly in silence. Neither of us is adept at small talk, and I can't imagine any conversation starting out with *Oh my God, you almost killed my kitten, not to mention yourself. What the hell was that all about?*

But I also can't stand this constrained half silence between us.

"You can take off the sweater," I tell her, finally, after choking down a bite of sandwich as dry as the Sahara despite the nearly half a jar of mayonnaise I spread on it. "It's not like I haven't seen your arm."

"It's not you I'm worried about."

A clump of tuna plops out of my sandwich onto the table. Does she know about Tom? How could she? Unless he called the crisis house after all. Of course. He has Cole's number . . .

Kat gives up the pretense of eating and shoves her sandwich away from her. "I don't like to see the evidence of my own sins."

"It wasn't a sin, exactly . . ."

Her voice takes on a singsong tone, as if she's reciting something. "I have trespassed against myself, my neighbor, and my neighbor's ass. Or in this case, kitten. Not to mention my husband and my family, and oh—let's not forget God."

"Haven't we all," I say, into the toxic waste of her words.

She shakes her head, avoiding my eyes. "Not you. Not like this. Here's the thing you won't believe. It seemed to make perfect sense that night. Somehow it was all lined up in my head as logical and right. Maybe even heroic. Save Rae from ongoing heartache and the expenditure of energy."

"Kat, don't—"

"It was totally selfish, not heroic. I see that. I can't even make sense of what I was thinking, and it's my own brain that thought those things. Like one of those weird-ass dreams that makes total sense at the time, but when you wake up you want to know what the hell was going on in your head. You know?"

"I know. Like the dream I had where it made sense to clean the carpet with a giant fish. Not a dead fish. It was sort of sucking up the dirt with its fins. I think."

Kat stares at me, and a tiny bit of the tension eases out of her jaw. "You're making that up."

"I'm not capable of making that up."

"All right," she says. "What I did made sense at the time, like cleaning the carpet with a fish. My new counselor suggests my behavior stems from a traumatic response to stillbirth, combined with postpartum depression. The same sort of mind-set that makes a woman kill her baby."

"Postpartum psychosis."

"Something like that." Her fingers worry at a loose splinter on the table. "You'd think it might help with the guilt, to say, 'Oh, I was psychotic. It's not my fault.' But it doesn't. It only makes me feel weak."

Of all the things I can think of to say, none of them are right, so I say nothing. The sun is punishing, straight overhead. I'm roasting, and Kat in her sweater looks miserable.

"Can we move?" she asks. "Out of the sun? My sandwich is turning into a tuna melt."

Of course we can't move, because I told Tom we would be here, and because my battery is now predictably dead.

"*You* are turning into a tuna melt." I stall. "Sun is an antidepressant. Strip off a layer, get some vitamin D."

"I don't tan. I burn." But she starts to shrug out of the sweater. I'm so focused on her that I forget all about Tom, who of course shows up the minute I stop watching for him.

Of all the versions of him I generated in my head, not one of them comes even close. I got the olive skin and the dark hair right, and that's as far as it goes. He's small and wiry, not much taller than she is. He has a round, sensitive face and wears glasses.

Kat freezes, staring at him like he's a ghost.

Tom crosses the distance between us. He reaches out his hand to her, as if he's going to touch her hair or cup her cheek, but instead he removes her half-discarded sweater. Kat lets him, as if she's suddenly boneless and incapable of resistance.

He turns her hand over to reveal the row of black stitches, ugly and harsh against her pale skin. His face spasms as if the pain of the wound is his.

"I should have looked for you," he says. "Right away, as soon as I realized you were gone. I thought you'd just left me. I thought I was right to let you go. I didn't . . ." His Adam's apple bobs. He turns her arm back over to hide the stitches and lets it fall into her lap. His fingers graze the bruise on her cheek while his eyes fix on the walker. "Jesus, Kat."

His tone makes the words a prayer, not a curse.

"Why did you come now?" Kat doesn't move, her arm lying exactly where he placed it.

"Because I didn't come then."

"Guilt," she whispers, glancing up at him and then away. Her face hardens, and the tone of her voice is cold when she speaks again. "You should know I can't have any more babies, Tom. They took my uterus."

"Thank God."

"What did you say?" Kat's expression says she thinks he's lost his mind.

"It was making you crazy, this thing with the babies. I'm glad it's off the table, so you can get on with your life."

Her mouth works as if she's about to speak, but nothing comes out. My presence feels wrong and faintly shameful, like I'm peeping in through a window on a private moment. Slow and quiet, I begin to detach myself, edging up from my seat.

246

"Don't you dare leave me," Kat snaps, her eyes crackling with an energy I've never seen from her. "You set this up. How dare you?"

"I think—" Tom begins, but she cuts him off.

"She called you, I'll bet. Dragged you up here. Don't deny it."

Tom glances at me, confusion clear in his eyes, and then back to her. "She called me, yes. I did my own dragging."

"But you wouldn't have come if she hadn't called." The implications of abandonment are naked in the space around her words.

"I came because I thought you wanted me. I stayed away because I thought you didn't."

"Even when . . . after. I almost died, and you didn't come."

The pain that twists his face at her words feels like glass in my heart. I remember all of my misconceptions, the anger I directed at him. It wasn't my place to judge. It certainly wasn't my place to bring him here, rub salt in both of their wounds.

"I couldn't," he says. "I was a coward. Every time I tried to even think about you under the tires of a car I ended up puking. I told myself you were better without me. Was I lying to myself? Or was it true? Are you better off without me, Kat? Tell me."

She shakes her head. "I can't do it anymore. I can't."

"It would be different now." He leans toward her, his outstretched hands closer to her side of the table than his own. "No more babies. I don't care about that. I never did."

Kat slams her hand down, her voice rising. "Don't lie to me! You said you wanted a baby. Our baby. You said it over and over. I saw you with . . . with the little one that died . . ."

"Ned," he whispers. "I named him."

"You see? That's the only son you're going to get from me. Death and grief and loss and—"

"I don't care."

"How can you—"

"Ten years we've been married. Ten years to love you and share space with you. Yes, I wanted a kid. I wanted to see what you and I could make together, like a child would be—I don't know—more than either of us alone. A brand-new being that we created together. But I can live without that. I'm not sure I can live without you."

His words, and the passion behind them, sweep me away. Tears are flowing down my cheeks, and I don't even care.

Kat is made of harder stuff.

"You've been living up until now. Seemingly fine. You look healthy. I suspect your mom has been feeding you—"

"Don't."

"Don't what, talk about your family? You are your family; your family is you. Maybe you can give up on having kids, but your mother never will. My mother will lament and rail against the fates, but I'm her flesh and blood and she's stuck with me. Yours will remind you that there are other women—"

"Not for me."

"You say that now." Her voice gentles, but her resolve doesn't falter. "You'll get over me. You'll move on. You'll see." She stops. Takes a breath. "I'm sorry. I'm sorry about everything, but if we're together it will always be like this."

"Katya." It's a plea, a cry, a prayer. His hand reaches for hers, nearly touches. I hold my breath, but at the last instant she snatches her hand away.

"Why did you *come?*" The dam holding back her tears breaks, and they burst out in a torrent.

"Katya," Tom says again. "Let me in."

She shakes her head, violently. Her words are twisted by sobs, but there's no missing them for all that. "I can't do this. I won't."

Painfully, she swivels her body away from us and reaches for the walker. "Take me back, Rae."

"No. You—"

"You did this. The least you can do is take me where I want to go. Or I can walk, if you'd rather."

"Walk, then. Or Tom can drive you."

Tears continue to pour down Kat's face, but my refusal jolts her out of her weeping. She stares at me, incredulous. "You *owe* me! You can't just leave me here."

Tom says nothing. He sits at the table, head buried in his hands. His shoulders are rounded in defeat. They begin to shake, and I realize that he, too, is utterly undone.

Remorse floods me. This is my fault. It's my responsibility to fix it.

A set of words surfaces from my memory and nudges me, demanding attention. I try to swat them away. *Not now, I'm busy.* But they are insistent, wedging themselves into the middle of the guilt-ridden answer I'm formulating. Instead of *I'm sorry. You're right. I'll lie down in the mud and you can both trample on me,* what comes out of my mouth is "Oh, now I get it."

"You get what?"

My attention is at least half on what's happening inside my head. Maybe they'll both think I'm psychotic. I don't care.

"I just remembered. I'm responsible *to* you, not responsible *for* you."

"What does that even mean?"

"I think it means that I should not have brought Tom here under false pretenses."

"Lies, you mean," Kat says. "Also, duh."

"I think it also means that since he is here, whatever happens between the two of you is between the two of you, and I don't need to be your dramatic exit."

"My what? Rae. Rae! Come back here! You can't leave me like this."

"Since I'm leaving you with your husband, who doesn't beat you and doesn't care if you have babies and really loves you very much, I think I don't feel bad about that."

She tries to pursue me, but of course she's slow and ungainly, and I'm driving away before she gets anywhere near my car. As she grows smaller and smaller in my rearview mirror she raises one hand, middle finger extended in a last gesture of defiance.

~

I show up for work a full twenty minutes early, a bit of a miracle for me, but blow the whole thing by standing out front trying to work up the nerve to go in. The emotions let loose this morning would suffice to fill an entire season of a soap opera, and I'm not at all sure I can handle whatever this shift has to throw at me.

Tentatively, I let my mind run back over the scene in the park, looking for my own wrongdoing. Guilt for lying to Tom, guilt for ambushing Kat. Check, check. Guilt for leaving her there with him? Nothing, zip, nada.

Corinne comes out to join me, the report binder tucked under one arm.

"Saw you on the security cam. Are we doing report out here now? I think that's a fabulous idea. A little hot, but if we sit over under the tree, it will be perfect. How are the kitties? They were so good for the residents, I think. Can't you bring them back? Or get another animal. Maybe another rat?"

She doesn't require answers from me before moving on, and I let her ramble, closing my eyes and turning my face up to the sun.

Cor's comfortable presence eases me, and I feel my muscles start to unclench, one at a time. Just when my defenses are down and I'm half drifting on a current of words and birdsongs, she strikes.

"What about that scrumptious Cole? Are you sleeping with him yet?"

"God, no." I jolt upright, eyes wide open.

"Why? Is there something wrong with him? He has got it for you so bad his tongue is practically hanging out of his mouth every time he looks at you. What is it? Is he married? Into kink? Not that kink would be so bad. I've always been curious—"

"Corinne."

"What?"

"I do not want to hear about you and kink."

"Well, is he?"

"Is he what?"

She sighs, elaborately. "Into weird stuff. Or married."

"No. At least, not that I know. It's complicated."

"Men are never that complicated. Food. Sex. Beer."

"Oh, come on. You know that's not true."

"Do I? Been married for thirty years, and that's pretty much what I can see. Oh, all right. Hunting, fishing, sports. A little porn, maybe." She pushes her lips out in a pout and flips nonexistent luxuriant locks over her shoulder. "Not that I mind porn so much, myself."

"Cor!"

"You're a prude. Who knew?" She laughs at me, then grows serious. "Come on. Let me play matchmaker. You like him, and he obviously has a thing for you. Where's the problem?"

"I said something I shouldn't have."

"Oh, a fight!"

"It was much more civilized than that."

She purses her lips. "How long ago?"

"Four days. He said he'd call. He hasn't. Also, he thinks I'm broken and in need of fixing, and I did something today that pretty much confirms his belief, so I think this relationship is doomed. Can we move on to report now?" I reach for the binder, but she holds it above her head, out of reach.

"Nothing is doomed. Call him."

Now there's a thought that hadn't even occurred to me. "No way. I can't do that."

"Why not?"

"Because . . . because . . ."

"See?" she says. "You don't have an answer. You're just scared."

"It's not that simple." I realize I'm repeating myself, and Cor of course latches onto that and runs with it.

"Everything is not so complicated. You think too much; that's your problem. What did you say to him? No, never mind. It doesn't matter. You don't even have to apologize, just make him think you're apologizing."

"Say that again." I turn toward her, laughing in spite of the loss that hits me every time I think about what I might have built with Cole if I hadn't ruined it.

"I don't need to. Look. He's a man. Sure, he's probably more complicated than my Charlie, but a man's a man for all that. Make him a sandwich. Add a beer for good measure. Tell him you're sorry—"

She holds up a hand to cut off my protest. "You don't have to be sorry for what you said. It was probably true, right? Right. That's the worst. Just tell him you're sorry you hurt him or whatever. Feed him. Alcohol him. Kiss him. Bam. Done."

"It can't be that easy, Cor."

"Thirty years," she says. "Take it or leave it. Oh goodness. Look at the time. Let me give you the rundown. There's been one sad development, not that I'm surprised."

I steel myself for the news of a newly diagnosed cancer or a resident accelerating toward death, but I'm not prepared for what she tells me.

"Mason called this morning. Said he's a coward and a drunk and couldn't face his mother. He has a flight booked for"—she checks her watch—"right about now. Said to tell you good-bye and that you're right. He's not from here. Whatever that means."

"Oh no! Nancy will be devastated."

Corinne sighs. "Men. What are you gonna do?" From there, with no more than a shrug and a half breath, she launches into a dizzying, whirlwind tour of what is going on with the residents.

My mind wanders, and I give up on trying to follow.

I shouldn't be surprised that Mason would skip town. It's in his character. But the news of his defection leaves me feeling like a cast-off sock. Tentatively, I probe at the emotion—*Rae, or not Rae*—and am taken aback to discover how deeply I, personally, feel betrayed and abandoned.

If Mason is a coward, so am I, and I put off talking to Nancy until it's time to check her blood sugar.

When I enter her room, the chair is empty. Her bed is neatly made. Books are stacked on the bedside table, the TV is off, and an untouched dinner tray sits on her bedside table.

In my entire time employed in this facility she has never once been out of her room at this hour. When I step into the hallway, Tia nearly knocks me over with an overflowing laundry hamper. She skids to a halt in the nick of time, soiled laundry swaying dangerously and wafting less-than-pleasant odors into my face.

"Seems to be poop night in this fine facility," she says, with a grin. "You were nearly a casualty."

"Speaking of casualties, have you seen Nancy?" I wince internally at the awkward segue, but she accepts it at face value. We don't have time on this job to worry about social finesse.

"Yeah. Saw her at about three. Flipping me a boatload of sass as usual."

"Any idea where she might be now?"

Tia steps around me to look into the empty room, her brow furrowed in concentration. "I have no idea. She never leaves her room unless somebody drags her."

"Maybe somebody dragged her."

"Hopefully a staff member," she says, and then realizes the implications of what she's just said, and an uneasy silence descends.

"That's probably it. Carry on with Mission Poopy Laundry. I'll find her."

I look in the dining room, the games room, even the chapel, as unlikely as that seems as a destination for Nancy. I ask all of the staff. Nobody has seen her.

Of course there's a protocol for runaway residents. Check with the family, call the cops and ask them to look for wandering strays. But escapees are usually patients with dementia, trying to get back to a home that no longer exists, or to find loved ones whose deaths have been forgotten while distant memory still burns bright.

Nancy can't walk, and she's not adept at rolling herself around in the wheelchair. Even if she was, surely somebody would have noticed and called in an old woman in a sparkly red dress rolling down the street in a wheelchair.

With sickness sloshing around in my belly, I remember her little stash of pills, her suicidal statements, and the way I dismissed them in my head as drama. Maybe she meant it, after all, and Mason's abandonment pushed her over the edge. Even so, where could she go? Where would she hide?

When you don't know what else to do, follow protocol. I call dispatch and give them the specifics. I try to call Mason, but his phone goes straight to voice mail. I almost feel bad leaving him a message, knowing he'll get it the minute his plane hits the runway in Chicago, but he deserves it, and I don't even try to be gentle.

The rest of the shift, I'm braced for tragedy. The only road leading away from Valley View is a steep descent. I picture a runaway wheelchair careening down that hill, gathering speed, carrying a screaming old woman in a scarlet dress toward disaster. I picture a car with an inattentive driver coming up that hill. A crunch, the horrible sensation of tires passing over flesh, and it's me in the car again with Katya in the road.

With that memory comes an attack of guilt-laced panic and a movie-worthy replay of the events of the crash and its aftermath. Did Tom get Katya back to the crisis house? As hard as I'm trying to avoid lapsing into feeling responsible for her situation, I can't seem to turn it off.

I try Mason's phone again. Still no answer.

Officer Mendez comes by to pick up a photo. "How do you lose an old woman in a wheelchair?" he asks, and I know he's thinking of his own father, who has quietly gone to bed without any trouble. He refrains from further judgment, promising to search the ditch on the sides of the drive, and to call the minute he finds her.

All night long the phone fails to ring.

At 10:35 p.m., while I'm in the office finishing up charts before giving report to Jennifer who comes on at eleven, the buzzer goes off for the front doors. They're open during the day, but we lock up right after dinner, when all the visitors are gone and the wandering spirit tends to grow stronger in our confused residents.

The aides are all busy, so I head for the door, thinking maybe somebody on the night-shift team has forgotten their badge.

But no. Waiting outside the door is an old woman in a wheelchair, and standing behind her is her delinquent son. Neither one of them looks shamefaced or repentant. Nancy waves an imperious hand at me, as if she's a queen on a throne.

"If you could just move out of the way, Rae, instead of gawking, we could come in and stop feeding mosquitoes."

Relief transmogrifies into anger, and I stay right where I am. "If you would sign out when you leave, we wouldn't have to waste time looking for you. Or file a missing persons report with the cops."

"The cops are looking for us?" Nancy whoops and cackles with outright glee. "I'm a wanted woman at my age. One more thing off the bucket list."

Mason swats at a mosquito on his cheek. When I step aside and he rolls his mother into the brightness of the fluorescent lights, I see his eyes are bloodshot. His face is pale, and despite the cool of the evening, a sheen of perspiration covers his forehead.

"I thought you were on a plane."

"Drove to Spokane. Made it all the way to the airport."

"And?"

"I decided I was tired of running away."

His gaze meets mine. Level. Something has shifted in him, but I can't identify the change.

"I've been worried sick. Why on earth didn't you tell us you were taking her out?"

He runs an unsteady hand through his hair. "She wanted to escape. I figured I owed her."

"The cops really are looking for her. How drunk are you?"

"Not drunk at all, God help me." There's a light of mischief in his eyes that matches his mother's. "Forty-eight hours sober. Librium on board. AA meetings located. I'm a new man."

"Wow. And your first action in this shiny new existence is to kidnap an old woman from a nursing home?" My anger is drifting away, mist on the wind.

Mason laughs, ruefully. "Here I thought sobriety was boring."

"Take me home, James," Nancy orders.

He touches his fingers to his brow in a small salute. "Yes, ma'am." Then he looks at me. "May I?"

Nancy yawns. "That's not a good expression for you, Rae. Your face will get stuck that way and you'll need enough Botox to kill an elephant just to undo the damage."

"You are incorrigible."

She sticks her tongue out at me, and that does it. All three of us are laughing as I step aside and Mason rolls her down the hall to her room.

~

Exhausted as I am, I toss all night like a ship at sea, and drag out of bed, feeling weighted and slow.

Last night's laughter has evaporated, and the moment of incredible lightness I felt at my wishing beach is a faint memory. I miss Bernie. I miss sitting down in her office and unloading everything, as if that somehow releases me from responsibility and transfers it to her. It's not her job to fix me, though. It never was. I can't imagine trying to catch her up on how much has changed for me since I saw her last.

Sitting down at the table with a mug of coffee, I find myself face-to-face with Tana's photograph of me, laughing under the tree with the golden orb above my head. Beside it, folded in half and almost hidden by a stack of unopened junk mail, is the loving-kindness meditation she printed off for me.

I unfold the paper and scan the words. Before I get to the bottom of the page, a crowd of people are already lined up in the wings as candidates for what reads to me like a blessing. Ignoring the instructions that clearly say to start with myself, I move on to a person for whom I feel strong, unconditional love.

Corinne.

Loving, good-hearted Cor. Holding her in my mind, I run through the phrases of the meditation.

May you be free from inner and outer harm and danger.

May you be free of mental suffering or distress.

May you be happy.

The meditation reminds me of skimming stones. The words quiet my mind and soothe my soul. Drawing a deep breath, feeling the irritable tension easing out of me, I move on to the next person on my mind.

Mason is not quite so easy as Corinne, but still, it is not difficult to wish all of these good things for him.

I know full well that Mason and Corinne are only practice runs. I want to stop here, feeling calm and easy, but Kat is waiting for me. My anger, my hurt, my guilt. Her darkness, the heaviness of her grief. I remember the wishing stone I tried to cast for her and the way it slipped through my fingers.

I think of all the ways I've failed her. All of the times she lashed out at me.

All I need to do is say the words, I tell myself. *How hard is that?* Nobody said I have to feel them.

And so I begin.

May you be happy.

May you be free of physical pain and suffering.

May you be healthy and strong.

As I recite the words they come alive, and I feel the knots that bind me so tightly to Kat begin to loosen. A sadness wells up in me, a loss, but there is nothing bitter in it. The tears that track down my cheeks feel clean, like rain washing away the dust after a windstorm.

In my mind I see Kat healthy and strong, hand in hand with Tom. She smiles at me, and I find myself smiling back, guilt and anger slipping away. I see her turn to Tom, leaning on his shoulder, and the two of them walk away from me into an obscuring mist.

Which leaves me alone with myself.

My relationship with Leila Elizabeth Blackwell Chatworth a.k.a. Rae is the most complicated and treacherous of all. If I'm not focused on saving somebody else, then what is there? Who am I? Why am I here? What do I want? If I were a cartoon character I would have big, empty bubbles hanging over my head where the words are supposed to go that answer these questions.

The words of the meditation are waiting, and I go back, finally, to repeat all of those wishes for myself, for crazy misfit Rae, for the Rae in Tana's picture, the laughing girl with the mysterious orb hanging unseen above her head.

May I be safe and protected.

May I be happy.

May I be able to live in this world happily, peacefully, joyfully, with ease.

Nothing transcendental happens. There is no sudden shift or epiphany. But I catch again that glimpse of a reality in which I have a purpose and a reason for being. Where I matter as much as Kat, or Mason, or Cole.

And this time the moment doesn't slip away from me.

When I'm through I feel quiet and almost reverent, as if the meditation should end with an amen and the tolling of church bells.

I also want to do something, to make a change, to keep myself from slipping back into the old patterns.

The easiest place to start is with right here where I live. I want a place like Tana's, a place that makes me feel reverent and joyful and invigorated. Maybe it will take me awhile to get there, but there's no reason I can't start now.

Taking action turns out to be a huge relief. I've got a box of giant trash bags left over from last fall's leaf raking. Holding the serenity of Tana's uncluttered space in my mind's eye like the Holy Grail, I whirl through my house getting rid of anything I don't need. Old clothes I haven't worn in a year, knickknacks, outdated kitten formula, all manner of miscellaneous gadgets that once seemed cool enough to alter the course of history but have not been touched in years.

At the center of this whirlwind sits my bloodstained couch, the elephant in the room. It's old-fashioned and heavy, a relic of the days when furniture was made with real wood and meant to last. When I brought it home, I bribed a couple of neighbor kids with pizza to help me drag it in.

Now, I don't know how I'm going to get it out.

Shoving the ruined cushions into trash bags is relatively easy, but the couch itself wants to be a permanent fixture. I can't drag it. But if I get behind it, bend my knees, and shove with my backside, I find I can budge it a few inches.

It takes an hour to move it as far as the door, and then I'm forced to admit that all the stubbornness built into my genetic code is not going to let me move that sucker outside without assistance, and even if I do get it out there, I can't leave it sitting on the lawn. My landlord will throw a conniption fit.

So I straighten my shirt, unstick my hair from my sweaty face, and open the door to go on a quest for male muscle, only to find it standing on the doorstep.

Cole's arm is raised, ready to knock.

"Damn. Do you have precognitive ability or did you hear me drive in?"

I'm not in any shape to deflect either the intensity of his focus or the expression in his eyes, so I blurt out the first words that form in my addled brain.

"You said you would call."

God. Nice opener, Rae.

"Your phone has been ringing busy all morning."

And a nice evasion on his part. He releases me from his gaze, and I manage to get a normal breath. His eyes widen as he takes in the wreckage behind me.

"I like what you've done with the place."

I can only imagine how it looks through his eyes. The naked couch right in front of the door. Trash bags randomly scattered around the room, some trailing contents out of their gaping maws.

"It's not exactly what I was going for."

"No? I thought maybe I'd missed something in decorating trends." His lips turn up in a grin, but it doesn't reach his eyes. His hands are in his pockets, his posture casual, but there's enough tension radiating from him to make my fingers twitch.

Generally, I'm polite about what I pick up from people. If they don't want to talk about it, I leave it alone. Today, God help me, not so much.

"What's wrong?"

"Nothing. Why?"

A lie and a deflection. All in one breath, he tumbles off the pedestal where I've placed him, right into the center of my heart. I give him a full-on smile.

"No worries. You don't have to talk about it. Help me with this couch instead."

"What exactly are we doing with the couch?"

"Removing it from the scene of the crime."

He assesses the room beyond me as if debating whether there really was a crime, and then he grins at me, a real one this time, his eyes lighting with amusement. "Where is it going?"

"I hadn't gotten that far yet. My goal was out of the house."

"Well, since I happen to have a pickup truck, maybe we could push the boundaries. It doesn't look like a Goodwill special."

"Dump, for sure."

"Let's do it. Does the rest of this go, too?"

Make a decision, Rae. No going back from this point. "The rest of it goes, too. Some to the dump, some to Goodwill."

He nods. "I'm yours to command. Let's get the couch first."

With him on one end and me on the other, we manage to force the monstrosity through the doorway and up into the bed of his truck. After that, the rest is easy. Bags for the dump in the back, bags for Goodwill in the cab.

"Good thing it's Saturday," Cole says as he shifts the truck into gear.

"Because we're not working?" I hazard, contemplating the expanse of bench seat that stretches between him and me. He has guarded with care the space boundaries between us, not so much as grazing my arm with his while passing me in the doorway.

"Well, yes, otherwise neither of us would be here. But also because the dump is open. Which it wouldn't be tomorrow."

I am ignorant of the dump and its ways, relying on the garbage truck to come and pick up my trash every Wednesday morning.

While we were busy and working together it was easy to pretend there's not a rift between us, but now a silence grows, ominous and difficult. Cole's fingers tap out a rhythm on the steering wheel. I sit on my own hands to keep them from some similar betrayal of my own unease.

My imagination takes me down a thousand different rabbit holes, trying to guess what's on his mind.

"Shall I play twenty questions?" I stare straight ahead, not looking at him. If this is about Katya, I don't want to see the judgment cross his face, the reminder that he thinks I'm broken and in need of fixing.

"What?" He sounds startled, as if I've called him back from his own random thought trail in a neighboring galaxy.

"This thing. Whatever is on your mind. I said you didn't have to tell me, but I think you really do."

His fingers pick up the tempo on his steering wheel drum solo. He catches himself and stills them. "That empath thing is a bit inconvenient." His tone is light, to soften his words.

"I dub thee king of the understatement. Sorry. Can't turn it off."

My heart sinks. This is going to be a good-bye conversation. One last good deed from the magnanimous hero, helping me dispose of the aftermath of war, and then he'll be out of my life.

He gives me the side eye. "Don't look so woebegone. It's not that I don't want to talk; it's that I've been trying to figure out how to say it."

"I'm a big fan of just spit it out."

"I've noticed." He laughs, but it's dry and brief. "I'm much more comfortable with getting other people to spill their emotions. Not so much with my own. Part of that whole hero complex thing you happened to notice."

A lump wells up in my throat. Here we go. "I shouldn't have said that," I manage to choke out. "I wish I hadn't."

"Why?" He glances over at me, his gaze holding for as long as safety allows before going back to the road. He sounds genuinely surprised.

"It's not like it isn't true. You put your finger right on the problem, in that slightly freaky way you have."

"And if I hadn't pointed it out, would you have called? Would we be this awkward with each other? That's why I shouldn't have said it."

He doesn't rush into explanations about why he didn't call. No excuses. No comforting lies. Finally, he shakes his head. "You pointed out what I already knew but hadn't found the words for. When you offered . . . when I said there were too many strings . . . that's what I meant. My hero complex. My need to rush in and rescue the damsel in distress."

I let this sink in, trying to see myself through his eyes and not liking the picture that emerges. Tears fill my eyes, and I focus on the road, trying not to blink in case that makes them fall. It takes a minute before I can trust my voice again.

"I don't need rescuing."

"Clearly."

"If that's sarcasm I hear, let me tell you—"

"It's not sarcasm. Damn it." I'm not sure whether the *damn it* is a natural part of this conversation, or because we've reached the dump and there is a line of five vehicles in front of us.

"Shouldn't your super feeling senses make this conversation easier instead of harder?"

"Ha. If that was the case, I'd wear a spangly unitard with a capital *E* on it. And a cape. A cape would be fun, don't you think?"

"Now who's being sarcastic?"

"That would be me. Look. The whole empath thing isn't fun for me, Cole. It's not a party trick. I can't turn it on and off at will, and so far it's torpedoed every real relationship I've tried to engage in. All I'm picking up from you is tension and unhappiness and anger. I assume it's directed at me."

"*At* you? God no." A vehicle behind us honks, and I see through a blur of tears that the line has moved up, but we haven't. Cole moves up behind the truck in front of us and its haphazard load of squashed cardboard boxes, an old mattress fastened on top with tie-down straps.

"Oh hell," he says. "I really like you, Rae."

"And this is a problem?"

"Yes. This is a problem." He takes a deep breath. "It's not you. It's me."

"God, Cole. You can do better than that. That brush-off was invented by a hairy guy in a skin loincloth carrying a club."

"It's not a brush-off." The truck ahead of us pulls through the gate and stops on the scales, leaving us directly behind a traffic signal, waiting for the green light.

"Okay. So it's not me and it's not you; it's both of us. You're a hero, and you think I'm a damsel in distress. Or a hobbit, maybe, and you're Aragorn the mighty warrior . . ."

"It was a hobbit who saved Middle-earth, if you care to recall. All right. Truth. When you got all tangled up with Katya, I thought maybe you had a tendency toward codependency, and I didn't want to . . . shit. I'm going to have to tell you."

"Light's not going to get any greener," I tell him.

"What? Oh right." He drives the truck forward onto the scale. A disembodied voice, tinny through a speaker, advises us that we'll have to drive around to the pit to dispose of furniture. Cole navigates the dirt road in silence.

"I'm not codependent in general," I tell him. "Only with Kat." Is this true or an evasion? It feels like truth. But maybe that's what my full-on switch is all about. Like I'm an alcoholic and just fell off the wagon, only my addiction is rescuing people instead of booze.

A muscle jumps in Cole's cheek. "You asked before why I do what I do—locking people up. And I didn't tell you."

I have this horrible feeling he's going to tell me now, and that it's going to be a thing I don't want to know. I cling to my image of him as healthy, balanced, untroubled by the usual baggage. Up until today his energy has felt blissfully clear and uncluttered.

"I changed my mind," I blurt out. "Don't tell me."

"What?"

"I just realized I like you as Hero, and you're about to shatter your image."

"You're a little freaky," he says. "I've mentioned that, right? How did you know?"

"This has nothing to do with being an empath." I sigh. "Now you have to tell me, though."

If there was any more tension in his voice, it would snap like an elastic band. "This thing happened in college. First year. First serious girlfriend."

"No high school sweetheart?"

He shakes his head. "A couple of crushes. And a five-day special when I was fourteen. No, Ashley was my first real love."

A little shiver of jealousy runs up my spine. "Where is she now?"

"Dead. She killed herself."

"Oh, Cole. How horrible." All of my protective instincts dive into the emotion pool at once. I reach out to touch his arm, the muscles hard and unyielding as stone. He doesn't look at me, or acknowledge my touch, and I let my hand fall to the seat between us.

"See?" he says, pulling the truck to a stop. "I tell you, and everything is different between us. Just like that."

I feel like the two of us are teetering on the edge of a precipice, and that my words are going to either steady us there or send our relationship plunging to its death on sharp rocks below. Silence, my old standby, is not an option.

Still, neither of us speaks. A warm breeze carries the pungent smell of decomposing trash in through the half-open windows. The buzzing of flies and the distant sound of heavy machinery fill the air.

"It's not a bad different," I say, carefully. "Better than half an hour ago when I thought you were mad."

Our world steadies as Cole draws a breath and lets it out in an audible whoosh. "Aren't you now feeling an overpowering need to fix me?"

I assess my emotional reaction, all of the feelings and the random jumble of thoughts. "I think I want to splint you."

He sputters at that. "You what?"

"You're not broken, exactly. Walking wounded, maybe, but everybody is."

"Splinting? Can't say I've heard that expression before."

"Sorry. Rae speak. When the body sustains an injury—not a break, but maybe a pull or a tear or a sprain—it tries to protect itself. The muscles all around the injured spot tighten up to shore up the weak area."

"Which works but maybe causes problems somewhere else. I think I see where you're going."

"Your girlfriend killing herself—you splint around that. And that leads to compensating. Like being a crisis worker. My guess is that it wasn't your fault."

"I should have stopped her. There were signs."

All the thoughts and feelings that poured through me when I ran over Katya, when I came home to find her bleeding out on my couch, come trooping back. My chest is so full of love and sympathy and sadness it's hard to breathe.

"How old were you?"

"Nineteen."

"Just a baby."

"Grown man, thank you very much. I was irritated with her for being a downer. I went to a party. She didn't come. I should have known."

"Because I'm sure by then you had all the signs of suicide memorized and integrated and at your fingertips."

"The signs were pretty obvious. I wasn't paying attention."

I've got nothing, no wishes I can pull out of my pocket to make any of this okay. We sit there, breathing in the disgusting stench of the pit, staring out at a vista of discarded refuse. I pick through the responses to his words, emotions, thoughts, trying to find a path forward.

Finally, I revert to fact gathering as the safest bet. "Were you always going to be a psych major?"

"Nope. Premed. Switched my major, and here I am."

"Doing lifelong penance."

"Never thought of it like that." He shoos a fly off the steering wheel, and it comes over to visit me.

I redirect the fly toward the open window, but it doesn't get the message and starts bumping up against the windshield, buzzing loudly.

"Are you allowed to be happy?"

"Allowed? Are there happiness police now?" He smiles, evading, but I've been well trained by my sessions with Bernie, and I wait him out.

Two more flies come in, and we now have a small fly gang. The breeze dies down, leaving the air heavy and hot. Sweat soaks the roots of my hair. The cloying stench of trash makes it hard to breathe.

Cole reaches out and delicately moves a strand of hair that is glued to my cheek, tucking it back behind my ear, and letting his hand rest on the side of my head. His eyes hold mine, burning, intense. Maybe he'll pull me over closer. Maybe he'll kiss me.

Another fly comes to join its buddies, making crazy circles around my head.

Cole's hand slides away, and his gaze falls to the seat. "I don't know. I'd like to think so." His lips curve up into a bare ghost of a smile. "Let's get rid of the trash, shall we?"

Getting the couch out of the truck is a far sight easier than getting it in. We give it a good shove at the edge of the pit, and it rolls once, before getting stuck with its bottom up, looking forlorn and unloved.

"Good-bye, couch," I say aloud, my throat unexpectedly tight. Cole tosses the trash bags down the slope after it, and the two of us climb back into the cab in a contemplative silence that lasts until we're out on the highway with the clean wind blowing in through wide-open windows.

"About that camping trip," Cole says. "I was thinking next weekend, if you still want to go."

He keeps his gaze on the road ahead, both hands on the wheel. I can feel his caution, the way he's trying to make it easier for me to bail, in case I've changed my mind. My feelings need sorting and my thoughts need organizing, but the answer to this question is easy.

"Yes."

Now he glances at me, his eyes a question. "You're sure?"

"I'm not going to pass on campfire-roasted hot dogs."

The smile that lights his face makes me feel like I'm one of my own wishing stones, skimming over sun-spangled water. His hand reaches for mine, and for a long time there's no need for either of us to say anything.

But even the best of wishing stones can't soar forever, and with Cole's next words the cold, dark waters of reality close over my head.

"Have you heard anything from Katya?"

My body goes cold, then hot again. My heart starts to beat out the command for retreat, but we're driving sixty miles an hour and there's nowhere to hide.

"Not in a couple of days," I answer, carefully. "How's she doing?"

"They discharged her from the crisis house a couple of days ago. I thought she might have been in touch with you."

"I haven't heard a word."

I'm telling the full-on truth, but it feels like a lie. Cole doesn't know what I've done, how I've meddled. The people who run the crisis house don't know, either. Fear envelops me in a fog that wipes away all memory of my fleeting moment of joy.

Even if she's fine, if she's gone back to Tom or somewhere else, safe and sound, this secret will always be an albatross around my neck. I'm going to have to fess up to Cole, and what that will do to the balance of a still-fragile relationship I don't know.

"Talk to me," Cole says, his fingers tightening around mine. "Second thoughts? What is it?"

"It seemed like a good idea at the time." I try to speak lightly, but my words are heavy as granite. My lips feel dusty, and I scrub at them with the back of my right hand. My left is still tangled up in Cole's.

He doesn't ask again, letting the silence speak for him. And so I tell him about my phone call to Tom, about our meeting in the park, about how it all turned out. When I'm done, he still says nothing.

This is it. The end. I start to pull my hand away, but his fingers tighten around mine, tight enough to hurt, not that I'm complaining.

"She made it back to the crisis house," he says as we slow down for the first stoplight into town. "Seemed fine, but applied for permission to leave. The crisis house is always voluntary, but we do assessments before they go. I talked to her myself."

"And you let her go?"

Worse and worse. If I've pushed her toward another suicide attempt, then I've also dragged Cole into the middle of it. Like he doesn't have enough weight to carry already.

"She seemed well," he goes on. "Not happy enough to ring alarm bells. Contemplative. Not so angry. And I've broken the confidentiality code telling you that much."

He releases my hand, and I make good use of it, wrapping both arms around my belly to hold myself together. "Did she say where she was going?"

"She did. I'll try to contact her. I can ask her to call you."

"Thanks. That would be good."

"Rae?"

I'm too busy fighting back a squall of tears to answer.

"Good call, getting those two together. I should have pushed her harder to be willing to meet with him."

"You're kidding, right?"

He shrugs. "Counselors are bound by all sorts of rules. We don't like to take risks, and we can break confidentiality under very limited circumstances. You did the sensible thing. She needed to hash that stuff out with her husband. Maybe it helped her."

"Maybe. You're not mad, then? Or—disappointed? Or thoroughly convinced that I'm hopelessly broken and in need of repair?"

We're driving down my street. Cole pulls into my driveway and shifts into park before he answers.

"I think maybe you need a little splinting." He unbuckles his seat belt and scoots a foot in my direction. "And so do I. So maybe we could—"

Before he can finish the sentence, I have my own seat belt off and am closing the rest of the distance between us. His arms go around me, his lips meet mine, and all of my shields evaporate with the intensity of our kiss.

Chapter Eighteen

"You went camping? On your first date?" Corinne's eyes shine with excitement and what might be a hint of vicarious lust.

"It wasn't our first date. The Oscar Event was our first date. And then he took me to meet his grandmother, and then we went to the dump. So, fourth date. Besides, just because we went camping doesn't mean we slept together."

She snorts. "That's a bunch of bull hockey, and you know it. He's yummy."

"And you are nearly old enough to be his mother."

"Which makes him extra yummy." She grins, unrepentant. "Please tell me you didn't insist on separate tents."

Heat creeps up my neck and into my face. It was decidedly a one-tent weekend. My body warms to the memory of strong hands, exploring lips, a—

"Hot damn." Cor slaps her thigh and bursts into a whoop of laughter. "Don't bother trying to lie to me."

I lift my chin and give her a dignified stare. "Are you going to give me report?"

"I was hoping for a report from you."

"Which you already got. So."

"Oh, fine. Be like that. There is nothing to tell. Everybody is exactly the same as they were on Friday."

"What about Nancy?"

"Except for Nancy. Nancy is moving out."

"She's doing what?" I blink, trying to imagine the home without Nancy. She's been here longer than I have.

Corinne leans forward, obviously savoring this bit of news. "Apparently, Mason bought a house. It's wheelchair friendly, and there's a suite of rooms for his mother."

"No." I shake my head, remembering all of the times I've seen Mason drunk. "He can't take care of her."

"Home care worker already hired. You and I both know she doesn't really need much care. She doesn't really need that chair, either—gets around just fine when she wants to."

At some point—sooner rather than later—every resident in this place is going to die. I know this. Nancy's death seems years away, though, and when I think about my life unfolding through the years, she's always in it, infusing my day with her special brand of crazy.

"He drinks. It will never work out."

"Currently sober and says he plans to stay that way. Besides, it's their decision, Rae. We don't have a say-so."

"I guess. I'm happy for her."

But as I go through my evening, despite the warm glow I get whenever I think about Cole, happy isn't what rises to the top.

When I go in to check Nancy's blood sugar, Mason is there.

He looks different. His eyes are clear and focused. His face looks leaner and firmer. "Oh good," he says. "Just in time. I have a favor to ask."

"Ask away." I'm always careful not to agree to favors until I know what they are.

"Can you show me how to do the finger stick thing and use the meter? So I can help her when I take her home?"

"Sure. My pleasure."

"No need for that. Give that shit to me." Nancy grabs both meter and lancet from my hands and lays them out in her lap.

"It's easy. Clean the finger with alcohol. Poke it with the lancet and make blood. Stick the strip in the meter, touch it to the blood, and bingo! Blood count in three-two-one seconds." She runs competently through the steps as she speaks, triumphantly showing me a blood sugar of 120.

"All this time." I glare at her, and then start to laugh. "All the nights I scrambled to find time to do that for you."

"I'm a drama queen. I require a great deal of attention. What can I say?"

Mason fakes a worried look. "I'm letting myself in for all kinds of surprises, I see."

"Be afraid," I tell him. "Be very afraid. When's the big move?"

"Tomorrow. No point waiting."

"Well, then." I shift my weight from one foot to the other, feeling suddenly lost and ill at ease. "I'll miss you," I tell her, realizing that I'm also going to miss Mason.

"No, you won't." Nancy sits up ramrod straight, in her most queenly manner. "You will be coming to visit. Bring a kitten."

Mason shrugs his shoulders at me, but there is laughter in his eyes. "How about Saturday? You're welcome to bring that Cole person. And Katya, if she's still around. And, of course, a kitten."

"To keep? Or to visit?"

"To visit," Mason exclaims.

"To stay," Nancy objects.

"Maybe since we're just getting settled, it would be best to—"

"Don't tell me what's best. I've got a lot of years on you. I think I'm capable of making decisions."

"I don't want a cat pissing in my brand-new house."

"Aren't you the same one moaning about how I deprived you of kittens when you were a vulnerable child? Forget the one-kitten thing, Rae. Bring us a litter."

I leave them bickering, but an idea follows me out of the room and dogs my heels for the rest of the shift.

When I get home, despite the fact that it's Monday and 2:00 a.m. their time, I call my parents. Payback is a wonderful thing.

My mother picks up first. "Leila? Is everything all right?"

"Everything is fine. I'm sorry to wake you."

She laughs. "We weren't sleeping. We thought we'd try online gaming and got hooked. Richard, save your place and come to the phone. It's Leila."

"It's only Monday," I hear him say in the background, and I can't suppress a smile. "Elizabeth, my dear," he says into the receiver, "how are you? How is Katya?"

"Katya doesn't live here anymore."

Silence on the other end, except for dramatic breathing. I know they are making gestures to each other, signaling their initial reaction to protect me and also deciding who will be pressed into first response.

"Oh, honey," my mother says, "we're so sorry. She seemed such a lovely girl, too."

"There will be other women," my father adds. "Although I imagine it's more difficult to find a same-sex partner. A smaller pool to choose from. Are there specific signals? Do lesbian women let you know somehow that they're, um, available?"

I'm tempted to let them go on believing, they are so much enjoying themselves. But I have to tell them the truth.

"Actually, I'm dating a man. His name is Cole. We went camping this past weekend."

The breathing on the other end of the phone turns judgmental. Before they can begin to voice their disappointment that I've cheated on my lover, I dive back in. "Katya was only a friend. You got that part all wrong. I ran over her with my car, and she needed a place to stay for a bit."

This really silences them. Now I can barely hear the breathing. Maybe I've given them simultaneous heart attacks. "Are you still there?"

"We're here." My mother sounds cautious, as if she's unsure whether being there is a good idea.

"She was suicidal and chose my car to ride in front of. So I wanted to help her."

My father clears his throat. "Why didn't you tell us? Either of you. You just let us go on."

"Katya was enjoying having parental units approve of her. Hers only wanted her to have babies. So she thought you both were wonderful, and you made her happy. I didn't want to screw that up."

It's my mother who breaks the silence. "I wonder—do you know how proud we are of you, Leila?"

I don't answer, can't answer, but sometimes silence speaks more loudly than words.

"I see," Mom says. I can hear the hurt in her voice and want to fix it, but of course there's nothing I can say. "We aren't good at saying these things, I suppose."

"We pushed too hard," Dad says. "Is that it? About medical school."

"A little. I'm not ever going to be a doctor. I'm asking you both, once and for all, to please give up on that idea."

Dramatic breathing on the other end of the line. I picture the hand gestures, the lifted brows, the shaking of heads. This time it's Dad who ventures in. "We noticed you're good with animals. Did you want to go to veterinarian school, then?"

"Not exactly."

I tell them what I do want. I argue, I placate. I present scientific evidence.

They listen. They ask some intelligent questions.

"What do you think?" Dad asks, deferring to my mother as usual.

"It makes sense, after a fashion. She might as well use the money."

"Agreed," Dad says. "She's not getting any younger. I say we put it in an account and trust that whatever use she puts it to will be right."

"Wait," I interject. "What money?"

"We've been putting money aside for medical school since you were a baby," Mom says. "There's a little extra now, what with interest."

"I'd been thinking you'd have enough to start a private practice," Dad adds. "But if that's not what you want, then you should use it for what you do want. We have no need for it."

My knees feel weak. "How much money are we talking?"

"What was it, dear?" Mom asks. "Something in the vicinity of five hundred thousand?"

"We put some in stocks. I'll need to ask Victor to finalize some numbers and see when we can get it out without incurring penalties. How much do you think your school will cost, Elizabeth?"

"It's Leila," Mom protests.

"It's Rae, and I don't need that kind of money, that's for sure."

"Everybody needs money, the way the world is going to wrack and ruin. We won't always be here to help you."

I bite my tongue to keep from reminding them that I haven't accepted any help in at least ten years.

"When you talk to Vic," Mom says, "make sure to ask about that other investment, the one slated for our retirement."

"Are we retiring? I was planning to work until I drop dead with a scalpel in my hand."

"You don't always get that choice, though, do you? Either one of us could come down with Alzheimer's or . . ."

They are talking to each other now, on the phone, probably sitting side by side on the sofa. No need for me to listen, and I've got plenty to think about. There's a certain wish of mine that could happen with that kind of money. Something that goes well beyond what I'd been thinking when I planned to go back to school.

"Mom?" I say. "Dad? Maybe you two kids can stay up all night, but I need sleep."

"Oh, of course," Mom says. "Good night, Leila."

"Good night, Elizabeth," Dad says. And then, unexpectedly, "Do you really want us to call you Rae?"

"You can call me whatever makes you happy." *I know who I am; it doesn't matter.*

"I hadn't really thought about the effect of the two of us fighting over your name." Dad's voice takes on its intellectual tone, and I know he's avoiding emotions in his usual way. "Might be a confusing thing for a child. I never thought about that until just now."

"Where did Rae even come from?" Mom asks. "I always wondered."

"Remember Grace?"

Silence. "Was she the babysitter?" Dad asks. "You know, the one with the butch hair and that VW bug car."

"No. That one had some weird name. Amalie or something. I always wanted to spell it with an *n*."

I interrupt their bickering. "It was the neighbor's cat, the big orange one. His name was probably spelled with a *y*. I thought they named him after a ray of sunshine."

"You named yourself after a cat?" Mom sounds thoroughly bewildered. Dad's got nothing.

"Animals were always easier for me than people."

"We should have had pets for you," Dad says. "We didn't see. I did like those kittens. Are you sure you don't want to try a kitten, Angela?"

When I hang up they are arguing with each other through the phone line. An unusual fondness for my unorthodox upbringing floods through me. They do love me for me. Not Elizabeth or Leila, or their dreams for me. It's not the money that tells me this, but the fact that my father almost called me Rae.

∿

It takes about a month to work out the details. When I tell Corinne I've given my two weeks' notice, shock drops her jaw clear to her chest, but for once no words come out.

"Breathe, Cor."

"You can't quit. We need you. The residents will all wither up and die."

"No, they won't."

"You never did have any idea about what a breath of sunshine you are. You light up their world. They'll all get depressed. I'm not kidding, Rae. Is it money? Ask for a raise. Or get them to adjust your schedule."

I start laughing before she's done. She's so earnest and energetic, and I've got a secret that makes me feel like I can fly.

"I don't see what's so funny."

"Because you haven't let me finish. Money is so not an issue. My parents have turned over all of the money they saved for medical school."

"That's nice, honey, but it can't be enough to—"

"Trust me, it's enough. You don't know my parents. Besides, just because I'm quitting this job doesn't mean I won't be back."

"Now you're talking in circles. Spit it out."

I look around the office where we sit to give report. It's cluttered, as usual, with paper and binders and sticky notes. There's a stack of faxes to go through.

"I'm going to be an animal therapist."

Cor stares like I've grown an extra head. "Like—a dog whisperer? Or one of those people who solves the behavior problems of cats? I read about a lady who does therapy with chickens. Can you make a living at that? In the city, maybe, but I don't know about here—"

"Cor. First, I really don't need to worry about making a living, at least for a bit. Second, I'll be using therapy animals to help people. I've already got two sweet cats lined up to live here at Valley View. And permission to bring a dog in for visits. So, like I said, I'll still be around."

I can see the wheels spinning as she tries to process what I'm telling her. "That's a thing?"

"It's a thing. I'll be training therapy animals, too, and placing them with people who need them. A matchmaking service for animals and humans."

She's still struggling to take this all in. "Where? Out of that little house you rent? What will the landlord say? Where will you find all the animals? Who is going to help you?"

"I've got it all sorted out. Mason helped me find the perfect place. Nice little house with a big heated barn. We're going to start a shelter. I'll work with the animals to train them, and if they've got the right temperament, we'll match them up with the people who need them. I'm starting now, but I've signed up to take an animal-assisted-therapy training so I can get certified and learn all the ins and outs. Cole will help."

Corinne grasps on to the mention of Cole as the first reasonable thing I've said in the last fifteen minutes. "You're still seeing him, then? What does he think of all this?"

"The delicious Cole is totally on board. He's making plans to stop doing the crisis thing and shift to private practice counseling. He says he might want to borrow my animals. It will be all right. I promise. If it isn't, I can always get another nursing job."

"I'm not worried," she says, tears welling up in her eyes. "I'm sad. I'll miss you. Whoever replaces you here won't be like you at all."

I think very carefully before I speak, because what I'm about to say still feels strange to me, even though in my bones I'm sure I'm right.

"We're friends, though, aren't we?"

"Of course. How can you even ask?"

"So, if we're real friends and not just work friends, then we'll see each other outside of work. You want to come see the new property on Saturday? You can help me figure out where to put things. And I need help buying furniture for the house."

She lights up like I've given her the secret to eternal youth or something. "Really? You want me to do that?"

"Of course."

Knowing what's coming, I take a deep breath before her arms go around me and my face gets squished against her bosom. "I love you, Rae," she says. "You know that, right?"

I make choking noises, and she releases me, laughing. Both of us wipe tears from our eyes.

"Oh my God. Look at the time! You get the abbreviated report tonight," she says. I listen with half my attention as she launches into a dizzying summary of the residents' status. My mind drifts, touching down lightly on one subject and another before drifting into the warm fuzziness of sleep.

I jerk awake to silence.

A blurry Corinne watches me, the corners of her mouth tucked up in what I have to call a smirk.

"What?" I blink and rub my eyes, trying to get her all the way in focus.

"You've been out for five minutes. Tell Cole he needs to leave you alone and let you sleep."

I pull the report binder toward me and open it as an excuse to hide my face. "I have a new batch of kittens." This is true. What Cole and I choose to do between feedings is nobody's business but our own.

"Sure," Cor says. "Feeding kittens. Is that what the kids are calling it these days?"

"I choose not to answer that."

She gets up and stretches. "You are running very late, Nurse Rae. Better get to work—you don't want to get fired before you get the chance to quit."

Before I can protest that she's the one who held me up, she envelops me in another hug. "Hey, speaking of kittens, how is that Wish cat?"

"I gave him to Nancy."

"You gave him to Nancy. Of course you did. Because that makes every bit as much sense as everything else you've said tonight. I'd better go get some sleep; I think I'm hallucinating."

I grin at her. "Sweet dreams."

When she gets to the doorway, I call her back. "Cor?"

"Yes?"

"This is a friendship, right? I mean the real thing. Not just work friends or sympathy friends?"

Her lips curve up in a smile that makes her look, to me, like an angel. "We've always been friends, you crazy girl. You just didn't see it. I'll see you tomorrow."

She blows a kiss in my direction, and I catch it in my hand and hold it fast. "I wish you happy," I whisper to her retreating back, and I smile, believing my wish will come true.

EPILOGUE

Rae Chatworth
846 Windy Lea Road
Colville, WA

Dear Rae,

I have thought about calling you but can't bring myself to do it. I owe you my life, and I'm not a fan of owing anybody anything. Especially that. Really, I just want you to know that I am still alive. Tom and I are talking again—mostly online at this point—but we might take a vacation together next month and see how that goes. He's ever hopeful, and it's infectious. Not that I'm an optimist, not yet, but maybe there's hope for that as well.

I've progressed to a cane, and the physical therapist thinks I'll be walking without assistance in another month or two. My mental health therapist (yes, I have one) shakes her head a lot, but she looks a little more relaxed than she did the first couple of weeks I came in to see her.

That's it, I guess. I wanted you to know I'm still alive and maybe even moving toward happiness of a sort. I forgive you for saving me.

Oh hell, I'm grateful. My love to your parents and the kitten.

Be well,
Katya

P.S. I am volunteering at one of the local shelters, meaning I brought an elderly cat home for some special care. I doubt he'll be returning anytime soon. I blame you for this.

AFTERWORD

My life was personally touched by suicide when my coworker and friend Jamie chose to end his life. He was in a very dark place at the time he died, unable to see how much he was loved for his beautiful soul, brilliant mind, kindness, uniqueness, and delightfully quirky humor.

If you are feeling the call of suicide, please know that even though you *feel* unloved and alone with your darkness, you are not alone. I urge you to keep fighting—for your sake, and for the sake of those who love you. There is hope. There is help. Even if you believe you've already tried every possible alternative and there's nothing left, you may be only a hairsbreadth away from finding what you need.

Reach out to a friend, call your local community mental health center, or connect with one of the resources below.

National Suicide Prevention Lifeline
Phone: 1-800-273-TALK (8255)
Website: www.suicidepreventionlifeline.org
Crisis Text Line
Text "HELLO" to 741741

ACKNOWLEDGMENTS

The idea for *I Wish You Happy* popped into my head during a late-night drive from the airport to home, born of a fortuitous intersection of sleep deprivation, a face-to-face conversation with my editor, and a random bicyclist I passed on the street. Now that the book is finished, though, I realize that tendrils of the plot and characters connect with a multitude of hidden nooks and crannies in my psyche.

I owe thanks for this book to every friend, client, or random stranger who ever shared their emotions with me, and especially to all of the brave people I've been privileged to assist during times of crisis. All of you are in my heart forever.

To my Viking—who not only believes in me and my stories but also has the courage to confront some of my pet plot twists and ideas—I love you. This book in particular was a partnership effort, from your input on the concept all the way through the treacherous minefield of your oh-so-important continuity read.

Susan Spann, thank you for being my kitten consultant, my critique partner, and always and forever my soul sister.

Kristina Martin and Janette Buba, I am grateful beyond measure for your willingness to read and critique under the tight timeline.

Love and thanks to Heather and Alex and all of the other friends who have been supportive and there for me during challenging times.

Mary Gaughin—thank you for introducing me to the world of orbs, and for giving me the inspiration for Tana. Beverly Scherette—I promised a character based on you, and I'm eternally glad I did. I owe you for Corinne, may she be forever and eternally happy.

Last, but never least, I want to acknowledge all of the clinicians out there doing crisis work. I know what it costs you. Never forget that your work is invaluable and makes differences you may never see.

BOOK CLUB QUESTIONS

1. Would you ever open your home to someone the way Rae does? Why do you think this might or might not be a good idea?

2. What do you think about Rae's eventual decision to cut her ties with Katya? Do you think that was a selfish or a healthy decision?

3. Why do you think Rae felt such a strong need to care for animals? Do animals often stand in for human relationships in your life, or in the lives of people you know?

4. Why do you think some people find it easier to relate to animals than to other people?

5. Have you ever met anybody who shares Rae's problem with watches and cell phone batteries? Have you ever experienced an event that was out of the ordinary, such as the orbs in Tana's pictures?

6. Both Rae and Katya are deeply affected by the conflict between what they want out of life and what their parents want for them. Do you struggle with the expectations your family has for you? What about the expectations you have for your own children?

7. Rae has difficulty finding a balance in relationships—what she calls "needing a dimmer switch." What is your experience with friendships? Is this balance easy or hard for you?

8. Why do you think Cole does the work he does? Is it penance, as Rae believes, or something else?

9. Many people make wishes—on a falling star, before blowing out birthday candles, et cetera. Have you ever made a wish that came true? If so, do you think this is because wishes translate to actions, or because there is some special power in wishing?

10. Rae is able to shift to doing work for which she is perfectly suited. If money was not an issue, what life work would you pursue?

ABOUT THE AUTHOR

Photo © Kerry Schafer

Kerry Anne King is the author of the international bestselling novel *Closer Home*. Licensed both as an RN and a mental health counselor, she draws on her experience working in the medical and mental health fields to explore themes of loss, grief, and transformation. Kerry lives in a little house in the big woods of the inland northwest with her Viking, three cats, a dog, and a yard full of wild turkey and deer. She also writes fantasy and mystery novels as Kerry Schafer. You can learn more about Kerry and her books at her website, www.kerryanneking.com, or by becoming part of her newsletter community at http://bit.ly/kerryanneking.